D1135241

Treading Water

Treading Water

Anne DeGrace

McArthur & Company
Toronto

Although inspired by the former community of Renata, British Columbia, and its residents, and although some historical references are based on fact, this book is a work of fiction.

First published in Canada in 2005 by
McArthur & Company
322 King St., West, Suite 402
Toronto, Ontario
M5V 1J2
www.mcarthur-co.com

Library and Archives Canada Cataloguing in Publication

DeGrace, Anne
      Treading water / Anne DeGrace.

ISBN 1-55278-526-2
      I. Title.

PS8607.E47T74 2005   C813'.6   C2005-903710-5

The publisher would like to acknowledge the financial support of the Government of Canada through the Book Publishing Industry Development Program, the Canada Council for the Arts, and the Ontario Arts Council for our publishing activities. We also acknowledge the Government of Ontario through the Ontario Media Development Corporation Ontario Book Initiative.

The lyrics to K-k-k-k-katy by Geoffrey O'Hara copyright 1918 (renewed 1946) appear by permission Warner Bros. Publications U.S. Inc.

Earlier editions of some stories have appeared in Canadian literary journals. The story titled "1932" appeared in the spring 2004 issue of *The New Quarterly* under the title "When the Moon Shines"; the story "1950" appeared in the spring 2005 issue of *Room of One's Own* under the title "To Bury a Horse"; and the story "1965" appeared in the spring 2005 issue of *Wascana Review* under the title "Smoke."

Design and Composition: Tania Craan
Front Jacket Image: Masterfile
Jacket Author Photo: Fred Rosenberg

Printed in Canada by Webcom

10 9 8 7 6 5 4 3 2 1

To the community of Renata, British Columbia, and to all communities who lost their land to progress but kept their stories.

Treading Water

1904

The axe lies against the chopping block to his left. There is no question: wood is required. He chooses not to think, but instead seizes the axe in a swift movement, the familiar shape fitting reassuringly into his palm. In a moment there is wood on block, axe in air, pieces on ground. But there is the slicing pain on the downswing, as if he has cut off his own foot with the axe, and with the biting shift of weight from foot to foot, the sharpness of the day rises, then falls. It is not the first time that day he passed out from the pain.

Later, Gus labours in the glow of the oil lamp, one side of him toasting from the freshly cut wood burning in the stove, the other catching the chill of the early spring. The boards of the table push up through the old ledger paper, teasing pen strokes into wild aberrations. This table was never meant for writing, stained as it is with the blood of animals. His leg on a bucket prop jack-knifes his torso as he bends forward. It's uncomfortable, and he welcomes this as a change from the relentless throbbing in his leg. From the corner, the steady drips from the leak in the roof echo as they hit the biscuit tin set beneath. As the tin fills, the tone changes, and so provides a musical accompaniment to pain, isolation, and the scratch of the pencil.

One, two, three, four, counts Gus, pausing. He writes:

> *I, Augustus Sanders, being of sound mind, do hereby leave all of my worldly effects to my partner Jean-Pierre Desjardins of Bear Creek, British Columbia in the year of Our Lord 1904*

He's unsure if this is how these things should be written, but it sounds right. He goes on, tapping the pencil on the table top as he thinks of the things he must list. Tap, tap goes the pencil. Drip, drip comes the sound from the corner.

> *Trapline, upper Bear Creek to Arrow Landing*
> *Four trapline cabins*
> *Traps, snares, tools*
> *My cabin at the base of Bear Creek by Syringa Cove*
> *Two good horses boarding with Frieda and George*
> *Hartmann*

No, he thinks, Frieda can have the horses...

Gus met Frenchie Desjardins at the Columbia Kootenay mine at Rossland. The Frenchman was loud, with great, sweeping gestures and big hands, black eyes glinting under thick brows, big voice, always singing on the job, even if nobody could understand what the hell he was singing about. And smart. Frenchie could smell a good deal just as he could sense a good man in a quiet demeanour, and Gus had such a demeanour. You could see it in the way quiet young Gus handled a workhorse, held a shovel, laced up a boot. After a while, there was no Gus without Frenchie, no Frenchie without Gus, like two sides to a penny.

Gus, oldest of a ragtag clan of grimy Sanders children, was out the door with a backwards wave of his cap by the age of fourteen. From the Portland docks he made his way to the British Columbia goldfields, his hard-working, quiet, likeable nature earning him friendly help and the occasional tip. In the Fraser the gold rush was booming, but he felt run over by the push and shove of it all; by 1893 he had moved inland, where there was word of good jobs to be had at Rossland.

On the day shift he shovelled muck and thought of nothing. At night, he dreamed of the tip that would lead him to the motherlode, when he dreamed at all. He would close his eyes against the constant shift and noise of the bunkhouse, sinking into a bed still warm from the last miner to lie there, gone on the next shift but leaving behind a pong of sweat and old farts. Took his boots off every other day to keep the rot out, slept with one hand over the bunk when he did, knuckles resting gently on the laces. Too tired to feel the bites from mattress vermin, he stayed comatose until the next shift clumped up the stairs and booted him down to breakfast.

He has a picture of them, taken outside the boarding house, spring of 1898. Gus is middle row, fourth from the left. His head is cocked, sandy hair emerging from a peaked cap. He eyes the camera thoughtfully, while beside him Frenchie, thumbs in suspenders, fixes the lens in a black-eyed stare, mouth rising slightly at the corners.

Frenchie told Gus about a trapline a buddy worked up the lake above Bear Creek. His buddy had returned to Quebec, and now nobody was working it. To Gus, who knew nothing about trapping, it sounded better than shovelling sludge.

It was almost a year after they first met when they caught a tug heading north up the Lower Arrow Lake. They sat and smoked with the driver, watching the shoreline pass, hearing tales of progress. The CPR was running big freight boats, sternwheelers that would move lumber, people, pianos, anything at all, the driver said. Farms north at Whatshan were already turning out strawberries, barging them down the lake. Seems like every week there's some new settlement, he told them: wharfs being built, buildings going up, and it wasn't just the mining towns like Sandon, Retallack and Trail; farming, orcharding and logging fed the boom. The driver swept his arm northward. The century is turning, he told them. There are great things happening.

Gus closed his eyes, imagined a lakeshore dotted with houses, two-storey homes with front porches and swings on them; a dog barking with a laughing child wrapped around its furry neck like a scarf. For a kid from dock-side Portland, it was a pretty thought.

Moving northward up the long, narrow lake, they rounded a bend flanked by soft mountains. An Indian canoe slipped down the shoreline on the west side. "Lakes," said the driver, and Gus thought he was talking about the water, but he was talking about the Indian. Ahead was a soft-green, treed lowland rising to a sunny plateau. A creek meandered down, running sluggish in the August heat, probably a gusher in the spring. "Bear Creek," said the driver as they pulled in by a gravel beach, the tug's shallow keel scraping gently. A deadhead served as anchor to a line of raw logs lashed together with mining cable. As the two men precariously made their way to dry ground, Gus noticed a curl of smoke rising from behind a stand of poplar. Frenchie grinned. "Dinner," he said, rounding out the word with a broad accent and a triumphant wave smokeward.

Standing there before an open fire in her long skirts, hair up in a bun, Frieda stared as the two travellers emerged from the trees. The smell of woodsmoke and venison wafted from a pot on the fire. Gus looked at the woman at the fire, her hands on her hips, waiting. Involuntarily Gus glanced up the hillside but there was no house, no porch, no dog, no child. There was a large canvas tent, from which a man emerged.

Frieda's mouth opened to speak, but instead it was her husband who spoke at that moment, the effect almost comical, like a ventriloquist's trick. It took Gus a moment to catch up and pay attention to the neat man with the German accent. He spoke, more to the older man than the younger, and Gus found his attention shifting back to Frieda's mouth. It was full and shaped as if carved from wood, with a warm, burnished grain. A corner twitched in amusement.

Raising his eyes to hers, he was met with a startling blue, and then she closed them briefly, a light extinguished. When she opened them, she was looking at her husband. "George Hartmann," he said. "My wife, Frieda."

George Hartmann's handshake was firm, a man in charge, a master of the household. Frieda's handshake said more. It said: I have great hopes for this place, this life. Welcome, it said.

It is snowing, the new flakes settling lightly on the rotting spring snow. Gus turns on the wood-frame bunk, shifting his leg carefully, and puts his head down for a moment on the grey wool. The thin red stripe of blanket stitch brushes blond eyelashes; the wool rasps the planes of a young face aged by three years of trapline winters. The cabin is cold, but fever has placed a sheen of sweat across his brow. He knows the wound is septic, and thinks he may be delirious but he isn't sure, just as he isn't sure how many days have passed. There are sharp moments of consciousness and long periods in which the measured dripping of water marks time, but tells him nothing.

From this angle, without lifting his head, he can see in a pinpoint vista: the pot-bellied stove, glinting embers through a crack in the seam; a good stove traded for the prime pelt of an unlucky lynx; on it, a deep, large iron pot with no handles, a blackened frypan and a kettle, his unwashed tin plate and cup; a row of biscuit tins for flour, baking soda, salt, oats, almost empty; on the table, an oil lamp, sooty at the base of the glass and a jar that once held Frieda's blackberry jam, now containing wire and springs for the traps; on the wall hang two leghold traps in need of repair, while on the plank shelf below, jars of scent, the trapper's secret.

He thinks about the scent that Jake Weider, who runs the store at Bear Creek, sold him. Mixed with rotten fish, it could lure an elephant all the way from Africa if the wind was blowing the right way. What the hell was that stuff? He remembers the summer he had it stored up in the rafters of the main cabin, getting ranker and ranker, pressure building. He was skinning a marten outside when the thing blew. He'd thought something was shooting at him, must've jumped a foot and almost took his thumb off. He'd had to sleep outside for a week. He laughs at the memory, and then begins to cry a little. He presses his head hard into the blanket, feeling like a little boy, and curls his fingers into the cougar pelt beneath it.

Outside, beyond his sight, lying tooth down and harmless in the snow, a bear trap. Leaning in the corner, a rifle. Ready.

Shifting slightly, he fumbles at his crotch and pisses into the bucket tucked half under the bed, congratulating himself on his presence of mind to place it there two, three days ago. The sound is fluid, a musical accompaniment to the percussive drip and an affirmation that this, at least, he can still control.

Later, he experiences a moment of strength and lucidity. He pulls himself up from the bunk, stokes the fire, and lays strips of rabbit, a little rancid, across the melting fat in the pan. There is still one piece of bannock. He pours water from the corner bucket, overflowing from the leak above, into the kettle, and brews a strong black tea. These small things have taken over an hour to accomplish, and now he is exhausted. He will rest a little, and then haul himself outside, again, to the wood pile. Frenchie must be on his way; is that him, now? In the corner the water drips, and he closes his eyes.

He awakes to smoke in the cabin. He has drifted off, not for long, but long enough that the rabbit is charcoal in the pan as he coughs his way to the door on one foot with the hot pan handle wrapped in a brown flannel shirt. He sets the pan on the woodpile, choking, and flaps the door back and forth. The snow has turned to rain, and now the rain has stopped. He pauses, looks at the trees, the glint of brief sun on water far in the distance. Everything seems needle-sharp: the hiss of wind, the diamond points of light, the ground at his feet, every rock and twig that lie against the dirty snow pocked with patches of wet brown earth. He leans against the doorframe and lets the cool air wash over him. *Frieda.* Her name is soft in his ear, yet nobody has spoken.

Frieda's warmth towards the two travellers cast a glow upon the clearing. After handshakes all around, George Hartmann invited Gus and Frenchie to join them for venison stew that day, with sorrel, onion, potatoes. Onions and potatoes, Hartmann told them, came with them from Manitoba, by horse and cart, then train. They had sold one horse, bought another, slaughtered a third. They had been here two months, he said. They had sent word to their Mennonite community: Come. They were expecting family—a brother, an uncle, cousins—at any time, but it was getting late; they may have decided to winter with another community. Frieda, not speaking, glanced at the visitors. It would be a long winter without family, alone on a partially cleared landing by a lake, the mountains looming in the winter light.

The Hartmanns would be finished their cabin in a few weeks, a log frame building set amid a copse of pine in stark shadow against the sunny flat behind, over which a crisp blue wind had arisen. Come, we'll show you.

It was not the front-porched house Gus had imagined. It was a two-room log cabin, the roof a crosshatch of uncovered beams, the trees cut from the land around them. The floor was dirt, but George Hartmann had plans for planking, being barged up from the mill at Robson, due soon. They were scouts for the new community; careful savings from the old would support the new, until fruit trees could be planted, begin producing. They had chosen Bear Creek for the broad plateau, perfect for orcharding. There were trees to be cleared, of course, but couldn't they see it? Here would be apples, pears and apricots. Here would be cherries. Here would be a rich life with families, children. Frieda smiled, whispered: *children.*

Dit es Heimat, Frieda spoke softly, looking at the two men who surveyed the expanse of uncleared timber.

Home. She wrapped her tongue reverently around the unaccustomed word. Her eyes were shining.

Three years have passed since that day and with them the cycle of seasons, the press of winter. Gus shifts again on the bunk, and pain spirals up into his thigh, interrupting his thoughts. For a moment, he can hardly see. The rain has eased, the drip decreased, the wood shifts softly in the stove. Gus Sanders, feeling much, much older than his twenty-three years, pushes himself up on one leg and, using the table for support, drops as much wood into the fire as can fit. When he is sure it will burn well, he moves the one pace necessary to get from stove to table to bunk and gently lowers himself: shoulder, hip, leg. Sleep.

Frieda was twenty years old when she first met Gus and Frenchie, who were the third and fourth people to arrive at Bear Creek. Children didn't come into the lives of the Hartmanns as she had hoped, but the other families did, and before long there was a settlement: John Fischer, who hoped to get the government contract to run the post office; Jacob Weider, who ran the one-room store; Birthe and Frederick Schroeder, Birthe a godsend with her happy, practical nature and skills as a midwife; the Webers, Mathilde and Klaus, who hoped, like she did, for a child.

Plattdeutsche, a Low German, was the language heard from the mouths of women stoking fires, and the men clearing trees. Chickens were barged up the lake, roosters crowed at dawn. Others came, too. Not the German or Dutch Mennonite stock, but hardworking as if they were: from the coast, from the States, from

England. Paddy came from Ireland, and brought music into every kitchen. There were Lakes Indians who came by, and sold or traded trout, berries, and baskets. It was a real settlement, with plans and aspirations. They called it Bear Creek, nobody quite sure who first coined the name. There was a creek, though, and there most certainly were bears.

Frieda, thinks Gus, now on his back looking at the square of rapidly fading daylight in a high window. Sleep has rejuvenated him a little. He sleeps so much, now, fever drenching the blankets. *Frieda. She smiles at you and it's the sun coming out.*

Gus and Frenchie repaired the three disintegrating trapline cabins they had inherited and a built a sturdy one-room main cabin, the one Gus lies in now. But Frenchie never did like to stay in one place. Attracted to quick money and town life, the girls and the saloons, he took on jobs as a teamster, hauling ore, taking him away for long stretches. It was Gus who bought the land, built himself a three-room cabin at Bear Creek, now sitting empty twenty-five miles away while he waits for supplies and salvation that should have been here days ago. Wherever work took him, Frenchie had always been reliable. *He should be here any minute.*

If Gus is very still, lying on his bunk, he can imagine a leg with no pain. He can shift his mind from now to before, pretend it didn't happen. He lets his painless leg walk the forest paths, rifle at his side. He remembers another time: a warm fall, a forest pool.

George Hartmann was a lucky man, and he knew it. That Frieda Neufeld even looked at him, fifteen years her senior, he felt blessed by the good Lord above. Smallpox had left him pitted, but he hid his face in a long, curling mustache, and distracted attention with an imposing gaze that demanded eye avoidance at almost any cost. Folks glanced away when they talked to George Hartmann, gazing after an osprey, gesturing to a plow blade; settling, if absolutely necessary, on the brown vest button set midway between his torso and his chin.

Because he did not understand why this willowy girl accepted him, a jealousy burned, and a sourness invaded bed and home. But Frieda knew tender moments with this man, and these she nestled and counted just as she counted eggs in a renegade nest; a windfall unexpected, a sweet surprise. He was like a spring wind, changeable, and it made her quiet, and careful. He was not a violent man, but neither was he warm.

It was a sultry Indian summer day three years after their arrival, and George was digging postholes when he realized that his wife had been gone on her walk a long time. There had been a grizzly sow around, her cubs growing, ranging farther. He had removed his shirt in the heat. Now he pulled it on, irritated when it dragged across gritty skin, bunched at his armpits. He was hot, and he needed a drink of water. He took a perverse pleasure in this physical justification of a deeper irritability. Leaving the jug in the shade, he stood sweating in the mid-afternoon sun, each annoyance compounding into a rising anger: at the bear, at Frieda, at hard work, at no children after these years of lying with his wife.

His rifle always at his side against a lucky shot and a meal—more than a few garden rabbits had met the stewpot in this way—he picked it up, enjoying the balance in his fist. He began walking.

When Frieda Hartmann reached the swimming hole, her clothes met branches piece by piece, finding their places with a familiarity born of repetition: dress, pale plaid, shot with green, a little worn, a favourite; underthings, plain. Her feet, sticky from the heat of her boots, were soothed when she stepped into the water across a massage of pebbles. It was delicious. She floated, her brown hair fanned out around her, small breasts breaking the surface.

The pond was really part of the larger lake, a sheltered inlet with a narrow neck. By September the lake level had lowered enough to create a separate body of water that warmed considerably. From one side to the other on its longest part, Frieda could swim a strong overhand crawl of exactly seventeen strokes; flipping onto her back and kicking against a rock to float gently backwards until the crown of her head gently knocked against a makeshift raft tethered to a pine. The pond was dappled with sun, serene, perfect.

George Hartmann watched his wife from the shadow of a birch grove above and to the west of the longer edge. He saw her sure stroke, her gentle, returning float, and marvelled at the beauty of her skin. He was acutely aware that he was a voyeur of a private moment. He felt as if he was looking at a woman he did not know. He shifted the rifle from his left to his right hand, leaned with his full weight against a tree. Above, a squirrel raised an alarm. Below him, the woman in the pond looked up, briefly.

Gus, standing on the opposite shore in dappled sunlight, above the pond and well into the trees, didn't see the other man. Pursuit of a deer had led him in this direction. Now, the deer forgotten, he stood still as an unsuspecting buck in a rifle's sights.

After twenty minutes, George left the grove quietly. When Frieda returned an hour later, skirts full of salmonberries, he said nothing. That night, he dreamed of a succubus that pulled him, taunting, into a warm lake. He awoke, aroused, ashamed. A good Mennonite husband should not have such dreams.

The next time George visited the pond was four days later. Again, his wife had drifted away from her tasks. Should she not be canning, drying?

Gus sat where he had stood before, above and to the left of what the local children called the Jumping Rock. On summer afternoons, chores done, they came in a ragtag handful of mostly boys. Now, the water was too shallow to jump; the only splash was the sound of a single supine body flipping fishlike, pushing off the rock when she reached it to begin a mesmerizing, gentle float that for Gus was five full minutes of beautiful, aching agony.

He had come every afternoon since the first day, taking guilty time from necessary work: cabin repairs, traps to be oiled, wood cut. He should be ready for the season by now, with time left still to make a little grubstake money at the mines downriver, but he stalled, returned again and again, each day relieved, disappointed. Now, he could hear a splash, a flash of skin caught in sunlight and then nothing but ripples on the water, until Frieda emerged from her dive some feet away. Sitting on a piece of deadfall, he contemplated a world in which he would approach the pond, and she would look up and see him, smile, step out of the water, droplets glistening on her freckled skin, and move towards him, welcoming him.

When the shot came, its sound triggered an instant reflex that catapulted him backwards over the log and into the tangle of brush on the other side. Bark sprayed from the massive cedar above him. A sharp branch had scraped his face, drawing blood. He touched it as he looked up at where the bullet had grazed the tree trunk. The birds, raucous a moment ago, were silent. The woman in the pool had stopped mid-pond, treading water, eyes wide.

He did not know where the shot had come from.

After a moment, one bird, then another, began a tentative song. Frieda emerged quickly and dressed, pulling clothes hastily over a still wet body, but Gus didn't see this. He had already slunk into the shadows, heart pounding.

By evening Gus had convinced himself that someone was taking a shot at a deer or something and missed. Frieda had returned home, saying nothing to her husband, who said nothing to her. George was not even sure he'd seen a man in the trees. That night, he made love to his wife with uncharacteristic tenderness, running his thumb softly across her cheek, placing a kiss on each eye, her throat, the sole of her foot.

Frieda did not go swimming for almost a week. The weather had changed, become cooler. The sun shone less, hiding behind mare's tails that joined to become a soft grey blanket through which the sun glowed eerily. But when one morning promised a summer's last gasp, Frieda hurried to complete her chores and headed out into the sultry afternoon, knowing that this would be the last time this season, and wanting to hold the summer a moment more.

Gus Sanders did not hear the tread behind him. His first indication was a sudden tightening of the cloth at his throat, and a lifting. Then, the contact of bone on cheek, the set of knuckles making fleshy contact that sent two teeth flying in a bloody spray. With no time to protest or defend, Gus went down, rolled in the needles and tried to peer up into the sun that framed the head of his attacker.

"You will not come near my wife."

George stood above him, foreshortened, almost comical from Gus's view were it not for the chill of the rifle half raised at his side. Gus scrambled to find footing and raised himself up, jaw thrust in a parody of a barside brawl, fists at the ready, blood on his mouth like lipstick. But George had turned his back, was pushing away through the brush, a German baritone trumpeting "Frieda!" as he descended to the pebble beach where his wife, eyes down, was fumbling into clothes like weights.

Swollen, gap-toothed, the next day Gus headed for the city where every whiskey he hoisted with a grin exhibited spaces that required explanation. He made sure the story changed each time he told it; a few drinks brought the words out, he found, quite easily. Over two weeks, it became somewhat of a standing joke at the Rossland Hotel, where new embellishments were expected, and encouraged.

When he came back with winter supplies it had turned sharply cold. He left two rabbits at the door of George and Frieda Hartmann, unsure of their acceptance. As he walked up onto the neatly framed porch he remembered his first meeting with George and Frieda, the tent, the cooking fire. He remembered George's plans for their house, and Frieda's plans for children. He waited until the Hartmanns had caught the steamer for town, waited until just before they were due back, hanging the rabbits high inside the covered doorway against the interest of predators. He was being neighbourly, he told himself. Payment, in part, for the boarding of Missus and Belle that winter, that is, if George would allow it, now.

When Frieda spoke to him next, it was to bring him a jar of blackberry jam.

She came up the hill, arms swinging, puffing up the slope in a sharp, cool late afternoon sun. The horses whinnied a greeting from behind his cabin, where they had cropped a great circle in the overgrowth.

Gus set down his axe, laying it carefully against the woodpile. He could not think what to do with his hands. He picked up a piece he had just cut from the round and held it like a shield with arm cocked. Set it down again when she held out the jar.

"I made so much," she explained in her soft German accent.

"Thank you."

She sat on the smaller of the woodpiles, stacked against the shed and stable against her weight. She looked at him, shaded her eyes against the sun behind his head. Her eyes were the blue the lake sometimes acquired, heralding a shift in weather. He thought this was remarkable, and because he was in thought, he did not hear her words at first.

"… a good crop this year," she said, "the first that has brought in money. Gravensteins did well. We are going to buy a cow, a pregnant cow, so she will birth in spring."

"That's nice," he said, and meant it. He lowered himself to the chopping block so she would not have to squint. She smiled. Around them, the wind blew the trees into soft whistles, high above. The clearing, a hollow a little out of the wind, was warm for the first time in a series of biting fall days.

"How is your mouth?"

He was grinning, like an idiot he thought, when she said it. He covered his mouth self-consciously against the gap in his smile. "It's fine," he mustered. He didn't want to talk about it and found himself reddening. He had said six words since she arrived in his clearing. Thank you. That's nice. It's fine.

"It's a nice house you have built," she told him, and to be sure, when he looked at the three rooms he had built, the neatly stacked wood, the shed, so different from his trapline cabins, it had the makings of a home. He remembered her word: *heimat.*

"Guess I'm getting settled," he said, smiling, and looked down.

She sat, clasped her hands in her lap, and looked up at the trees swaying against the sky, half their leaves still clinging goldly. His hands were clutched around the jar; a place to put them. They hadn't moved since they found it. Now, he held the jar up to the light, a small epiphany: here was something to talk about.

"It looks real good."

"Yes."

"Mrs. Hartmann," he began. "Frieda." The woods, the sunlight, her neat, sturdy shoes on dust and pine needles, everything became sharply focused into this moment, and then a roaring took over, as if his head was swept suddenly under a waterfall.

"Well," she said, rising, "I must go. George does not know I'm here."

Gus stood also, confused by the noise, by the sudden brightness of the day. She leaned forward, then, and kissed him on the cheek, a moth on its way to a lantern. He watched her back descend down the path between the tall grasses.

The kiss lingered on his cheek that day and the next, and the week after, and followed him up into woods that rained leaves around him as he hiked the twenty-five miles to number one cabin. The kiss distracted him, so that an hour, two hours would pass as he walked, heavy pack swaying, and he could not remember the route, or how his feet had found the way. It lay there, ghostly, on his cheek the night he first heard the grizzly on the porch, chuffing, snorting, and knocking over things.

He stayed put, that first night. He figured with the coming winter the bear would go to ground, leave him the hell alone. Several days later Frenchie came up from Bear Creek with some traps and dry goods, laughed at his story about the bear, poured him another glass, and sang a raucous bar song in French. It was warm in the cabin with a grouse in the pot and fresh supplies unpacked on the table. There was no sign of any bear.

"Just the same, order in a bear trap, wouldja?" Gus had said, and Frenchie laughed, nodded. "Sure," he said, "sure."

Frenchie had good work at the mine in Trail, better money than the trapline, and Gus, in his third season as a trapper, felt confident to work it alone. Frenchie was a good partner: reliable, solid, if talkative. Gus knew he owed everything to Frenchie: this trapline, this place, this life. And yet, the anticipation of quiet and solitude lay ahead like a cool lake on a hot day. With a promise to bring up fresh supplies by February, Frenchie said goodbye and the partners parted amicably over potato moonshine on a late October evening.

"Don't let that bear get choo. I see you in spring, then," he said. Then a laugh, a slap on the back like a fish on a plank. "Goodbye, *bonne chance*," he called, and then the quiet of the forest closed in.

She was a problem bear, larder-raiding, unpredictable, certainly not hibernating in any meaningful way. She would not leave him alone. Once she had kept Gus in the outhouse for an hour, her snuffsnuff punctuated with grunts, just outside the door. It was a mild winter; she came back five, six times, tearing into pelts and pulling down a fresh deer hanging in the cabin porch.

Another trapper, cutting through Gus's line to his own, brought the news of the big trap's arrival on the Sternwheeler *Minto*. After leaning on the door frame, watching the departing back of the first human he had seen in many weeks, Gus packed up and trekked out from midway in the fifty-mile trapline on snowshoes over crusty February snow. The trap, big, toothy and hair-trigger, drew a small crowd when he unpacked it in the Bear Creek store. He thought briefly of the damage those teeth could do to an unsuspecting bone.

"Shoot the thing," said Jake at the store, looking over his shoulder. "I'll help you. Hell, take my gun, it'll get 'er good."

Gus looked up from the gleaming teeth. There should be nothing easy about this. "My bear, my problem," he said, grinning. "My solution."

He bought supplies, just enough to pack up comfortably; when Frenchie came, he'd bring enough to see them through to March thaw. He bought shells for the .22, the .303. He put the new trap down in the corner of the main cabin. There was no sign of the grizzly, and he thought: maybe she's just gone. But he didn't really believe it. He saw her when he slept, slipping around the corners of dreams, scratching at the edges, chuffing, clacking her jaws, looking at him with an inscrutable eye. There is no knowing what goes on inside the head of a grizzly. Twice she chased him through the landscape of sleep, leaving him breathless in the dawn light. In the morning, dung on the porch, warm.

He was skinning a weasel, taking the fat off with the pelt taut against the board, drawing the knife with an expertise that pleased him. He had become quicker over this long winter, more adept. He liked the smooth efficiency he applied to the task. He liked the mounting inventory of furs, including two lynx, caught in the same day.

When the bear came into his clearing, broad feet splayed on the packed snow, she came fast. Not running, but there was no meander to her gait, no: *just checking things out, moving through, don't mean to bother you*. She strode with purpose, head swinging, fixing the scene with one eye, then the other, enticed by the smell of guts that lay at Gus's feet as he sat, frozen. She smelled like a bear; she smelled like aggression. She was thirty feet away, but it felt like three. There were only six or seven feet between the edge of the porch where he sat and the cabin door. It was only when he was on the other side, panting, that he felt the beat of his heart, the pain of it trying to leap from his chest and scuttle under the bunk. From outside came the wet sounds of a large grizzly consuming the entrails of a weasel.

That night, as Gus dreamed, she was there again, pawing at the door. Heart pounding on the other side, he kept pushing back at it, but instead of the hard resistance of pine it was soft, rotten, decayed. It bowed under his weight, came away in his hands. It thinned to parchment, until he could see the steely eye of the sow as if through glass.

He awoke to stillness in the cabin, but he could feel her out there. The sun was breaking.

He tracked her backwards, across a creek and up the trail he used to check his smaller snares. He cut down two saplings at what he gauged was the height of her head, tied the points together, making an X over the place where he would set the trap. On the sides, for ten feet leading up to the spot, he laid freshly cut brush pointing outwards, creating a barrier against detour, against any approach other than the one that would plant her squarely in the path of the leghold trap, securely staked to trees from two directions. From the crossed branches, he hung a rabbit, partly gutted and smeared with rotten fish.

He had taken the .303 with him. Coming back, he crossed the open creek, traversing the deadfall bridge he used daily. When the sharp crack came, he thought first it was the bear, charging him from the creekside brush and he whirled wildly, looking first for the bear before feeling in horror the shift beneath his feet. But it was the fallen tree, rotten and thawing, cracking beneath him. He kept his footing, but lost the rifle.

He went back to the cabin, spooked, loaded the .22 and waited, knowing the rifle was too small to shoot a grizzly. He filled his time with cabin chores, chopping wood, gun close. The day went by. At dusk, he lit a fire, cooked some beans, one of the last cans. He stopped, put a little more wood on the fire, listened again. He went outside to piss, listened, looked up at a clear sky, at a million stars, past lodgepole pines that swayed, nudging one another like gentle conspirators. He walked up the path to check the trap, knowing absolutely that checking bear traps in the dark was not good trapping practice. He approached cautiously, but in the brightness of the clear night could see only the rabbit hanging like a rosary between branches joined like praying hands.

He slept, without visitation from dream bears. What woke him just before dawn he couldn't say. He lay in the dark, listened, heard it again. Chuff, chuff. What sound would a bear in a trap make? Would she roar? Wouldn't she? Would she bang into trees, try to pull the trap free, gnaw at her foot, tear at the underbrush? He was listening too hard; it was only the scrape of branches on the cabin roof.

He rose in the dark, pulled on heavy leather boots, lit the lantern, and hefted the rifle. He had to see that the trap was still there, the rabbit still in place. He knew he would not sleep, in any case. From the cabin porch, no sound. Raising the lantern, he swung it towards the path, but could not see far enough to know for sure. This is the hardest light to see in, he thought, that moment at dusk or at dawn when the eye can't find the balance between dark and light, and objects are indiscernible from one another. He stepped off the porch softly, as softly as you can in a heavy miner's boot, laces untied, dragging, thick wool socks keeping the cold from creeping up his pant legs.

There was the trap, the crossed branches. The rabbit was gone, he was sure of it, and he moved forward to see if the trap has been sprung, thinking, how can this be? From beside the track, a crashing, and then she was there, all teeth and claw and fur, and he cocked the rifle and shot wildly, stepped back and at first he thought that the bear had him, somehow got her teeth around his ankle, pulling at it.

A crashing in the brush receded as the bear retreated at the sound of the rifle. His fall had knocked the crossed branches to the ground, and one hand closed in its fall on a partly gutted rabbit smeared with rotten fish. How could he not have smelled it before? He looked down, saw the jaws of the trap closed across the heel of his boot, teeth embedded into the rubber and leather and, on the top side, into his heel. He thought, briefly, how lucky to have been caught at such an odd angle, the boot heel absorbing the brunt of the bite. Then he passed out.

He cannot quite remember how he returned to the cabin, how he pried apart the jaws of the trap, how he removed the boot. He believes it all took some time. He remembers thinking, at first, this is not so bad: a jagged gash almost to bone across the back of his heel, but everything intact. He poured in iodine, passed out, closed the flaps of skin, clung to consciousness as if by tooth and nail, sweating, crying. Wrapped it up. Prayed.

He knows the bear returned some time later for the rabbit, lying on the snow like a meal for a dog. He knows she's been back since. He's not sure how long it's been, or how many times, or when, exactly, that god-damn Frenchman is supposed to show up. Everything is on fire, and he envisions flames that have crawled from the stove, across the plank floor, sneaking like small animals up the bed leg where they wrap themselves in the blanket and begin to gnaw at his body with sharp, hot teeth.

A noise outside and he's sure it's Frenchie. It's past time.

But there is no Frenchie, no booming, jovial greeting. Gus catches a movement through the single window, sees a brown, furred hump passing along the sightline of the frame, hears the unmistakable scratching of claw on wood, feels his heart accelerate. It comes again, and he knows it to be the rub of a branch on the roof, but now his hearing has sharpened to a razor point as his mind repeats the sound he heard, replays the vision he thought he saw, analyzing, unsure. He closes his eye, looks into the tiny eye of the bear, feels her hot breath on his face.

Twice, in moments of panic and desperation, he tried to walk out, but pain and the weakness of fever drove him back. He feared he would pass out in the woods and nobody would find him. He cannot stand the thought of not being found, of being picked apart by coyotes and crows, and somehow this is worse than the notion of the dying itself. Stay here, he told himself. It's only a matter of time, he'll come whistling up the path, be surprised to find me here like this.

Since it happened he has been outside for firewood, to shit. He has eaten most everything in the cabin, but for days now has had no appetite, just a powerful thirst, kept quenched by the bucket in the corner when he could still get over there. Seven feet away, it felt like a hundred, might have been in Spokane for all he knew. Days ago he had pulled up his pant leg, could barely stand his own touch, to find blackened, weeping skin from calf to toes and a stench like a rotting carcass oozing from under a bandage soaked with blood, stained with tincture of iodine. He lay back on the cat skin and lost consciousness, or slept, one or the other. Thoughts tumble together, images. Traps. Wood, axe. A jar of jam.

A pond, and a splash of water. Frieda. A baby. When he went to get the trap, Jake told him Frieda was going to have a baby.

Can't believe George had it in him, old bastard.

He wants these things for Frieda: the house, the porch, the dog, the child. *Frieda,* he says. *It should have been different. It should have been me.* Now he's talking to Frenchie, saying: *Where the hell are you?* Now he's talking to a bear that drifts by his window, claws at his door, gnaws on some bone outside. His bone. She is gnawing on his bone.

Give it back. It's mine.

One. Two. Three. Four. Dripdripdripdrip.

chair, table, stove.

one deep iron pot with no handles

a blackened frypan

kettle

tin plate and cup

Biscuit tins, for drygoods, empty

oil lamp, sooty and dark at the base of the glass

jam jar

rifle.

There's another sound, now, too. Gus wants to open his eyes to see what's making it, but he can't, they won't open. He is blind and his ears have become all of his senses, all at once. There is the wind in the pines outside, and it sings like Paddy's pennywhistle when he wants to make it cry. There is the drip of water, making different sounds as it hits now the tin, now the rim, now the floor. There is the sharp last gasp crack of embers in the stove and the shift of timbers in the cooling cabin. A chipmunk, heralding spring, chitters outside, scolding. They are musical scores overlapping. They are everything, and they are nothing.

1905

Frieda

On the day of Ursula's birth I dreamed of waterfalls. I dreamed I was standing beneath a stream of water that fell straight down from a great height. I stood in the fall of cool water on rounded, slippery rocks; on the bank a carpet of brilliant green moss, soft and fragile, broke away when I tried to hold on. I felt myself slipping, and there was no purchase, nothing to stop me as I swept downstream, the water becoming warmer as I descended. Ahead, the roiling, warm, flowing water dropped from sight over a precipice I could not see, but only sense.

When I awoke, the water was beneath me, around me, warm, and from my own womb. The baby had started.

My husband George awoke at once, immediately angry. Who knows what dreams my flood interrupted? When he saw my eyes, wide with the moment, full of so many emotions, his own filled with sudden understanding.

"Frieda, now?"

"Yes. I think so," I said, sitting half up, my heart suddenly jumping about in my chest. I watched George struggle into his pants, his suspenders hanging, pulling on one boot, then the other, no socks. I had seen many births, both human and animal, and yet the first pain, when it came hard on the heels of the gush of water, which I would not, after all, be floating away on, took my breath away.

"Now, George," I said again and he was gone, the front

door banging behind him. I felt in the chill air the absence of his kiss, and thought: an oversight in the excitement, that's all. For certainly he wants this baby just as much as I do. Outside, I could hear the crow of the rooster, the lowing of the cow. The baby was early.

When we lived in Manitoba, water had shaped my days. It had to be pumped, heated, drawn, wrung out, distributed. It washed, quenched, watered, scrubbed, cooled, and cooked. In the winter, we chipped the ice off the surface of the water pail. In the summer, we watched the level of the well while we watched the sky, praying for clouds to appear in the endless blue. I counted: the number of times to the pump for laundry, the number of buckets to fill the steel tub for George, the number of trips to the woodstove to heat that water, the number of pots and plates one could reasonably wash in one pan of water. I counted buckets of water like I counted the underthings and handkerchiefs, shirts and dresses that I washed and hung flapping in the prairie wind behind our house. On wash days, we five wives got together at one house or another—Birthe, Anna, Agatha, Katharina and myself—and scrubbed and pounded and laughed, and I counted the days until that day for the fun and talk it brought.

I watched while they washed the baby things, and counted the days between my monthly times and wondered how long since my last.

George counted, also: days with rain, to coax the shoots from the soil; days until harvest. He was always counting, gauging the best time to plant, to cut, and watching the clouds collect in a tease of rain, then scamper off like children, laughing at him.

When we came to British Columbia in 1899 George's eyes grew round as my own at the abundance of water: lakes so big and wide they would never dry, and days and days of rain. We came for the pull of the west, for the newness of it. We among our village came first; we were young and strong with no babies to slow us down. Another family was to come with us, but illness in that family prevented the journey. For the company, I would have waited, but George had hopes for this new place, and was anxious to come without delay. We had purchased land from an agent, Harry Stoddart, not a Mennonite but a good German name. He told us about this place, halfway between the cities of Calgary and Vancouver, in the mountains. He told us about the flat bench of land, perfect for orchards. He did not tell us how big the trees were that must first be cleared, or how many. The day we arrived we stood together, holding hands, gazing at the blue of the lake, the sway of the trees, the emptiness and the fullness of the land, the possibility and the impossibility of it all.

Later, Birthe and Frederick Schroeder came, and their young ones of course, and Anna and Gerold Martens arrived with their boys, and others came. But of our little washing group, I have not seen Agatha or Katharina again. Sometimes in my mind I see them, laughing together as they hang diapers on bushes in the prairie sun, and I feel very far away. Would they know me now?

After I have sopped the pool of my own warm water with flannel and dressed myself in my newer nightgown, I set the old in the corner basket for washing—when?—and pull off the bedclothes before laying down the oilcloth and the old sheets I have saved for this time. As I put the water on the stove to heat, the pains become regular, just as they were with my mother, whose babies always came very easily. The pains have been gentler since the first, and I think that I may have sent George to fetch Birthe too soon.

I pause when a pain comes, and my hands on the back of the spindle chair are white and freckled and seem very far away. Looking up, the kitchen in the early light is a stranger to me. Here is the woodstove, freshly blackened. And here are the pots shining on their nails; here is the faded cloth, embroidered by my mother, on the wood table, everything as neat as I left it last night when we went to bed, and yet whose kitchen is this? My feet beneath me grip the smooth boards, confident of the gentle ridges they know from the paths they have daily worn, and then another pain grips me and it is as if there is no floor beneath me at all.

Birthe

Birthe means *bright*, and as a child I was teased because my hair was so blonde as to be almost glowing. When I grew up and followed my mother's path as a midwife, I was teased by the women I helped who were not of our village, who cried and then laughed with joy and relief, exhausted and holding their newborns, for my name sounds like birth in English, and that is what I was there for.

In an old German legend, Birthe is the White Lady who slips into nurseries to rock children to sleep. She is also the terror of naughty children. This I tell my children, just as my mother told me, as I tuck them into the beds they share. They snuggle down and know the warmth of a happy home. But when there are chores to be done, they feel the White Lady watching, and so the stories of my childhood are useful to me now, so many miles away from my mother's country.

I have four boys, one girl. Frederick, named after his father, Horst, Jacob, Hannah, and Albert. They are good children: they do their chores and obey their father. Frederick is a woodworker by trade, and is not suited to orcharding, although we planted young trees like so many who have come to Bear Creek. Now, he and Jack Armstrong clear both holdings of timber with Jack's horse Ace and our workhorse Gabi. Sometimes we borrow Gus Sander's horses and put them to work as well. There are so many rocks and stumps to haul. There are plans for a mill to the south of the townsite, and my Frederick may work there until our trees bear enough fruit. He is thinking, too, of the boxes needed to ship fruit. There is little money here, but many possibilities. Frederick is always happy working with his hands.

The first time I met the Indian woman I was in the woods with my three boys and Hannah, my girl; Albert was not yet born, but he was inside, just beginning, making me feel sick in my stomach in the mornings and sometimes all day. It was May and we were picking wood lily shoots, which make a good spring vegetable.

I don't know how long the woman watched us from the trees. With the sunlight slanting through, sending bars of shadows across the forest floor, it would be easy to stay hidden just by standing still. We had seen the Indians before, but they were like ghosts drifting by in their canoes. I had never spoken to one.

It was strange to see her watching us, alone like that. There is a village not far from here, a summer camp to which they return each year. I have heard that the flat land of Bear Creek was also a village until we came. There has been more than one argument between ourselves and the Indians; now, they keep away, and so the presence of this strange woman in her long, dusty skirts and her braids, standing there with a rifle at her side, made me drop my pail. In truth, I threw it into the air, scattering the shoots across the moss. For a moment, I thought I heard her laugh at my surprise, but I could have been mistaken. The children stood beside me, their mouths agape.

I do not speak much English; Frederick is the one who talks so earnestly with Jack and I cannot follow. But I know many words, and with them can make a sort of conversation. I decided that I would not be afraid of this dark-skinned woman. I had been taught from the time I was a small child by my own mother to trust my feelings about things, and I felt no reason to fear. But I was also curious, for here was a woman when there were really not so many women in our little settlement. When I spoke, it was in English.

"Hello!" I said, and cupped my hand above my eyes because to look straight at the woman standing above us at the edge of the woods was to look straight at the morning sun behind her. She looked at me for a full minute, serious. She did not approach, but raised her hand a little and then turned away.

We went out again the next day, looking for more of the new shoots, moving farther afield and up the hillside. Again she stood, quietly, as if waiting, and I drew closer, the children behind me. She beckoned to us with a motion of her hand, and then gestured to a patch of the shoots that grew beside her, nestled together on the forest floor, bulbs pushing through the moist soil. The shoots are difficult to see, although later there would be beautiful orange flowers all through the woods. Now, they are the gentlest green, and so they need a good eye to find them. The word she uttered as she looked at me was unlike any I had ever heard. It sounded like "kick-san." I could feel Hannah beside me, her blonde head at my elbow as she cut the blood from my hand with the pressure of hers. I could sense the boys, wary. But I could sense, also, no threat from this person, and so I smiled at her. When she smiled back, she pointed again, but did not pick the shoots herself or offer to help. Instead, she reached forward, and with a brown hand, touched Hannah's blond braids and then her own black ones and laughed.

"Justine," she said, touching her breast with one hand while the other still hung in the air against the ghost of Hannah's braid, now hidden behind the small head that peaked around my skirts.

"Birthe," I replied, and she tested my name on her tongue, curling it. It sounded funny, and I smiled, and Hannah giggled. When our eyes met, there was friendliness there.

Later I told Frederick about our meeting.

"She must be the one," he said.

"What one?"

"The woman whose husband was shot, by that man, John Hamilton. That would explain why she is alone."

Frederick recounted the news heard from passengers travelling on sternwheelers and barges, collecting produce and lumber, dispersing supplies and gossip. This is what I came to understand:

John Hamilton had been clearing trees on the land he

had purchased honestly and to which he believed he had a right, having paid cash for it. He had built a small cabin, and he was pulling the stumps of the trees he had cleared using his shovel as a lever. Like so many, he was lured by promise of rich soil on which a man could build a small empire, take a wife, raise children. He was alone, without wife or rich soil, instead faced with a quarter section of uncleared land and few provisions to see him through.

When the Indian approached, he spoke to the white man with English words plucked from a small vocabulary, but the meaning nevertheless plain: this is our land, this is where we hunt. You must leave. The settler said he would not, that he had bought the land fair and square and that he aimed to stay. The Indian went away.

But Hamilton was nervous about the exchange with the Indian, so he took his rifle when he worked, and for several days he was undisturbed as he moved rocks and stumps. I imagine him sweating, alone, wondering what had possessed him to leave his old life and come to this place, looking up for the hundredth time at a sound in the forest around him, expecting the shadow of the Indian to fall across him.

When the Indian returned he was with his wife, the two of them taking a detour from their path to see if the white man was still there. He had told his wife about the earlier meeting, and she followed reluctantly as they descended the hillside. On her back she carried the one rifle they owned.

Nothing was said. No words were exchanged. As the Indian man stepped from the trees, the white man looked up from where he worked to loosen a stump. Perhaps he thought that his eyes deceived him as they had so many times before, when, in his imagination, a rustle became a savage with murderous intent. He reached for his gun, and, leaning against the stump, raised it. He could see two figures approaching rapidly, saw a swift movement, took aim.

As the Indian reached for the rifle strapped to his wife's back, she turned, removing the gun from his reach, unwilling to allow this violence. Perhaps she had witnessed these altercations before, knew no good of it ever came for her people.

The force of the bullet knocked the Indian backwards, shattering his chest; for all the white man's fumbling attempts at homesteading, he was a good shot. The Indian's wife fell to the ground beside him, crying out.

Justine told me this later, in words and gestures. What John Hamilton said in court was that he and the Indian fired together, but the white man's aim was better. Although many would say that my allegiance should be to my own race, I am sympathetic to Justine's story. She has made me understand that for this time of mourning she must live apart from her people. It's the Indian way, she tells me. And I have come to understand that she is young and terribly lonely in her solitude, and so seeks my company, perhaps despite herself. And we have something in common, we have found, and that is in the birth of babies.

Frieda

The pains have softened, and my early panic subsides. I muster my strength, reminding myself that women in our village in Manitoba kept working in their early labours, because labours can be slow at first. Because it is an easy chore, I resolve to collect the eggs from the chicken coop attached to our house. The pains are just a tightening, now, and I must stop for a moment, but only that.

As I leave my front steps I look carefully for the bear, but there is no sign of her today. But I have watched her from a distance, a female. She's not like the black bears we see so often, but a grizzly, and yet I don't feel afraid of her, only for her, because George would shoot her if he saw her. The dawn air is full of the conversational call of crows.

When I enter the yard, the chickens, my beauties, all run to me. They are all colours, and they have become my friends. Strutting in the background is the wild turkey that appeared one day in our yard. He is so comical! He thinks he is a chicken, and has become a joke among the village: "they are raising wild animals at the Hartmann place," they say. He is a sight, to be sure, but George says he will make a good Harvest dinner, and so we keep him, feed him, watch him grow fat. Every day George looks at him with the chopping block in mind.

The speckled eggs are warm from where they have nestled beneath the chicken. I hold the warm egg in my hand, life inside, and as I do another tightening, another pain, comes and I think I should finish up, go inside, rest. But for now I lean against the laying shelf, and think about life, and death.

Two months ago we all gathered on the flat we have set aside for a cemetery and said a prayer for the young man who perished when an accident on his trapline took his life. It was Jack Armstrong who found him. Out hunting himself, he followed a smell, thinking: carrion.

He was careful, half hoping to shoot a predator at the kill, a cougar, maybe, or a bear. Instead he found his way to the cabin of Gus Sanders. He would not speak of what he found in the cabin, but spoke of evidence of a large animal about, a grizzly. He buried Gus there, and then burned the cabin to the ground.

Gus Sanders was a nice man, quiet. Polite. I think about the jam I brought him, to thank him for the rabbits he gave us, and to say something else, an apology, because of what happened when George caught him watching me in the pond. I told Birthe about it later, George snorting and stomping like an old bull, eyes bulging. He looked so funny, but of course I didn't laugh at the time.

Later, we heard the news that travelled on the steamer about the explosion at the powder house at the Centre Star in Rossland. We have not seen Mr. Sander's partner, the Frenchman who was called Frenchie, but Jack thinks he was working at that mine. So, two sad things, close together, and one joyous one that just now has me more frightened than excited, for the pains are coming faster and I think that this gathering of eggs was a foolish idea. But here comes Birthe and with her the Indian woman, they are coming up the path, George trailing, and Birthe is scolding me, her voice falling like cool rain.

Justine

Raspberry tea, when labour begins, helps to open the woman so the baby can be born more easily. The white woman, Birthe, has her own name for it, and tells me, waving her hands and speaking slowly in English, that her grandmother picked it in her land, too. After the birth, yarrow tea is restful, restores strength, and helps to heal.

I set about making tea in the kitchen of Frieda, Birthe's friend. I do this for Birthe, who is my friend, and who wants me here. The husband does not want me here, I can see it in his eyes, but he does not want to anger Birthe. All this I can see without language. In the next room this man walks back and forth, back and forth, his boots hard on the wooden floors. Birth is women's time, soft floors of pine boughs and soft voices in our women's hut, the quiet gathering of strength. This is not right.

This Frieda does not want me here, either, but Birthe has asked me to stay, and now I hear her talking to her friend in a low voice, explaining. To help in childbirth is hard, it is better with another woman. But I am not comfortable here, I want to leave, this is not my place, and I am afraid of this white man with his hard boots. Now Birthe sits with her, listens to her belly, tells her: things will be fine. And I stand there, my hand on the kettle, with one foot wanting to stay, the other to run.

Frieda

There is a time when the pains subside. Birthe and the Indian leave me for a time to boil water, make tea, murmur softly in the kitchen, and I hear my George in the shed on the other side of our wall, moving about. I can feel his anger: George does not like for things to be out of his hands.

I close my eyes and think of my own mother. Eleven children, three born in Russia, and all lived except for the twins, who were born after the ship to Canada, and who died when they were still babies, and my sister, Gertrude: Gerdi. The twins, she lost them in Ontario, before the family moved to Manitoba. She was new, she spoke no English, and she was very weak.

Gerdi had just turned thirteen when she died of brain fever. She was oldest, and she looked after all of us, she was like a mother herself. Before she slipped into the long sleep before her last breath, she prayed to God to look after us all, and God did; we all survived. We had nothing to bury her in, so my mother cut up the wedding dress she had brought with her and made her a new dress. As I think of this now, I begin to cry. I miss my mother, who is now also with God. Birthe hears me crying, comes to hold my hand, to soothe my brow.

I hear the Indian woman in my kitchen, adding wood to the stove, saying something to herself in her own language. She is so strange, and I whisper to Birthe, "make her leave," but Birthe tells me in Plattdeutsche that she is her friend, that she has nobody, that she will make her go if I say she must, but that she knows many things. I see that Birthe wants her here, and Birthe is my friend, so I nod my head. Outside, George makes enough noise for a herd of cows. He wants me to know he is there, but he doesn't know what to do, and I don't know what to tell him. Each time I think of something I must say, a pain comes and takes my words away.

Justine

I have tea to soothe, roots for pain, nettles for bleeding. I carry the medicines of my people with me, for a woman needs a place, and that place with my own people is being one who helps women have their babies.

In our tradition young people, before girls become women, boys become men, go into the forest for a few days to find their spirit guides. For a woman to be a healer, a strong spirit guide is needed. After some days the spirit guide makes itself known, and this guide you hold close to you as you go about your life. It is not something shared. So I will not tell you about myself, but I will tell a story about another girl who went to find her spirit guide.

This girl was the only child of her father, for her mother had died giving birth to her brother, who also died. She was only young at the time of her brother's birth, and yet she can remember the long night and day and night that followed, and the moans of her mother, and the women who came and went from the reed-woven shelter. She can remember curling up by her mother's hot side, then being drawn away, cuddled by an aunt, spoken softly to.

Her father loved her, and wanted her to be strong. But as she grew towards womanhood, it was the women who took her aside and explained that now was the time to go and find her spirit guide. They wished her a strong guide, and the gift of healing.

She had been in the forest, alone, for four days when her spirit guide appeared. She had fasted and she felt light, as if she might float up off the mountain and over the valley, where she might wave to her father from the sky. So when she heard a noise, a panting, she felt so light as to feel no fear, and stood to look for the source of the noise, confident that she could float away if needed, out of reach of any danger.

It was a she-bear that came to her, with light fur and a glinting eye and it looked at her while she felt a rock of fear lodge in her throat. The sun shining behind the bear formed a halo, and the bear began to sing. The girl was afraid, but did not run away, and in a moment the bear turned and left, but the song remained in the ears of the girl as she descended the mountain.

Upon her return, the other women dressed the girl in fir boughs and a mountain goat's–wool blanket, and the camp celebrated the new woman among them. They could see that she held in her eyes the knowledge of her spirit guide, and her aunts began to teach her the ways of women and childbirth, the plants to use, the things that may, and may not, be done. And as she learned she carried the strength of the she-bear.

These white settlers are very strange. They don't understand the forest, and they want to make everything flat. They cut the trees, and now the places where the food plants grew are gone. Sometimes, it means killing whatever gets in their way, whether an animal or a tree or a husband. I do not understand why the spirits do not kill them for these things that they do.

I am almost at the end of my period of mourning. It has been a lonely time, with traditions that must be followed: I may not gather food at this time, and so my people give me food to eat. I am accepted at the fire but not welcomed, because I bring the scent of death with me. Soon, I will be released from this. When the leaves fall I will travel south with my village, and leave the scent of death behind me. But now I wander the forest, listening for the rush of wings, or a movement in the undergrowth; a flash of fur, a whisper: we are here. We are still here.

Birthe

Sometimes a labour will start this way. Strong, like that baby just can't wait to come out, then it wants to take a little rest, think about it all for a while. So Justine and Frieda and me, we sit in Frieda's kitchen and drink tea. Justine and I have learned to use our hands to tell stories. Justine is quiet at first, shy around Frieda, but after a while she responds to the gestures I make. We are familiar with this, but Frieda so often looks confused, she raises her eyebrows right up into her hair and this sets me and Justine, together, laughing. I have not seen Justine so light before. Usually, she carries with her a heaviness, and I think it is because she is alone, she is grieving for her husband, who died almost one year ago.

My own husband has gone on the steamer down the lake to get us a cow like the Hartmanns have bought, and will be gone two days yet. I am lonely with just the children. Stay, I told Justine, although Frederick would not approve. She would not stay in the house, but must have stayed nearby because when George Hartmann came to get me a little before dawn she was there, and when I beckoned she followed with her satchel. George looked at her.

"We only need you, Birthe," he hissed, his mustache trembling, eyes narrow. Behind me I could sense Justine standing still the way she does, watching. I have never liked George Hartmann, but I love Frieda like a sister, and I want the best for her.

"I need her," I told him, looking back at Justine, whose face remained expressionless. I remember George as a boy; I am a few years older. His nose was always running. We stared at each other, and then he strode on ahead.

"Come," I said to Justine. "Please." She nodded once, her eyes following George's back as he strode up the hill.

I told my oldest, Frederick, to wake the other children and make the oatmeal, and to send Horst and Jacob to collect the eggs. I told him to take the younger ones to Anna's, that I may be gone the whole day, maybe longer.

Now, in Frieda's kitchen, we talk a little about the two recent deaths, Gus Sanders and the Frenchman, but Frieda doesn't want to talk about death, and of course, it is bad luck to talk about such things at the birth of a child. So we talk about other things. I want to tell her about my own baby inside, but I think, I will wait, it is early to tell, and bad luck to tell if anything goes wrong with this birth. Justine knows, I think.

"What will you call the baby?" I ask, instead.

"Oh! George if it is a boy," says Frieda. "George Heinrich Hartmann." She says it proudly, head up, thrusts her chest out like a proud father. Then she makes a face, laughs.

"I am very happy for George to have a son, and of course he is so happy about the baby. And a boy, first, would be good. But a girl, a girl...I have a special name for a girl, but it's a secret."

"A secret!" I put my hand over my mouth, my ears, my eyes, an exaggerated gesture, to make Justine understand. But Frieda has stopped talking now, and takes several shallow, rapid breaths, followed by a deep sigh. Her forehead creases, drawing freckles together, and then relaxes a little.

"I think I would like to lie down," she says, and I settle her into the bed. Justine hangs back, unsure, and I beckon her closer but she stays in the doorway. This is not her place, she wants to flee, but she may be needed and she will not abandon a woman in childbirth, this I can tell. She makes me feel less alone in this. I have helped at many births, but always I was with an older woman, my teacher. Every child is a blessing from God, my mother told me. I must put my faith in God and as God's servant, put my whole heart into my hands as they do His service. Two hearts, four hands: with Justine, I am stronger, and I believe she is God's servant, too, whatever she believes herself.

This will be the first child born in our new home.

After a while I coax Justine into the room, and there is not so much difference between Justine and me as we listen at the belly, rub here, touch there, give sips of water, make soft sounds. It doesn't matter what we say. I can see Frieda relax between pains, almost asleep for a small moment, and that is how it should be. A woman should rest completely so she has strength when she needs it.

George moves about the cowshed, which, like our traditional homes on the prairie, is attached to the house. The cow is tethered in the shade, and now George is sharpening a blade on the stone in the barn. I know this rasp, rasp sound, and sometimes the scream of the blade makes Frieda jump, and I don't need to see him to picture in my mind George bent intently over his work to the exclusion of the activities in his home. But he is not thinking, really, of the blade or the stone.

I rise, rest my hand on Frieda's shoulder, say: "I will be right back." But when I step into the doorway of the barn to speak with George, he is standing, hands at his sides, not moving. He stares at me, searching for words.

"Why are you here?" He shouts at me. "Why are you not in there with my wife?" His fists are clenched, and the veins stand up in his neck, twitching. "She should not have her hands on my Frieda," he spits, his voice a little lower, but I know they can hear him through the wall. I can feel my hands tremble at my sides, my heart in my throat.

From inside, a low, long moan. His eyes widen, grow wild, and I see for a moment the boy in the man. Whatever I had thought to say is gone. I touch his sleeve.

"This is women's work, George," I say gently.

He strides away without speaking, almost running, and I watch him disappear into the woods. A birth is a confusing thing for a man I think as I turn to hurry back to Frieda's side. He will come around, soon enough, because the first baby changes everything.

And then suddenly everything does change, because here is Jacob, running up the path. "Horst! It is Horst! Come quickly!" he cries, panting in the doorway, and although he can barely get the words out, I understand. Horst wants to be a big boy, he took the axe to chop the wood, like his papa, his older brothers, and there has been an accident, blood, I don't know how bad.

I turn to run, then stop mid-stride and run back into the house, where I take Frieda's hand while Jacob stands in the doorway, big, sobbing gasps coming from him. I am there only for a moment. "There is time, Frieda," I say. "I will be back, you are not ready yet, don't worry. Justine is here."

Frieda

She is gone, and I am left with the Indian, her brown hands on my body, and George, George is nowhere and I want my husband, and my friend. I look at this woman and her teeth are not good and her eyes are black as night and then she smiles and there are crinkles at the corners. I am waiting for the next pain, and my thoughts are everywhere. I can hear a crow outside my window, making those noises that they do, they sound like they are talking. I can smell the breath of the woman beside me, and it smells musty and sweet, and she is holding a cup of warm tea and it is bitter but the warmth feels good and the bird flies away and then there is another pain and she is talking, talking in her language, and as the pain subsides I find I am glad that she is here with me.

Justine

For a time there is just the woman Frieda and me, and she pants and rests and I stroke her belly and say the words we use when a woman is in labour. Birthe has run out the door, pulled by her boy, there is an accident. I didn't understand the words. I think of my spirit guide and ask for the strength of the bear for this woman. Strength, and trust.

The baby begins to come very fast, and the white woman is working very hard. She is moaning, deep moans that come up from her belly, like an animal. This would be a shameful thing for our people, and I draw back. I hear her husband come back once, walk back and forth, back and forth on the porch. A cry comes from Frieda as a new pain takes her, and I hear her husband's footfall stop. Frieda looks at the door, and I can tell she wants him, doesn't want him, doesn't know. Then the steps are back again, on the porch, and a loud thump, like a fist hitting a wall. Frieda jumps slightly, but is again taken by the force inside her, and I think he will go away, will not come closer. Frieda looks at me, lost in herself, sees me and doesn't see me. I can tell she is ready to push the baby out, and I tell her to push hard, and now there is no difference in language, she knows what I am saying.

Then the husband is in the doorway, a presence big as a grizzly. But I have the strength of a grizzly, and I look at him with that strength and tell him to go away in my language. We stare at one another, there is hate between us, and I tell him again, my words coming strong. Then there is a lunge, the rushing of predator at prey, and I raise my arms to ward off the blow I know is coming.

From the white woman on the bed, a cry that comes from deeper place than either of us has known. And as the white woman pushes against the force that seizes her, there is Birthe at the door, rushing to crouch beside me at the foot of the bed. There is blood on her dress, but she is saying something over and over and we are both there as the blue head crowns.

Birthe

As I run towards the house, I can hear the cries of childbirth. In the doorway is George, an animal presence tense in fury, but the moment is bigger than the confusion and anger of this man, the husband of my friend, and I push him aside. I hear him growl, like an animal of some kind, but he does not move.

Later I will explain about the axe, and Horst's fingers, and how I didn't know how bad, and that Justine knows so much, that I knew Frieda would be fine. But now I am here, by the bed, and I'm saying "it's all right, it's all right," and I don't know if I mean Horst or Frieda. And the head is there and Justine looks at me, and I let her take the baby's head and gently ease the shoulder's sideways, and there is the wide-eyed pant of Frieda and there is George again, in the doorway, a look on his face like none I have ever seen.

I look at Justine and she does not even see him, one hand on Frieda's swollen, moving, heaving stomach, the other cupped to catch the blue, blue baby that is coming now, and all of the anger and fear leaves the room on the wings of angels at the miracle of this moment.

Frieda

It is wave after wave and I am swimming against them, and sometimes they pull me under. I am a small girl and I am at the river, catching minnows, my feet slipping on the clay. My mother on the bank, grabs my hand with hers but her palm is wet, she has been washing, and mine is wet and slippery and there is a moment when our palms slide past one another like swimming fish and I can hear her call out but then I am under. There is water in my ears, my nose, my hair is all around me like a swaying weed and my toes find ground, slip, catch again on a rock and slip again and I am under, moving, a slave to this river that pulls and pulls and pulls.

I am drowning, and I want the sky and the air and this is enough, if this is a dream I must wake up now. Now. My skin is somebody else's, and if I could I would shed it like a snake and swim away, start again.

And then I come up against something hard, and I push against this thing and suddenly it gives, and I am laughing and sobbing and Birthe is holding up a blue and pink fish for me to see, Justine wiping my face and saying "girl, girl." And she is not talking about the girl in the river, she is talking about the girl in my arms, and there is a fish mouth at my breast and we are all wet and slimy and full of tears and laughter.

"Ursula," I say.

"Ursula," says George, now gentle at the bedside, "is a fine German name."

He is thinking about tradition, and our past, and the country of our parents and their parents. But I am thinking about the first child to be born in Bear Creek, our home, our *Heimat*. This, I also wish to honour.

"Ursula."

Justine and Birthe make tea in the kitchen, this one for bleeding and for strength in the womb, Birthe says. Mostly, they are giving George some time alone with me, and he is crying, my George.

"Ursula. Frieda. Ursula." He says it again and again, a whisper. He is another man, one I have not seen. So many men today in this one man, my husband. He looks at Birthe, then, and I see the thanks in his eyes like a prayer. And then he turns his gaze on Justine, and there is a look I cannot read. When she nods to him, an understanding passes between them, and this is plain in the room. I see this all from my bed, and yet what I see most clearly is Ursula, George, my family. It is later I will remember this, talking quietly with Birthe while her children play and I nurse my baby.

"Ursula," said George, again.

I had thought about her name for a long time, through the winter and into the spring, and by the time the first ferns were poking up I knew I would name my daughter after our home, after Bear Creek.

Birthe has wrapped the afterbirth to bury it, deep enough so the animals will not smell it. I wonder what Justine would do with such a thing, what happens in her village, with her people, but we do not have a language between us for me to ask.

George will kill the turkey and take it to Birthe, he tells me, and this pleases me. Birthe and Frederick have such a big family, and the turkey will be a wonderful dinner. It is a proper way to say thank you, to give something you, yourself, covet. And with little Horst having lost the end joint of his finger, a feast is a good distraction.

But George does not know how to thank Justine, or what to say. Handing over the heavy, dead bird, he asks Birthe where to find her, and Birthe tells him what she thinks. But George cannot find her; the camp is empty. I imagine George standing by the shore for a long time, still, like a statue, the way he can sometimes be, staring at the circle of cooking stones, the empty clearing. He is hearing the water as it kisses the shoreline, the wind in the trees around him.

At home I lift my baby, hold her against my breast and press my lips to her hair, gently kiss the spot that pulses.

1915

The hole in the rock was the size of a ten-year-old's fist, several inches deep, and cold inside, as if it belonged to some other place or time. When Ursula withdrew her hand it held an arrowhead, carved in stone. She felt the chiselled black surface, and then looked around quickly. Below the bluff on which she stood the lake sparkled in the late May sunshine; around her, the pines swayed like drunken dancers, creaking. There was no one.

There were no pockets in the dress she was wearing, so she bent down and tucked her prize into the hole in her stocking, feeling the cool descent of the arrowhead as it slipped down and settled above the bone in her ankle. When she returned home, she would put it in the wooden tea box she kept under her bed with the other things she found in the rock: an osprey feather; a rusted iron key; a 1905 penny—the year she was born!—with King Edward on the back. A button the colour of goat's milk.

When she came down the path she saw Jake Schroeder, fishing rod in hand, walking home. A Saturday, his chores done, he had a little free time.

"I've got a secret," she said to him as she drew up alongside, stretching her own stride to match the older boy's. He looked down at the blonde braids, thinking again that Ursula Hartmann was sometimes more like a sister than his own, thinking, also: If only we were the same age. What a girl she'll be when she grows up! He waited for her to go on, smiling.

"Guess where it is," she said.

"At your house?"

"Hmmmph."

"In your head?"

She shook it.

"In your ear?"

"Ja-*kob*!"

"Okay, where?"

"It's in my stocking," she said, laughing.

"So, what is it?"

"You have to guess." They were rounding the bend in the dirt track, approaching the point at which the road forked, the Hartmann house on the east side of the dock on the waterfront, the Schroeder house on the west. The road bisected the two halves of the small community of Bear Creek, British Columbia.

"Is it bigger than my head? Or smaller than my hand?"

Ursula held up her thumb and index finger an inch apart.

"Only that big?" said Jake. He thought for a moment. "I had an arrowhead about that size once. I found it on the beach, in one of those dips where the sand washes away from around the pilings at the dock."

"What colour was it?" asked Ursula, eyes narrowing.

"It was— reddish, like clay." They had stopped at the fork. Jake rested the end of the fishing rod on the ground like a walking stick, waiting. Ursula smiled a small, smug smile, feeling the presence of the arrowhead in her stocking.

"Didn't you get any fish?" She pointed to the fishing rod.

"Nope. I was over at Herb's. He glued this for me, clamped it overnight." He showed her the crack in the wooden reel, the seam hardly visible.

Herb Crane and his parents were new to Bear Creek, the family having bought the Martens' orchard. Among the first non-Mennonites to settle in the community, the Cranes were an amiable, capable family. Jake, drawn to their easygoing worldliness, found himself spending more and more time in their company. At seventeen years old, Herb was good at so many things—skills different than those the Schroeder boys were expected to learn. Exotic. Jake ran his thumb over the curve of the reel, feeling for the crack.

"Look," Ursula was saying now, reaching into the hole in her stocking and snaking her hand down to retrieve the arrowhead.

"You're making that hole bigger. Well." Jake turned the arrowhead over in his hand. "This is a fine one. Where did you get it?"

"Nowhere," said Ursula. Jake raised his eyebrows under his fringe of hair and dropped the arrowhead back into her upturned palm. She closed her fingers around it and with a wave ran down the track towards her own kitchen and the dinner that was waiting.

At Jake's house, Birthe Schroeder was putting borscht on the table. The big slabs of buttered bread were already placed and Hannah was setting out spoons.

"Call Papa, would you, Jake?" She said. "And Fred and Horst, they're out back."

As Jake turned to call his brothers and father, Albert, the youngest, crashed into the room the way he always did, kicking off his boots in his hurry to get to the table. In this family, a call to dinner was always answered promptly.

As they ate, Jake wondered how to introduce the subject most on his mind. He didn't need to.

"I hear there is to be a number of boys going to enlist next week," said Frederick Schroeder. "Not the Mennonite boys, of course."

"Herb's joining up," said Jake, not looking up from his bowl. He waited a heartbeat. Two. Three.

"He's not old enough," Birthe said.

"He's eighteen this month, Ma. He's going to go to Revelstoke to enlist. They're putting together a Kootenay Battalion. There's money to be earned." He looked from his mother to his father and back again. "He's going to see the world."

Frederick Schroeder was looking at his son; Birthe looked at Frederick. The Schroeder siblings were watching their father's face as Jake went on.

"Pete and Hubert are going. And Wally. They're all going together, on the Saturday boat. If they enlist together they'll keep them together. Wally's cousin down in Nelson said recruitment officers came to the high school, said every boy there is enlisting or is going to enlist as soon as he turns eighteen."

Jake stopped suddenly, drawn to the pull of his father's gaze. Nobody spoke. His older brothers, Fred and Horst, looked at one another, spoons halted midway from bowl to mouth. Jake looked down.

"We are not to judge the conscience of another. But we came to this country to serve God and to live by our convictions as Mennonites. We will not harm another nor aid in the act of war. Don't you forget that, Jakob."

"They fight so that we may live by our convictions." Jake spoke to the table, softly.

"What did you say?" The silence around the table was palpable.

"Why should *they* fight to protect *our* freedoms?" his voice rose slightly, but the beating of his own heart, he thought, must surely be louder.

"Jakob," said his mother.

"He's going to see the world, Mama."

"Tonight," said his father, "when we read from the Bible, you will hear the word of God."

"But—"

"Jakob." His father's voice, a knife edge in the room. Then: "Any son of mine who would enlist will be a son of mine no more."

Jake held his father's gaze until his own faltered, and he looked away.

Herb Crane was chopping wood when Jake arrived, his own chores done for now. There were always more. Always more wood to chop, fences to mend, cows to milk, trees to pick, fruit to pack, branches to prune.

"Phew. Time for a break," said Herb, swinging the axe heavily into the block.

They sat on the porch step. "Not much longer," he said conversationally, and yet his words were weighted with import. Jake could feel the fire behind them, this ember of possibility and adventure he was denied.

"You're catching the Saturday boat?"

"Uh huh. Mum's still crying about it, but heck, even Dad would go if he could. Times are so tight, they'll be glad for the pay I send home. And anyway Billy's still home, so it's not like I'm leaving them all alone." Herb's words hung in the air. Jake could feel his excitement like a live thing.

"Come with me, Jake," he said. "We can train together.

Come on, they won't even ask how old you are and anyway you're eighteen in July. And you know what? You
even look older than me."

Jake's long legs were stretched in front of him. He felt
old enough. I'm ready, he thought. If Herb goes without
me, when will I get another chance? To Herb he said, "I
tried to talk about it at dinner today. Now it's going to be
the centrepiece of tonight's Bible reading."

Herb looked at his friend sympathetically, clucking his
tongue. "You know what they're saying about conscientious objectors. How can you have everyone looking at
you like that? They'll think you're a German sympathiz-
er, especially with your name."

Jake had heard it: Jerry-lover. Worse. "Mennonites
don't fight," he said. "It's— it's hard to explain. But that's
why my grandparents came to Canada, so we could follow our beliefs." He felt like his father talking. "Fred and
Horst won't go. They'll stay on the orchard. That's what's
expected. There's some from our church joined
Alternative Service, like my cousin Cornelius in Altona.
Ma and Pa wouldn't even talk about it when they got the
letter, but I read it once they'd gone to bed. His parents,
my aunt and uncle, they wouldn't speak to him at all
when they found out."

"What's Alternative Service?"

"Medical, that sort of thing. Like stretcher-bearers. Or
drivers. Things that don't involve combat." Jake had only
the barest idea of what Alternative Service was, especially
with none of the parents willing to discuss anything to do
with the war. In a town of less than a hundred people,
with sternwheelers delivering news and mail twice a
week, it was hard to get any information at all. "Ma and
Pa don't believe in anything that helps the war go on."

"But then who's going to fight the Jerries? What if the enemy wins?"

Jake knew what his parents would say, what his community believed, but these things seemed weak against the patriotic enthusiasm of his friend.

"Well, lots of farmers don't go," offered Herb. "'Course, there's three other boys at your house."

"But what if I *want* to go?" Jake spurted the words he'd been wanting to say for weeks.

Herb looked up, a new spark in his eye. "Will you? What would happen?"

"I don't know. It would break Ma's heart, I guess." But in his mind's eye the uniform looked good on him. As if reading his thoughts, Herb punched him in the shoulder, saying: "You know what they say about girls when they see a man in uniform."

Jake blushed.

In the weeks Jake had been leaving presents for Ursula Hartmann to find, something that started on a whim but had become a habit, there had never before been anything left in return. He unfolded the lined schoolbook paper and read:

> *The arrowhead was very nice. And the button.*
> *Who are you?*
> > *Cordialy,*
> > *Ursula Hartmann*

Jake smiled at the word *cordialy*. He had not seen the word spelled out before, thought there may be a letter missing, and in any case could not imagine where Ursula could have heard such a formal word, and yet it was just like her, somehow. He had no pencil with him and could not have mustered a reply without a little thought, so he tucked the paper in his pocket and extracted the piece of blue glass he had found at the site of the old cabin, the one Jack Armstrong burned down after he found its owner, a trapper, dead. It was a bit of a legend, now. Jake sometimes liked to poke around there, and had once found a perfectly good axe head that needed only some sharpening and a new handle. He held the glass to his eye and imagined Ursula looking at a world turned blue. As he put the glass in the rock, he felt something else, and laughed. *I am your secret admirer* he wrote on the back of her note with the stub of pencil she had left for him. Then he wrapped the paper around the glass and tucked it in the hole with the pencil. He was late for supper, and Bible reading.

When Ursula opened the paper she turned it over twice, and then traced her finger over the round, strong letters. She was a good reader and filed all the words she read into boxes in her mind, waiting for the right sentence. "Admirer," she said out loud as she looked through the blue glass at the lake. It looked like a fairy tale, swathed in cobalt hues.

She caught up to Jake after Sunday service.

"I have an admirer," she told him.

"Do you now? And who might that be?"

"I have a *secret* admirer," she said.

"So it's a secret, then?"

"Yes. You won't tell?"

"'Course not. That's what a secret is." He grinned at her. "Any secret of yours is a secret of mine, little buddy. That's what friends do."

When Frieda Hartmann called her daughter in from the road, she thought, not for the first time, how much the two looked like brother and sister. It's not that they look alike, she thought. But there's something there. And she wished, not for the first time, that there had been a brother or sister for Ursula, for an only child is a lonely thing to be.

Jake didn't mention Herb's plans or anything else about the war in Europe for the next few days. He helped Hannah and Albert with their schoolwork and Fred and Horst with the orchard. He felt his parents watching him.

On Tuesday when he went to get the mail there were two new postings up at the post office. The first announced that the Kootenay 54th Battalion had been authorized by the Militia Department in Ottawa on the first of May, 1915. Men in good health, ages eighteen to forty-five and living in the Arrow Lakes region were encouraged to enlist at the Revelstoke Legion. *Your King and Country Need You*, it said.

Frank Preville, who had just taken over as postmaster, smiled at the middle Schroeder boy. "Exciting times," he said. "'Course, the war's almost over. They'll be beaten back before the year's out. Still, if I was young enough I'd sure be there."

It was the second poster that held Jake spellbound. A soldier rode his motorcycle over the top of a rise, its front wheel in the air. The image was mirrored by the knight in armour behind, his rearing horse aligned with the motorcycle, as if the soldier of today was watched by the courageous warrior of the past, bathed in the light of a brave new dawn. A line of soldiers marched proudly in the background. *Canada's Army Needs Men Like You*, it said.

Like me, thought Jake.

That night Jake lay in bed, his little brother breathing softly beside him. He thought about the soldier on the motorcycle, the pride and courage in that image. He drew the blanket up around Albert's sleeping form and lay back, looking at the rough wood of the attic ceiling in the darkness. He could sense around him the dreams of his parents, his brothers and sister. He could feel the house breathe with their presence. He imagined the wide world beyond: how very big it was, his own world so small. Here was family; it was everything, and it wasn't enough.

After school on Wednesday Ursula changed her clothes and ran down to the wharf. She remembered what Jake had said about finding arrowheads in the hollows by the pilings on the beach, and she thought perhaps she could find one of her own to leave in the hole in the rock for her secret admirer. As she poked about in the shadow of the dock she thought about the Indians who had once lived there. She imagined she was an Indian girl, her canoe close by. She would paddle down the lake, exploring new shores and different mountains.

Footsteps on the wharf above her made her draw farther into the shadows for no particular reason except that you never could tell what people might talk about when they thought no one was listening. The May sun warmed the sand, but the shadow under the wharf was cool. She was going to slip away—her mother would be wondering where she was—when Jake's voice stopped her.

"I saw that poster up at the store," Jake said. His voice

seemed lower somehow, and full of purpose. "I'm not going to be a C.O."

"What will your folks say?" Herb Crane's voice.

"Plenty, I guess, but I'll be gone. I'll write from Revelstoke. Herb, this is my chance."

There was a short silence, and then what could only be the sound of a slap on the back.

"I'm glad, buddy. I'm really glad. It's going to be swell, you and me."

Ursula tried to listen to the conversation that followed, but the voices were often lost in the lap of water. She heard the word *France*, and *training*. The voices rose again as the two walked back towards the shore, their footfalls directly above Ursula where she crouched.

"I'm not going to spend my life pruning trees and milking cows," Jake was saying.

"Damn straight," said Herb, and he sounded older, like a grown man.

By the time they had left the wharf Ursula was no longer interested in finding an arrowhead for her secret admirer. She ran home and found her mother in the kitchen.

"What's a See Oh?" she asked, breathless.

"Who have you been talking to?" Frieda asked her daughter, alarmed at her wet shoes and flushed cheeks. "Where have you been?"

"Nobody. Nowhere. But what is it?"

"A conscientious objector is somebody who will not fight in a war because he knows it is wrong to harm another person," Frieda said, stroking her daughter's hair. "Mennonites believe it is not for us to fight because we believe in a peaceful way of life."

"But what if someone is fighting us?"

"It is not for us to fight back. That is not what the Bible teaches us."

"What if I had a brother and he wanted to fight in the war?" She raised her soft grey eyes to her mother's blue ones.

"You do not have a brother, my little bear. But if you did, he would stay here to look after you, because that would be the right thing to do."

There was nothing in the rock on Wednesday evening when she reached the bluff as the afternoon light was fading. Thinking that maybe her secret admirer was hiding in the woods, she shouted: "Come out!" but only the trees creaked in response. After a while she whispered, pleading: "Please come out."

Back at home Ursula opened the kitchen door. The conversation between her mother and father, soft tones in the sitting room, fell silent. Her father called her over, the edge behind his words causing her step to falter as she crossed the floor.

George Hartmann placed his big hands on his daughter's shoulders. "Have you been talking to Jakob Schroeder? What has he told you?"

"About what, Papa?"

"If Jakob is thinking of joining up, it is not right to keep it a secret."

Ursula didn't know exactly what Jake's secret might be, but she thought that if he had one, it should be his to keep. After all, he kept hers. That's what friends do. But Papa's question confused her, and the tone of her father's voice made her lip tremble as she spoke.

"Joining what, Papa?"

"She doesn't know, George," Frieda pleaded, and

George relaxed his grip on the girl's shoulders. He looked away, grunting. He hadn't meant to hold her so firmly, or to scare the girl, but then, Frieda was always getting in the way, her feminine softness taking the edge off the sharpness he so cultivated. He was no match for these two.

"If she knows, she had better tell us," he grunted, rising to go outside.

"Tell what, Mama?" asked Ursula, and her mother smoothed her hair and sighed.

Jake had his cousin Cornie's letter in his pocket Thursday afternoon when he found Horst behind the barn shovelling manure. He could not talk to Fred about his plans; Hannah and Albert were too young. But when Horst, a year younger than Jake, had lost a finger chopping wood, it was Jake who ran with all his might to get his mother from the Hartmann's. It was Jake who helped Horst form his letters in school in spite of the missing digit, and Jake who would not allow the other kids to tease him. Horst smiled as his older brother approached, his smile widening as Jake took up a shovel from where the blade hung suspended between two nails and threw his weight into it. Jake stepped into the ease between them as if into a warm pool of water.

"Thanks," said Horst, grinning. "This'll take half the time, now."

"Do you ever get sick of it?" asked Jake, not looking up.

"Of manure? Well, sure. Of course."

"Don't you ever think of going away, of doing something else?"

"What are you saying?" Horst had paused, leaning on

his shovel, to regard his brother carefully. The ease felt a moment ago was absent.

"I mean, Fred, he'll be here forever. That's what he wants. But what about you? What about me?"

"What *about* you?" Horst looked at his brother, who met his gaze evenly. Neither blinked. Then: "You're joining up." The statement, cold, hung between them.

Neither spoke for a moment. "It's going to kill Mama and Papa," said Horst finally.

"I have to, Horst."

"You're wrong, Jake. It's wrong."

"Please." He meant, please understand. He meant, please tell me you'd go too, if you were old enough. "You can't tell."

"You can't just go. You have to tell them. If you don't, Jake, I will."

"I'm going to tell them," said Jake.

Later, when Jake went up to the bluff to think, he had nothing with him to leave in the rock. Patting his pockets, he found the letter from his cousin and felt alarmed that he had not returned it to its place on the kitchen windowsill. Perhaps his mother would think his father had disposed of it, and his father would think his mother had done the same, feeding the offensive words to the kitchen woodstove. The olive one-cent stamp showed the noble profile of King George V, embraced by the words Canada Postage, maple leaves, and the British crown. *For King and Country*, he thought, and tore the stamp from the corner of the envelope and tucked it in the hole for Ursula to find.

He was sitting, thinking, fifteen minutes later when Ursula came up the path onto the bluff. It was late in the afternoon, the pines casting long shadows across the ground. She had been watching her own shadow grow tall and didn't notice Jake sitting quietly on the top of the rock until she was almost underneath it.

"Want to come up?" he asked her, and she started, and he laughed. Her hands itched to reach into the hole, but she resisted. Her secret.

"Here, give me your hand. I'll pull you." When she did, her hand felt small and warm in Jake's big one. She sat beside him and stretched out her legs, her boots reaching as far as his calves. Fine hairs on his face shone in the yellow light.

"What are you doing here?" She asked.

"Thinkin'."

"Thinking 'bout what?"

"Ursula, do you ever think about how big the world is? I mean beyond Bear Creek or Arrow Lake or British Columbia or even Canada?"

"Sure. We study other countries in school." But when she thought about it, they were just coloured areas on a map, except that some had jungles, and elephants.

"I'd like to see an elephant," she said.

"Me, too."

They were quiet for a while.

"I think there are some people who can live in one place their whole lives, and there are people who have to see the world," he told her. "You know?"

She nodded.

"I think some people can be happy on the farm, and some people have to do something completely different. Like go to different countries and learn new things."

"Like French? Or how to play cricket?" Ursula had read a story in a school reader about an English boy playing cricket.

"Yeah, like that. And other things."

71

As they spoke, Jake bent the letter from his cousin Cornelius into an airplane, and Ursula watched him. The torn corner where the stamp had been removed made one wing tip uneven. "That won't fly," she told him, and he folded it up and put it into his pocket.

"I think somebody who wanted to go away to learn things could always come back," Ursula ventured after a while.

When he had gone she reached into the hole in the rock. She fingered the stamp torn from the corner of the envelope, tracing the arch of the frame around the picture of the king, and smiled.

Friday morning Jake had still not told his parents of his plans. Bible reading the night before had been especially pointed:

> ...and many nations shall come, and say: "Come, let us go up to the mountain of the Lord, to the house of the God of Jacob; that he may teach us his ways and we may walk his paths." For out of Zion shall go forth the law, and the word of the Lord from Jerusalem. He shall judge between many peoples, and shall decide for strong nations afar off; and they shall beat their swords into ploughshares, and their spears into pruning hooks; nation shall not lift up sword against nation, neither shall they learn war anymore...

As their father read, Horst spent the time staring pointedly at his brother. For Jake, the concrete examples of pruning forks and ploughshares only put in mind the very things he so much wished to put behind him. He caught Horst's eye to let him know he would be talking to Mama and Papa after the younger ones had gone to bed. And yet, when the moment came, he could not. He went to bed thinking: if I am too cowardly to tell my parents what I want to do, how can I be a soldier? From his room he heard his parents talking below, in low voices.

"Any son of mine who goes to war will no longer be a son of mine," he heard his father say again. He didn't doubt the sincerity of the words, and he felt himself go cold. Albert rolled over beside him, his breathing ragged in dream. Jake could not hear his mother's reply.

When Ursula picked up the mail for her mother, she saw the recruitment posters on the wall. She liked the rich colours and the knight rearing on the horse behind the soldier on the motorcycle. She thought of the hole in the rock, and how the poster would fit perfectly if it were rolled up tightly, as she turned to ask for the Hartmann mail. Behind the counter, Mr. Preville's back was turned away as he was tried to read through a thin envelope held against the window's light to see who was writing to Muriel Crane all the way from Ontario. When he turned to see Ursula looking at him, he was so startled he almost dropped the letter he was holding. Instead, he fumbled it into the Crane mail slot, his face reddening.

"What do you want?" he barked. Mute against his outburst, she pointed to the poster on the wall. She had not intended to ask for it, and was even more surprised at the postmaster's behaviour than her own.

"Take it, then," he said, making shooing motions with his hands. "Go!"

Ursula was out the door and heading up the path with the poster under her sweater long before Mr. Preville could change his mind. She had completely forgotten to collect the mail. At the rock, when she rolled the poster tightly it fit in the hole just as she'd hoped it would.

Friday evening Jake found his mother in the kitchen. Hannah was at her side peeling potatoes, the long peelings falling into a bowl Jake knew would later make their way to Pansy, this year's pig. It was Hannah's job to tend to the pig, and so Hannah also got to name the pig, much to her father's disapproval lest she become too attached to the animal. A practical girl, she never did, and ate the cured ham with the same enthusiasm as her brothers. Jake looked at Hannah's twin brown braids and felt a sudden attachment of his own for his only sister. He stood looking at them both for a minute, feeling acutely the living, breathing presence of the three of them in the kitchen. Birthe turned and looked at her son with a measured glance, then spoke to her daughter.

"Hannah, that's enough potatoes, I think. Finish that one and then go see to the pig, will you?"

When Hannah had gone with the bang of the door behind her, Birthe sat at the table and faced her son. He remained standing.

"Ma," he said, but she held up her hand. Then she looked at him, taking in this height, the shape of his jaw, the down growing on his upper lip, and the way his chest filled his work shirt before speaking quietly in a tone that did not allow for interruption.

"There is a time in life when a boy must obey the rule of his father. There is a time when a man must honour his faith and his family, and must put first the wishes of those who love him most."

Jake looked away from his mother's gaze, his eyes settling on his hands where they rested on the back of a spindle chair.

"*Honour your father and your mother,*" she quoted, "*that your days may be long in the land which the Lord your God gives you.*"

Jake knew what he had to say, if he was ever to say it at all. He felt himself falter under the pull of family and faith. There were only a few moments before Hannah would be back. "Mama," he began, unsure of the words that would follow. No further words came. He heard the long intake of breath before his mother continued.

"When I was about your age there was a young man I wanted to marry more than anything in the world. My family forbade it." She watched as Jake's eyes found hers again. His mother never spoke of anything before Bear Creek. She rose and turned back to the sink, and there spoke to the cross-stitched prayer that hung above it. "There are times, too, when you must follow your heart."

He stepped forward and she turned to embrace him. When, after several moments, Hannah came back in with the empty bowl, they pulled apart. Hannah, confused by the fog of emotion in the room, stood before her mother, facing Jakob as he moved away. Jake could see tears in his mother's eyes, but she did not cry. Instead, she placed her hands on the shoulders of her daughter and gently drew her close so the two stood as one.

"I'll be back for dinner. I won't be long," said Jake as he turned to go, his own eyes wet.

Although the evening sun still glittered on the lake, the rock was in shadow when Jake approached. The poster, when he unrolled it, gleamed with its own light, the shining knight rising above the brave soldier. He looked up, expecting to see Ursula at the edge of the trees, or behind the rock. How did she know? He turned the poster over. On the back was written, in her precise ten-year-old hand,

> Dear Secret Admirer,
> I hope you will see the world.
>> Cordially yours,
>> Ursula

Jake ran his hand through his hair and wondered what he could possibly leave as a final gift.

The Mennonite people of Bear Creek went about their business at the dock when the *Minto* arrived, acutely aware of the young men leaving the community to enlist with the Canadian military. They did not stay to listen to the boisterous lot on the deck, men who had been picked up at one landing or another, who looked at the lake and mountains and saw, instead, the heady excitement of battle in a strange country. Frederick Schroeder stayed away, having no business with the boat that day. When the whistle blew he was building a rock wall in the back field with his eldest son. His younger children were doing their chores as children should. If he wondered at the whereabouts of his second son, he gave away nothing. Birthe and Hannah were making pies when they heard the whistle. Birthe flinched, and Hannah watched as her mother passed a hand across her brow and returned to the pastry she had rolled on the table, her lips moving in silent prayer.

Horst stood at the landing, hands in pockets, watching while his brother approached Herb Crane, watching as Herb slapped Jakob on the back like a comrade-at-arms. Jake had not yet seen his brother, and Herb could not make his throat effect noise to draw his attention. He watched as Ursula Hartmann rushed forward past the small knot of villagers to thrust a folded piece of paper into Jake's hands.

When finally Horst turned to walk away he was almost at the end of the wharf before Jake's voice reached him.

"Horst! Wait!"

And then they were facing each other, hands on one another's shoulders. Jake looked at his brother, their eyes level. He's as tall as I am, Jake thought.

"Tell him I love him, Horst," he said.

"I'll do no such thing. You tell him yourself."

"I love you too, little brother," but Horst could hear, behind the words, the excitement of the day, of the adventure ahead. He felt angry, betrayed.

He held his lips together tightly against the warning tremble. "See you, then," he said, and walked away. Jake watched, unable to move.

And then Herb was there, hauling Jake and his duffle towards the boat, laughing. The Cranes hugged their son, his mother crying, his father stoic, and then, because there was no-one there to hug Jake, they embraced him, too. Ursula was gone, or at least, Jake couldn't see her. Those gathered at the dock waved and shouted at the young men on the deck who waved and shouted back. Herb, caught in the excitement, grinning like a wild man, punched Jake in the arm playfully and gave him a little cuff across the head.

"What happened to your hair?" he asked, tugging at a piece of Jake's brown forelock, cut near the root and standing on end. "Got too close to the hay scythe?"

But Jake wasn't listening to Herb, or to the shouts around him, or the final whistle of the sternwheeler as she pulled away from the dock. He could see a figure up on the bluff, and as he waved saw the gesture returned in the pale sweep of an arm above a white face. He unfolded the paper he still held in his hand and looked at a soft wisp of hair the colour of the sun.

When the telegram came, Ursula pulled the wooden tea box out from under the bed and lined up its contents on her windowsill: an osprey feather; a rusted iron key; a 1905 penny; an arrowhead; a stamp, torn from an envelope. A button the colour of goat's milk, and, folded into a scrap of paper, a lock of brown hair. When each treasure was placed back in the box and the box returned to its place beneath her bed, Ursula walked up to the bluff.

The hole in the rock was empty, and cold, as if it belonged to another place or time. She knew it would be, but she had to put her hand inside just the same.

1919

Isobel Gray, the young woman, and Ace, Jack Armstrong's new horse, arrived in Bear Creek at the same time. They didn't arrive on the same boat; Ace arrived on a barge, Isobel on the sternwheeler *Minto*. As usual, half the village had turned out to greet the sternwheeler, but most of the attention was now directed at the barge. The big roan, terrified to get on the barge in the first place, was now wholly unwilling to disembark, arching his neck and rolling his eyes. Jack Armstrong spoke quietly to his new acquisition; the barge driver looked on, impatient. A good hard swat to the backside was the way to go, the driver obviously thought; Jack preferred a better first impression of home for the horse.

From the deck of the sternwheeler just pulling in some distance away, Isobel Gray looked down from the passenger deck and watched the tall man speak gently to the red horse, who reared its massive head suddenly, looking sideways at the noisy laughter of small boys for whom this event would be today's highlight.

"Hoo, boy, hoo, take it easy," said Jack. The horse, situated as he was at the head of the barge, required unloading before the crates of store supplies and the big iron stove heading for the Hartmann's kitchen. On the wharf, Frieda and George Hartmann also watched, more interested in the stove than the drama of Jack Armstrong's new horse, but fourteen-year-old Ursula thought she had never seen a more beautiful animal, and told her mother so.

"Yes, he is a beauty," agreed Frieda, "but awfully skittish, isn't he?"

Having disembarked, and enjoying the feel of dry land beneath her feet, Isobel sympathized with the horse. Water travel was foreign to her, and, although she considered herself a relatively fearless young woman, cause for a vague unease. This she attributed to her Prairie upbringing. Her friends had expressed surprise that she would travel all the way from Winnipeg to the wilds of British Columbia to help a sister burdened with twins and unwell since their birth. She was a city girl; what would she be doing, chopping wood, hauling water, milking the cow, butchering the pig? She won't last a week, said her friend Lisbet. Not a week.

"You want to leave all...*this*?" Lisbet had said. They were talking over tea in a makeshift print shop in a downtown basement, sleeves rolled up, piles of leaflets stacked around them. Lisbet's tone was joking, but there was an underlying reproach.

"You know the motto: deeds, not words..." began Isobel, but was interrupted with a hoot of laughter from Maeve, who gestured to the stacks of paper.

"We're doing pretty well with the word part, so far," she said.

"My point is, she's my sister. Even Mrs. McClung preaches the importance of family," said Isobel.

"Our work is in educating the people about the importance of votes for women. Isobel, we're so close!" The small round table shook with Lisbet's words. It was 1919; Canada had survived a world war and now was moving forward. So far, six provinces had given women the right to vote, and the long and frustrating battle continued. Tensions were high. When the tea in their cups had settled, Isobel tried again.

"I won't be gone long. She needs me, 'Bet."

"Think of your father…!" Lisbet said again. She let the sentence hang in the air, making Isobel feel as if her late father, social activist, was standing behind her waiting for the correct response. How *would* her father have felt: about Isobel's work in the movement, about her sister's marriage to a Mennonite homesteader, and about Isobel's choice of one or the other, now, when the momentum was there and the cause so close to success.

"He'd want me there," she said with more conviction than she felt. She had not seen Helen for four years; even when they were young they were not close. "He'd want what Mama would have wanted. I'm all the family she's got, Lisbet."

Within a week Isobel had left the intensity of the Winnipeg suffragette movement to head into the woods to help a sister she scarcely knew anymore, under the imagined gaze of a dead father whose commentary from the grave remained a constant companion.

"Now, Ace, easy Ace, good boy, forward now," said Jack gently, and the horse, calmer, took a step into the sudden hush from the dockside audience. Parents held the shoulders of their children, willing them silent. Then, "Isobel!" called a male voice. A hat waved above the small crowd. Late for the sternwheeler's arrival, Joseph Kroeker wanted to make sure his sister-in-law was not standing there thinking she had not been met. As he shouted, the horse reared above the crowd, knocking Jack against the barge railing with a crack. A bruise the approximate shape of Arrow Lake would bloom there within an hour.

The horse, smelling the scent of earth beyond the crowd of people, gathered his back legs for the spring and bolted from the barge, scattering the onlookers. Isobel paused to watch. All eyes were on Jack, John Fischer, and Fred Neufeld who were tearing up the road after the departing horse, a ragtag bunch of boys and one or two girls of varying ages running after them.

Joseph reached his sister-in-law, confused by the scene but more concerned with what he had to tell her.

"I'm so glad you're here," he said, touching her arm shyly. "She needs you, Isobel. The twins are dead, eleven days, now." And with that he threw himself on his sister-in-law, despite the fact he had only met her once before, and sobbed.

"I must have missed the cable," Isobel murmured, staring past the collar of his dark wool jacket, unsure of where to put her hand. He pulled away, looking down, ashamed of his outburst.

"I'm so sorry, Joseph," she said, but could think of nothing more to say as, busying himself, he turned to gather her luggage from the collection accumulating on the wharf. She pointed mutely at the two leather suit-cases she had brought along, thinking of the unsuitabil-ity of the clothing they contained. The crowd at the wharf had turned their attention to the unloading of the stove and the greeting of other passengers. Those who noticed poor Joseph Kroeker and the stranger in the city clothes—Helen's sister from Winnipeg it must be, they would think—left them in peace.

Bear Creek had been largely spared the Spanish influenza epidemic of the past year, and owed much of this to relative isolation. But the community had not been untouched; some had lost relatives elsewhere, and fear remained high. It was not clear to those in Bear Creek if the death of the twins was the 'flu or a hard birth, a small size, a weak mother and a shaky future. And so well-meaning neighbours had left hot food and pies, but fear of infection framed a distance unusual for a community that prided itself on Christian charity.

The twins had come as a surprise, Joseph explained as he and Isobel walked up the road towards the Kroeker home. Birthe, the midwife, had missed the second heartbeat. They were so small, Joseph told Isobel quietly as they rounded the bend that brought the house into sight. Isobel looked at Joseph properly, then, for the first time, saw the grey circles beneath his eyes, the drawn expression. He continued to talk, as if unable to stop himself now he had begun. The orchard was producing well, the cherries almost ready to pack. They had expected that, by now, the babies would have been two months old, and Helen recovered and able to help. Now, he told his sister-in-law, Helen was in despair and barely able to leave her bed. He would hire some boys to pick, he rambled on; there was nothing else to be done, for if the cherries didn't go to market, there would be no supplies for the winter. Isobel felt the heavy weight of need before they even reached the house.

At the doorway, Helen, leaning against the frame, watched the two figures approach. When Isobel mounted the last step, Helen would not unfold her arms, and Isobel found herself awkwardly embracing what felt like a sister made of wood.

At Jack Armstrong's eight-room hotel, Jack, postmaster John Fischer, and Birthe's husband Fred Schroeder sat in the shade of the porch. The men were drinking last year's cold cider from the root cellar. Each had his feet on the railing, tilting backwards in homemade wooden chairs. The horse was nowhere in sight. They could hear the shouts of children in the woods above the settlement, still looking; Jack had offered a quarter to the one who could report Ace's whereabouts.

The hotel was empty of guests, in part because the end of the war meant the end of viable copper production at the Mountain Chief mine, in part because the influenza epidemic had all but stifled travel. Jack was not concerned; he was more interested in being an orchardist than a hotelier, and with a small inheritance had made a little money buying and selling land and thought that with the two, he might build a comfortable living for himself. His new horse, bought at auction in Nelson, was part quarterhorse, part workhorse, bought both for his size as a working partner and his adaptability as a mode of transportation.

John, making finger trails in the condensation on his bottle, glanced at Jack. "They'll find him." He took a pull on his drink, relishing the cool tang of it.

"Oh, I know." Jack was just glad to be sitting down after a long and frustrating run, and he shifted slightly in his chair, his hip still smarting. "He's a good horse. And young, he's got some years left in him."

"How do you know he's a good horse?" asked John. "You just bought him. You don't even know him. And he ain't here, now, is he?"

"Could just tell. We just looked each other in the eye, knew we were a match from the start."

Fred grinned. He had long admired Jack's infectious optimism. Now, it just seemed foolish. "Not much eye-to-eye happening now."

"Well, you can't send him back," said John. "You'd

never get him back on that barge. You'd have to ride him all the way, if he'd ever stand still long enough for you to get on."

There was a pause while the men considered this.

"What are you going to call him?" asked Fred.

"Ace, I think. My Ace in the hole."

"Hah!" John laughed. "What, like a flying ace? That's a fit, the way he took off! Ace, Jack. What are you doing, stacking a deck? Get yourself a queen, you'll have a pretty good hand. Question is, who gets to be king?"

From above came the shouts of two young boys, Harold Weber and Frank Klaussen, tearing down the hillside path that came out close to the back shed.

"Mrs. Toews says," Frank leaned down, hands on his knees, to catch his breath, "to get your damn horse out of her garden."

"I'm so glad you're here," Joseph Kroeker repeated to Isobel as he set her bags in the small room off the kitchen. The room, once storage, had been freshly painted. There was a hooked rug on the floor; in the corner, a commode with a basin and jug. A small window looked out onto a fading forsythia. This would have been the baby's room, Isobel realized with a small shock. Joseph explained he had borrowed the iron-frame bed she would sleep on from Frederick and Birthe.

"Their oldest children are grown, now, and moved away," he said softly. "Except for Jakob, killed in the war."

For the next few days, Isobel tried to talk to her sister, who showed no interest in conversation or comfort. It was as if there could be no comfort for her. Joseph picked cherries, packed cherries, carried on, and Isobel watched him work, understanding his need to keep busy, although certainly there was no shortage of work to be done in any case. Although money was short, he'd hired the boys, Frank and Harold, to help.

"It's not enough," he told Isobel one evening as they sat on the porch, Helen asleep as she was so much of the time. "The orchard's not enough. There is talk of a government wharf to be built; there would be work there, perhaps, close to home. But I don't know when that will happen." He took his hat off, wiped his brow across his sleeve, and looked so despairing Isobel could think of nothing to say that wouldn't sound trite. None of her political work, in defence of the weak, towards the betterment of society, had prepared her for such despair.

"Thank the Lord you are here," he turned to her. "I can work in the orchard, and know that you are with her." Isobel wished her presence made some difference to Helen; it didn't appear to, but she said nothing to Joseph.

Isobel's work for women's suffrage—meetings, rallies, and the printing of pamphlets—was tireless and brought with it the rush of power that comes with battle. After the first celebratory rush when women won the vote in Manitoba there was still much to be done, and she warmed to the cause. Until she received the telegram, she had not given any other life a second thought.

It had always been hard for Isobel to fathom her older sister's life and the choices she had made. Here, in Helen's world, life was so different, and yet there were battles daily: water that came in from the wooden pipes from upper Bear Creek had to be heated on the stove; there was an outhouse, not a bathroom. But these, at best a trial for a city girl, were nothing compared to the weight of depression that hung in the house. Helen would see nobody but Joseph and Isobel, and with them she barely spoke. She slept alone on the daybed, couldn't bear to let her husband touch her, save the moments when she would suffer to let him hold her hands and speak softly to her.

On the fifth day, Isobel slept late, emotional and physical exhaustion exacting a toll that forced her body into sleep. When she awoke, Joseph had gone out to the orchard after leaving a pot of tea and a cup on a wooden chair pulled up beside the daybed for Helen. The tea was cold, and Helen was weeping quietly as she lay on her back, hands folded in a parody of the dead, staring straight up at the ceiling. Isobel pushed aside the chair, kneeled beside her, and began to stroke her hair. Helen turned her head away.

"Just go home," she said to the wall. "Oh, why don't you just go home?"

"Helen." Isobel's hand was suspended in the air above her sister's turned head.

"Just go home," she said again, a whisper. "I don't want you."

There were several beats of silence, Isobel's tongue unable to form words. "All right," she said.

Isobel headed up the dirt road without quite knowing where she was going, into upper Bear Creek and the paths into the forest beyond. She was wearing Joseph's pants and shirt, both too large but better than her own clothing for life in Bear Creek; she had always cared little for social convention, in any case. She needed time to think, what with Joseph begging her to stay and Helen telling her to leave, never mind the pull she felt from her work at home. As she passed Jack Armstrong's empty hotel, Jack, fixing a railing on the porch where the horse had pulled it loose, saw her go by. He raised his hand to wave. He thought she had not seen him at first, then saw his wave returned, and thought to himself that Helen Kroeker's sister from Winnipeg was a fine cut of a woman, even in pants.

Jack's new horse was proving a challenge, as well as a fine subject for conversation in the village and a good joke. "He's got that Ace up his sleeve," he overheard John tell Henry Martens. "Trouble is, looks like he's lost his shirt." Since Ace's arrival, it was clear that the horse had a mind of his own, and would not be held by tether or fence, or the best intentions of Jack Armstrong.

On the first morning after Ace's rescue from Agnes Toews's vegetable garden Jack arose, cheerful. It was a beautiful day, he had a new horse, and there was work to be done. The night before he had tethered Ace under the large Spanish cherry tree, then stood back admiring the long shadows of the evening and appreciating his holdings. He had been lucky, he thought, with good land and a sturdy log-frame hotel to show for his labours, and now a good horse. But when Jack came out of the hotel whistling and looked towards the cherry tree, Ace's absence glared. Swearing, Jack swung around and marched through the gate, storming up the road, looking for the shadow of a big red horse in a garden, behind a shed, lurking amid the swaying, sun-bleached sheets on a clothesline.

"Hey, Mr. Armstrong!" Called Harold Weber, passing by with Frank, grinning.

"Hello, Harold, Frank." Jack kept up his long, determined stride.

"Looking for your horse, Mr. Armstrong?"

Jack whirled around, sending up a small cloud of dust. "You've seen him? Where is he?"

"Eating Mrs. Hartmann's carrots," laughed Harold, as Jack broke into a lope. The Hartmann place was on the far side of Bear Creek. Frieda would have a fit.

But Frieda was not home when Jack pulled up, panting. She was with Birthe Schroeder, visiting an expectant mother. Fourteen-year-old Ursula sat on the porch by herself, the soft nose of the big red horse in her palm. As Jack approached, a green carrot top disappeared from view, and Ace swung his huge head around, looked at Jack, and blew through his nose. Ursula laughed.

They led the horse back together, Ursula talking a mile a minute the way she did, exclaiming upon the wonder of being awakened by a horse at her bedroom window. She hid him in the orchard, she said, until her mother left and her father was out of sight.

"It wasn't hard to hide him with that pile of early falls behind the barn," she told him.

If Jack was worried about colic from all those green apples, he didn't need to be. Ace exhibited a formidable constitution as he ate his way through porch railings, fence posts, all manner of rope and leather harness, pig slops, dog scraps and a still-warm freshly baked cherry pie set in a windowsill. As time went on it became apparent that Ace was indeed a wild card: no gate latch was a match for Ace's prehensile lips, no rope or harness strong enough when faced with his sturdy yellow teeth. If Jack hobbled Ace, Ace slipped the hobble. Locked in a barn at night, by morning the door would be swinging in the breeze. Fenced in the pasture, Ace could jump anything.

Most people figured Jack would just sell the horse and be done with it. But Jack loved a challenge. Even more than a challenge, Jack loved a good joke, and Ace was a horse with a sense of humour and therefore a horse after Jack's own heart. Nevertheless, he was an expensive horse, and not a very useful one. He had already made more than a few people angry.

Jack wrote in his diary nightly. His entries were cropped sentences that gave away nothing, and yet when he looked back at them, the words were a doorway into a day he could remember in detail, his own private stereoscope. The night he collected Ace from the Hartmanns he wrote:

Ace escaped again. No keeping him, it seems. Helen Kroeker's sister visiting from Winnipeg, helping out after Kroeker babies died.

Then he wrote:

Ace the Horse arrived by boat, the day was fine, and folks took note

That if Jack claimed he was the Master, Ace, the horse, was somewhat faster.

Isobel and Helen stood on the outcropping of rock overlooking the community of Bear Creek and the lake beyond. It had been all Isobel and Joseph could do to convince Helen that a walk would be good for her. Now, she hugged her cardigan around her, although the air was not cold.

"I'm sorry," Isobel said gently. "I really am."

"I know." Helen looked across the lake, eyes fixed midway up the mountain.

"Do you still want me to go?"

"Yes. No. I don't know," Helen turned and looked at

Isobel for the first time. "You don't know how I feel. You can't know what this is like, to lose your babies."

"Of course I can't really know, Helen. I just want to help, that's all."

"Why now, Isobel? You weren't there for the wedding. Hell, you weren't even there for Daddy's funeral. It's always one cause or another. All your *work*." The quiet bitterness hung between them, a live thing.

In the silence that followed Isobel fought emotions for words. She thought of their father, liberal thinker, union activist, gifted public speaker. Caught in the icy grip of a heart attack on the way to a rally, with nobody on the railcar who knew how to help. *You're a smart girl, Isobel Gray,* he always told her. *Make a difference.*

"I'm making a difference," she said now, defensive. "I'm doing it for your children, Helen. The ones you're going to have."

Helen walked away, then, and Isobel stood, wishing that her father had taught her when to keep her mouth shut.

That evening Isobel prepared dinner, and the three sat and ate in relative silence. Afterwards Helen retired early to the day bed and Joseph and Isobel sat on the porch in the evening light, talking quietly.

"She's a little better today," observed Joseph.

"The walk may have helped. But I think it could take a long time, Joseph."

"I lost them, too," he said, and she could see the full toll, then, when he looked at her. Here was an abandoned man, who in an instant had lost his children and his wife. She had not fully considered this. He went on: "They died, within hours of one another, but you know that.

They had so little strength. They wouldn't nurse. We were feeding them sugar water, and the midwife, Birthe, had tried everything. Even goat's milk, warmed, a rag dipped in, and they wouldn't suck. We had Jack—did you know he's a lay minister? We had Jack baptise them. We named them Thomas, after your father and Mary, after my mother. When the second one died, the girl, Helen let out a wail I can still hear, in my dreams." He paused. "You know, she won't let me touch her, she won't hardly talk to me."

"She wants me to leave," said Isobel.

"Please stay," he said. "Please."

Jack sat on the porch of his hotel the next evening with Paddy, who blew a soft reel on his pennywhistle. He was a good worker, Paddy was, and Jack had just offered him some logging work if he could ever get his horse to cooperate.

"If you can ever get him to stick around at all, you mean," laughed Paddy. He reached for a cider, and Jack leaned over to pass the hunting knife. As he pried off the lid, he grinned at his friend. "Never saw the like."

Jack had indeed managed to harness Ace, who had been good-natured about the whole thing, and they had spent a day piling deadfall and clearing a path to haul the trees he would cut down to the mill. It had not been a bad day's work, considering that the first half had been spent trying to find the damn horse. He was eventually spotted in the upper pasture with the village cows, grazing as if he'd found his herd at last.

Jack could hear Ace, now, tethered in the yard, gnawing on the wooden fence railing and shifting his big hooves on the hard ground.

"He's a good horse. He's just getting his legs under him, that's all. He'll adjust." A soft nicker from the other side of the fence offered concurrence, and Paddy laughed.

"Sure, he is. He's a good horse, sure enough. And sure enough, you need to be doing something else, now, Jack. I don't see a lot of takers for your rooms, and you don't look about to make a killing as a saloon-keeper, you giving away last year's cider to every bugger who comes a-calling."

"Yourself included, Paddy."

"'Course."

"I've given up on the hotel. For a while, now. I might sell, I don't know. It's too big for me, eight rooms, Lord knows I don't need that much."

"Get married," said Paddy. "Fill it up with wee ones. What's stopping you?"

"Hmmph," answered Jack. They sat companionably, drinking, enjoying the evening. After a while Paddy took up the pennywhistle again, blew a few reels, and said: "Hand us another one, Jack."

The next morning Jack was just heading out to look for Ace when the horse appeared, strolling up the lane like a poodle on a leash, led by Helen Kroeker's sister, the one who had arrived the same day as Ace. She wore a brown walking skirt and plain shirt, her wavy reddish hair pulled back in a loose bun. She walked with a confident stride. Beside her, Ace tossed his head and pulled at her collar with his lips. She laughed and pushed him away, slender hand against coarse hair.

"Did you lose this?" She asked as she drew closer.

"Did I lose what?"

"This. This horse."

"What horse?"

She laughed, and he took hold of the rope halter. "Thanks," he said. "He is a problem."

"So I've heard. Isobel Gray." She held out her hand.

"Jack Armstrong. Can I get you something?"

"A glass of water would be lovely. But I've come to ask you something else." Jack gave Ace a swat on the rump and the big horse ambled over to the apple tree, where he happily munched green Pippins, leaves and all. A small, older tree outside the orchard rows, Jack decided to let the horse have it.

"I've come to inquire about a room," Isobel began when they were seated on the porch. "In the hotel, here."

"A room!" Jack could not have been more surprised. "This really isn't a hotel anymore. I don't know about a room."

"Well, you have rooms, don't you? I mean, rooms that are empty?"

Jack considered this. "Why do you want a room?"

Isobel looked at her glass, wondering how much to say about the private lives of her sister and brother-in-law. But she considered straightforwardness to be a personal hallmark, the sign of an independent, free-thinking woman.

"Helen and Joseph need some time alone," she said. "Things have not been...good. Helen would have me gone, but Joseph doesn't want me to leave Bear Creek, so I'm looking for a compromise. I thought, a week out of the house but close by in case I'm needed, and then if things looked good I could go back to Winnipeg."

"Why on earth would Helen not want you, after all that's happened in that house?"

Isobel shook her head. "This is the best way, I think."

"There are people who would let you have a room. Families. Birthe and Fred, they've got lots of room, in that big house, half their kids grown up." Jack was thinking of the empty rooms in the hotel behind them, the two of them there, alone. How would it look?

But Isobel wasn't interested in social conventions, and preferred the independence offered by a hotel room over boarding with Birthe and Fred.

"I prefer to stay here," she said, with a firmness that startled him.

"I'll think on it," Jack reached out, offered his hand to help her off the step. "I'll let you know." Isobel waved him off, descended the somewhat rickety steps easily, and strode towards the gate. If this was the best she could get for now, it would have to do.

"You stay put, now," she called to Ace, who whinnied from beneath his Pippin tree.

"Where was he?" Jack called after her, an after-thought. She turned at the end of the path.

"He was looking in my bedroom window. He woke me up, in fact."

The porch of Jack's former hotel was full that night. Paddy Doherty, John Fischer, Fred Neufeld and Fred Schroeder had come to pass the time, lured by talk in the town.

"Pretty canny, getting yourself a horse that likes women," said Paddy, tossing back a cider. "Nice he's going for the unattached ones."

"He's not all that discerning. He also woke up Ursula Hartmann a few days ago. She's a little young for me, I think," laughed Jack. He decided not to tell them about Isobel's request for a room. He had not quite figured out what to do about that. From the barn, Ace nickered. Jack had decided to lock him in for the night.

Later, he wrote: *Visit from Helen Kroeker's sister Isobel. Wanted to rent a room. Held her off for now. Nice evening on the porch with the boys. Ace still a problem.*

Isobel brought Ace home three times in the week that followed. Jack had still not decided about her request for a room, and stalled her, saying that, really, the place was a mess, and surely Helen needed her. Isobel could not shake the feeling that she should not have come at all, that the sooner things were back to normal in that house—as normal as could be—the better. She was anxious to return to her life in Winnipeg; duty called. For now, Isobel had taken to long evening walks, leaving Helen and Joseph time alone.

As she walked she could hear the talk and laughter from the old hotel porch and quelled her urge to join the group, knowing that the sudden appearance of a woman would end the conversation. The thought irritated her. She missed her friends, the political meetings, the sharp banter, the cunning plans. Here, without traffic and bustle, matters of the heart were far too close.

Jack was leading Ace down the dirt road that ran parallel to the lakeshore. He'd found him at a beach picnic at the far end of the shoreline where beach met rock, a favourite place for adolescent boys and girls to meet on a summer's evening. Ace had Peggy Klaussen and Betty Epp stroking his broad neck, one on each side. Jack noticed the horse stayed well back from the water's edge. As Jack approached, Ace had swung his head around to look at him as if reproachful of the intrusion, but he came along good-naturedly enough. When he saw Isobel on the road ahead of him, he picked up his pace and snorted a greeting, so the horse, at the end of a halter rope, arrived at Isobel a few steps ahead of Jack.

"Ace, you old scoundrel," she greeted him like an old friend. "And Mr. Armstrong. It's nice to see you out walking on this beautiful evening."

He laughed, and as he did, he took in her easy stance, the fiery hair escaping from the loose knot at her neck, the strong hand on the horse's soft nose. Ace butted his head against her shoulder for a scratch, and she laughed and obliged.

They walked together for a bit at a leisurely pace, the horse between them, the clop of Ace's unshod hooves providing a percussive counterpoint to their own soft footfalls. Jack peered around Ace to say something, and then ducked under his horse's head so as to put himself between Isobel and the horse, like a jealous lover cutting in on a dance.

"You live in Winnipeg," offered Jack conversationally. Like most Bear Creek people, Jack knew a fair bit about Isobel already, but feigned ignorance.

"Yes," she answered. No help there.

"And how is Helen holding up?"

"Things are a little better. She's begun to talk with me now. She wouldn't before. You know, I thought I was coming to help with a baby—not that I'd have known what to do. Joseph had cabled and asked me to come."

Jack hadn't known this. "So it was a surprise for you, then. The twins' passing."

"Yes. And I'm glad to be here for my sister. But it was hard for me to leave Winnipeg, you know. I have…work there."

Jack decided the best approach with someone like Isobel Gray was straightforward, and he liked this woman, who, after all, seemed to like his horse. "So I heard. The vote for women."

Isobel looked at him, surprised, and found him smiling, interested. "Yes," she said. She waited for the challenge, the cutting remark. It didn't come.

"Always thought it was a good idea," said Jack, scratching Ace under the chin.

It was the first of many walks, and a gentle courtship that lured the two back to an empty porch in the evenings, suddenly and curiously devoid of its usual visitors. Jack had always prided himself on being abreast of news, of embracing a liberal viewpoint, collecting the papers from Nelson whenever the boat would stop with the mail. And so he was not alarmed by an opinionated woman, but rather charmed. Paddy was not so sure.

"Trouble, that," he offered, catching up to Jack at the post office. "She won't stay."

"No," agreed Jack. "She probably won't."

The letter, addressed to Isobel Gray, piqued the curiosity of John Fischer when he sorted the mail.

"Run this up to the Kroekers," he told Ursula, in to collect the Hartmann mail. As she spun out the door with the letter in hand, "report back," he said under his breath. Even if she didn't tell him directly anything she found out, he knew it would get back to him eventually. Everything got to everyone in Bear Creek eventually.

Standing politely at the Kroeker door, Ursula waited to see if Isobel would thank her and send her on her way, or ask her in. Isobel, thinking a young visitor might be just the thing for Helen, did the latter. Helen was up and dressed in a housedress and cardigan, peeling potatoes at the sink. When she saw Ursula, she smiled slightly.

"I have a casserole dish to return to your mother," she told the girl. "Tell her thanks."

"I will."

"Iced tea?" Isobel stood with her hands on her hips, her letter tucked in the pocket of the pants she had borrowed from Joseph.

They sat at the kitchen table, Helen joining them. Ursula, unsure what to make of the strange quiet in the house, made circles on the table with the damp from her glass.

"I just brought a letter for Miss Gray," said Ursula.

"Isobel," said Isobel.

"Who is it from?" asked Helen, looking at her sister. She looks old, Ursula thought. She looks much older than Isobel, even though Mama said Isobel is the older sister. She waited for Isobel's answer.

"I didn't look," said Isobel, then, to Ursula, asked: "How's that horse of Mr. Armstrong's behaving?"

When Ursula had left, Isobel opened the letter. "It's from Lisbet," she told her sister.

"Your suffragette friend?" Helen's emphasis on *suffragette* suggested distaste.

"My suffragette friend," replied Isobel matter-of-factly. "She wants me to come back. There's to be a rally. She thinks it will be huge."

It was nothing specific, Isobel thought, perhaps just exhaustion, but things had eased in the Kroeker household. Sooner or later you have to join the world or leave it altogether. She had heard of women who never recovered from the melancholy that sometimes descended after childbirth, even when the baby was healthy. How must it be, then, to lose two babies? As Helen and Joseph fell into a gentle, shared grieving, Isobel felt relief and then impatience; perhaps it was time to go. Then came a morning when Isobel awoke to find the day bed had not been slept in. Thinking the two were still in bed, she crept out for an early morning walk. She came upon Jack weeding carrots, the sunlight, barely over the mountain, casting slanted rays across the garden.

"You're up early," she said cheerfully.

"That'd be two of us." He stood up, shading his eyes with an earthy hand. "When were you going to tell me you were leaving?"

"I can't stay here. I watch Helen go from chore to chore; I see Joseph worrying, constantly, about money, and they'll have more children, and with each child the first thought will be whether or not they'll live to see their first birthday. This isn't the life for me, Jack. It just seems so futile. I want to make a *difference*."

"You make a difference to me," he told her.

"That's not enough."

That morning she came back from her walk to find Helen on her hands and knees scrubbing the kitchen floor. Helen looked up at her sister's step at the door. "Helen, let me," she said, kicking off her shoes and reaching for the scrub brush.

"No. It's all right, Iz. I can do this."

"You shouldn't." On her knees beside her sister, Isobel reached for Helen's arm.

Helen jerked it away.

"Why? Because I've just had twins? That was a month

ago, Isobel, and they're cold in the ground. I thought you were going home. So—go home," she said, her voice catching.

As Helen scrambled to get up she slipped on the wet floor and fell back against the counter, then slumped against it, tears flowing. Isobel crawled across and sat beside her, leaning her head against her sister's as they had done as girls, red hair against brown.

"I really need you to go home," said Helen, her voice small and damp. "And I need you to stay. I'm afraid to be alone again with Joseph in this house. Oh, Iz, I don't know what I need. I do know I need to get on with life somehow. I just don't know how to get there."

Isobel spoke into Helen's hair so her voice came out muffled.

"You'll get there, Helen" she said.

The next evening Jack and Isobel came across Helen in the graveyard. The two had been walking in uneasy silence for over an hour in the coolness of the evening. Helen was sitting beside the little wooden cross that marked the single grave of her infant babies. Her arms were folded around her knees as she looked out over the lake. Jack turned as if to move away from this private moment, but the sound of their footfalls had alerted Helen, who stood up, shook the grass off her skirt, and approached them. Jack could see in her eyes a weariness, and a tentative peace.

"I heard there might be something going on with you two," said Helen.

Jack turned to Isobel, eyebrows raised. "I didn't tell her," she said.

"Tell me what?" asked Helen, expecting a declaration of engagement.

"I am leaving. I was going to tell you tonight. It's time for me to go back."

Helen looked at her sister in surprise. Winnipeg, she realized with sudden clarity, was a long way away. "I'm sorry about what I said before. I need you, Iz. Please stay."

"See?" Jack looked at Isobel. "See?"

Later, Jack's pen hung poised above the soft paper of his journal.

Will ask Isobel Gray to marry me. I don't think she will.

Isobel Gray, champion of causes, city woman, independent thinker, walked under a sky the colour of a bruise. Her clothes were folded and ready to pack, the house dense with low barometer and high emotion. A walk was necessary, and she had slipped out before Helen could ask to come along. She walked up to the ridge, taking a wide route to avoid Jack's place. She had to think for a while before going to talk to him. At the final ascent to the lookout, she was startled by a noise in the trees. She caught her breath, expecting a bear. When she caught the glint of red-brown through the pines, she laughed. Ace looked up, whinnied, and ambled towards her, pushing his big head up against her chest.

Jack had been around to the Kroekers' house, and had not found Isobel there.

"I don't know where she's gone," said Helen, "she just left."

When Jack returned home, Ace was gone, which was no great surprise. He thought to go looking for him, but saw a movement in the shadow of his porch and approached the hotel.

"Why haven't you asked her?" Paddy's voice surprised him.

"It was you who told me to stay clear of her," Jack replied, settling against the railing. "And anyway, she won't stay. You can't tell her anything. You don't know her."

"'Course I don't. She spends all her time with you when she's not at the Kroekers'. Or with the horse."

They were interrupted by a noise above and back of the hotel. Both heard the clomp of hooves, and a female voice.

"Be seein' you," said Paddy, and nipped around the side of the building and away up the far path.

When Isobel and Ace rounded the corner of the hotel, Jack was seated in the cane chair on the porch looking generally unconcerned and quite comfortable, as if he had been there for a long time. Isobel gave Ace a smack on the rump and he trotted off through the gate and into the near field, where he began to crop the grass with a singular focus.

"I *am* leaving," Isobel told him, anticipating his words before they were spoken. There was a distant rumble of thunder. The sky had darkened.

"I didn't say you weren't. In fact, I think you should."

"You think I should."

"Yes, I think you should." He reached for her hand, and she gave it to him. "You're right, you'll need to get out of that house for Helen to take charge of her life again."

"Well, I did try," she told him. "But you wouldn't rent me a room."

"And anyway," said Jack, running his thumb gently along hers, "there are things you should be doing in this world, and that's not staying here with an old codger like me."

They sat in silence for some time.

"Of course, if you did stay with an old codger like me, there are things you could do. Here."

"I just need to make a difference," Isobel said, as she always said. As she had been saying for years.

"You have nobody in Winnipeg," Jack pointed out. The thunder cracked, closer.

"I have friends."

"No family, then."

"What, precisely, are you saying, anyway?" Isobel looked at Jack, caught in a flash of lightning.

"It's a big world, Isobel Gray, and there are many ways to make a difference."

And the rain began, then, suddenly and in torrents.

That night Isobel lay in bed watching the moonlight stream through the tiny window. The clouds had cleared. She watched as the moon moved through the sky until its glow fell across her face, and then she closed her eyes against it. *Loony*, she thought. *Moon madness.* The old wives' tale she learned in her mother's lap seemed appropriate now as she contemplated exchanging an old life—happy, full, meaningful—for a new. What was there for her in Bear Creek? So removed from the world, so isolated. Look at Helen, she thought. Adrift in grief, how have the choices she made resulted in happiness? A light cloud skittered across the moon, darkening the room. *Jack*, she thought, and felt the familiar, physical, gentle blow just at her breastbone, there for a moment, then gone.

In the hotel Jack, too, was unable to sleep, and had arisen, pulled on his trousers and, suspenders flapping, padded across to the small table by the window where he'd moved to light the oil lamp, then set down the unlit match. The full moon streaming in the window made a light unnecessary, and he rested for a while in its glow. After a few minutes he poured a shot of whiskey from the bottle he'd left on the table and pulled towards him the list he'd made of things to get on his next trip to Nelson. Four inch nails. Coal oil. Tea.

He turned the list over and wrote:

Isobel Gray arrived by boat, the day was fine, and Jack took note,

That if the sun was half as bright, we'd all be blinded by its light.

Early the next morning Isobel awoke, a pale streak of dawn barely visible through the leaves of the forsythia bush outside her window. As she lay picking out features of the small room as they emerged in the growing light, she felt as if she were poised at the corner of two streets. Never had she felt as if any decision she made would so influence the course of her life. She thought of Lisbet, her black eyes, her pixie face, writing letters at the kitchen table in a circle of women, missing Isobel. And suddenly, she wanted to be right there among them. It was, after all, what she said she would do. Solidarity. Support the movement. Women unite.

When you make a decision, see it through.

Helen was up, now, and whistling—whistling!—in the kitchen. She heard the screen door bang and Joseph's clomp on the front step, heading for the barn. She put her bare feet on the cool floor and reached for the travelling clothes she had left out, hanging on a nail the night before.

The boat was due to arrive at nine o'clock, but Isobel asked Helen to walk down with her alone, a little early. A time to talk, a last opportunity. The storm of the night before had settled into a soft, steady drizzle. There was a thin fog, a rarity on the lake in summer. It would burn off by noon, but for now, it gave everything a ghostly appearance.

"Thank you," said Helen, as they walked hand in hand, a suitcase apiece. "You have been a help. I *am* glad you came."

"Well, that's something, I guess," Isobel smiled. Then she stopped, threw back her head, and laughed.

"What are you laughing at?" They were approaching the dock, now, past the store and post office. People had not yet gathered to meet the boat, and so they were alone. Helen could make something out towards the end of the dock, and she whispered suddenly, in recognition: "It's Jack's horse!"

Ace the horse nickered and carefully picked his way towards them in his slow, horsely gait, planting his big hooves dead centre along the wharf's length.

"Take him home, Iz," said Helen. "There's time. I'll wait here."

Isobel and the horse met Jack on the road, midway between the old hotel and the dock. Isobel and Jack stood for a while looking at one another. When Helen finally came after her sister, Joseph waiting back at the dock to say goodbye, the *Minto* was loading mail and passengers in the bustle of the morning. Jack and Isobel had been kissing for a long time. Ace was several feet away methodically stripping a Lambert cherry tree.

"It was the only way for me to keep the horse at home," Jack told Paddy much later, sitting on the hotel porch, feet on the railing, cider in hand.

"And it was the only way," Isobel, from her seat on the step, smiled at them both. "I could ever get a room in this place."

1921

From where he crouched beneath the desk at the front of the classroom, Richard North could see twenty-seven pairs of shoes ranging in size from very small to almost as big as his own, in styles from hooks to laces, and states of repair from nearly new to barely shoes at all.

He stared blankly, trembling, as one pair detached itself from the very back of the neat rows and came towards him, cautiously. Tentatively. They were female shoes, delicate in shape, but practical for passage over dirt tracks, for ambling through fields, for running from the teasings of adolescent boys.

"Mr. North?"

As his last name took the upward inflection of a question, another blast shook the floor. He whimpered, clasping his hands tightly over his head.

At that moment, Richard North cowered in a Passchendaele trench. Around him exploded a bombardment so furious that its violence rendered him frozen, deafened, beyond thought. There was burning, a sharp, toxic stench that overrode the smell of loam and blood. There was screaming. He was having trouble separating the sounds, and so it took some time for him to realize that the screaming was his own and that the hot, wet mass in his hands belonged to his hometown friend Roger, who had fallen back into the trench on top of him, nearly severed at the torso.

"Mr. North? It's just dynamite, for the stumps."

In his arms lay Roger's upper body, an expression of surprise on his face. North, still screaming, let the body drop, registered the rolling of the head, the alarming red of blood and organs, threw his gun and helmet aside and began to scramble up the trench wall, either to commit suicide or to kill the Jerries with his bare hands, he didn't know. He felt a violent pull to his leg, a blow to his head, and as he fell saw the set face of the soldier beside him, rifle butt still on the downswing.

"Mr. North, it's just my father and Mr. Armstrong, blasting stumps. It's just some dynamite, Mr. North." Ursula spoke as if to a deaf person as she peered under the back of the desk at the white face of her teacher. At sixteen, she had reached her last year of school. North peered into her arresting grey eyes, unsure of their place in this nightmare, and suddenly returned to the present. Rising abruptly, he hit his head on the underside of his desk, sparking nervous laughter.

He stood, straightened his jacket, and, without looking up, rearranged papers on his desk, hands trembling. To his right, Ursula stood, unsure whether to return to her seat or not. From the back of the room came the derisive laugh of Harold Weber. North, still shaken, registered the sullen presence of the young man. He raised his eyes, felt the tears pool in his lower lids, and looked at Harold, who smirked at him and held his gaze.

"Class d-dismissed," said North, although it was only 1:30 in the afternoon. With a cacophonous scrape and bang of chairs and tables and slamming of books, the students tumbled out into the grey October day, much to the surprise of the two men in the upper field, causing them both to pause in their work and scratch their heads.

Ursula, still rooted to her spot, felt an odd responsibility for her teacher, but, helpless, stood curling a strand of blonde hair onto an index finger. He turned to her, nodded curtly, repeated: "dismissed."

When he heard the door slam behind her, he sat, put his head in his hands, and wept.

Later, the talk at Weider's General Store and Post Office was all about the teacher, and what was to be done. This was not the first time the new teacher, Mr. North, had behaved oddly.

"One day last month he didn't even show up until it was gone eleven," said John Fischer, leaning up against the grey shingle, scraping mud and cow shit off his boot with a stick. Frederick Schroeder and Jack Armstrong sat in the two porch chairs that were seldom unoccupied, the store being a favoured gathering place. Jacob Weider stood in the doorway, smoking.

When Frederick grunted his displeasure at North's behaviour, Jack looked away. He liked Richard North, and knew he'd had a bad go of it in the war. When Borden brought in conscription in '17, Jack's Mennonite neighbours had been exempt from service; Jack himself, thirty-seven years old and with an irregular heartbeat that alarmed doctors, was off the hook. But the stories of the horror were everywhere, sixteen thousand young Canadian men lost at Passchendaele alone. It must have been absolute hell, he thought.

"He forgets what he's saying in the middle of a lesson," offered young Harold, leaning up against the porch railing. Harold, they all knew, had been held back in the classroom. "He forgets what he's saying in the middle of a *sentence*."

John Fischer looked at Harold for a long moment, taking in the surly slouch, the curling lip. Here was a kid who didn't have anything good to say about anybody, never mind that he'd been through a rough time. You want to feel sorry for him, Fischer thought, but he doesn't make it easy.

Fischer wished he hadn't brought up the subject of the teacher at all. He wasn't happy with these incidents; he had three children in North's class, and felt that an education should be an education, and that children, if they were not doing something useful at home, should be getting one. Still, he didn't like to be on the side of Harold Weber, who had all the markings of a trouble-maker. If it were his kid, he'd have had him out of school and working full time at the shake mill, make him so worn out by the end of a day he'd be too tired to be nasty.

"He stutters," said Harold. "He can't even talk. He should be fired." Harold spit. He caught the eye of four-teen-year-old Josephine Epp as she walked by, looking back over her shoulder to see who was gathered at the store. Harold grinned at her, glad to be caught in the company of men, and she rewarded him with a charming little upward turn of her mouth. He adjusted his stance to be as adult as possible, turned back to the men, and said again seriously: "He should be fired."

Later that night, his wife curled against him in the quiet house, Frederick Schroeder said into the general dark of the room: "They are saying he shouldn't be teaching."

"Mr. North?" Birthe pulled herself up from the sleep into which she had been sinking gratefully. "Who is saying that?"

But Frederick rolled over, said nothing more. He wasn't sure why he'd said anything at all.

In a small community of fewer than one hundred souls, telephone lines were not necessary for the dissemination of information. Richard North's nervous disposition soon became the topic of conversation at communal gatherings: the butchering of a pig, or an apple schnitzing. Harold started the buzz among the young people, and was especially successful with the quieter boys for whom friendship, or at least acknowledgment, with the older, tougher boy was an advantage. In truth, Harold wanted out, but his parents wanted him in school one more year, especially since his cousin's death the summer past. They felt another year would help him recover from the tragedy. Harold wanted to work for his uncle in the shake and box factory full-time, earn some money of his own, and leave Bear Creek for good. His general dissatisfaction was reflected in everything he did.

Richard North heard the rumbling, felt the silence descend when he entered the post office. At school the next day, things carried on as usual. Ursula, he thought, was especially solicitous, a nice girl. He thought about them one by one, turning over their personalities like pennies in his hand. Hannah was quiet, and on his good days, he would try to draw her out; on his bad days, it was all he could do to keep control of both himself and the classroom. There was Harold, smouldering in the back. Albert, dimpled, tow-headed, as charming as a boy could be, would be a killer with the girls soon, he could tell. Horst did well even with half of his right index finger lost. He mastered his letters with more dexterity than most. Dieter was not a good student, at so young he could see that, but he was smart all the same. It was hard for him to master letters, words, sentences, and yet he could remember every city, every lake on the map.

North's eyes grazed the rows, tallying the people who were his charges in this one-room school. It took him some time to become aware of the shifting, the giggling, the general uneasiness in the room.

He caught Harold's eye from the back of the room, where the boy glowered with hatred. Meeting his teacher's eyes, Harold leaned sideways and spit on the floor. And suddenly North was angry, both at this act of insolence and because he had not come this far to be tormented by a stupid adolescent boy.

"Mr. Weber, stay after school, please," said North in a flat tone, without tremor.

Later, as Harold chopped wood for the stove—wood not even needed, there was plenty already stacked—he thought of dropping the axe and walking away into the late fall afternoon, but he finished the job. Mr. North would only speak with his father if he didn't, and he didn't want that. Resentment crouched in the blade of the axe, compounded itself with every blow, wood flying.

The previous summer, Harold had managed to get a little work driving the village cows to the upper Bear Creek grazing pasture. He had wanted to work at the mill, but his uncle had put him off: Next year, he had said. Grow a little more. Besides, there are too many men who need to feed their families right now.

For a dollar a head each month, Harold would walk through the village at dawn and pick up the cows. They would be at the gate, milked and waiting: the Hartmanns' Jersey, the Neufelds' black-and-white, a ragtag bunch of mooing, smelly animals who would whack you with a tail full of shit given half the chance. By 7 a.m. they were all happily munching clover, and Harold would return home to help his father tend trees or mend fences against garden-loving deer. In the heat of the afternoon, there would be a few scant hours of his own, and then in the evening the damn cows had to be driven home, deposited at their own doorsteps. Luckily, they would do this on their own; once in town, they ambled purposefully to their own gates, giving him baleful looks over their shoulders, a last tail swish to remind Harold who, really, was boss.

It was on the first really hot day, the cows happily pastured and already congregating under the spreading poplars in little bovine gossip huddles, that Harold hurried through his chores and begged the indulgence of his father to quit early enough for a swim. Permission granted, he jogged over to Frank's place, flicking his too-long black hair out of his eyes and feeling the summer heat adhering shirt to skin. Frank was restless, ready to go. His father, in a good mood, grinned at them both, waved them away. Kids should be kids, he thought.

Frank was ready to head for the swimming hole, but Harold had more ambitious ideas.

"We'll take the boat. We'll head down the lake, to Baker's Landing where they load the ore from the Mountain Chief. I want a job, Frank. I don't want to spend my whole goddamn summer pushing cows uphill."

The boat was a lovely little Walton with a solid motor. It belonged to Jack Armstrong, who had bought it in Nelson right from the builders. The *Lanark*, named after his hometown, was Jack's pride and joy, second only to his horse Ace. But since he married Isobel Gray the boat had been sitting idle. His new wife was not partial to water. There it sat, pulled up on boards a good distance away from the wharf, under a grove of trees and out of sight of lakeside comings and goings, resting under an oilcloth.

"He'll never miss it," said Harold, pulling off the tarpaulin. "We'll be back in a couple of hours. I just want to ask for a job."

Frank, sandy-haired with a big, friendly face, was slow moving but quick to take a risk, most times. Now, he just looked at his friend. Moving an outhouse six feet over in the dark was one thing. Taking a boat worth ten years of obnoxious cow herding—or their very lives, if caught—was another thing altogether.

"We'll pull in, have a swim, come back wet, so it will look like we just went swimming," grinned Harold. "They'll never know."

Frank, too, wanted a job at the Mountain Chief. Neither wanted to return to school, and in these times, a good job was a good excuse. They were fifteen years old. They could read, write, do sums. What else did they need? More, they wanted to be freed from home chores and village life. They could make a bundle, send some back home, be their own men. Together, they pulled back the oilcloth, flipped the boat, set the motor, resting underneath, onto its bracket at the stern. Harold pulled the stiff oilcloth into peaks to approximate the shape of the little boat. He hoped that, from a distance, it would look as if the boat still rested there. Harold had swiped gasoline from his father's shed. The two boys, pants rolled up, pushed the craft along the water's edge until a stand of shoreline trees shielded them more fully from view. They paddled awkwardly until they dared to prime the motor and pull the cord.

With the wind in their hair and the sparkling lake

around, the two felt freedom in their teeth, their eye-lashes, the pores of their skin. Saying nothing, they smiled into it, eyes almost shut against the air in their faces. With Harold at the rear, they took a shoreline route slowly at first and then, well away from the settle-ment, headed out into the main lake just to feel the space around them.

Frank pushed Harold with his foot. The wind took his words away, and so he had to shout three, four times.

"Better steer back to shore, Hal. The *Minto*'s due in, somebody from Bear Creek will see us, sure. There she is now!"

Harold could see the great swanlike sternwheeler rounding the curve at the narrows. The Mountain Chief mine was behind her; she had already made that stop. Why hadn't Harold thought about the timing? He hadn't even stopped to consider what day it was! The only thing to do was to head for the shoreline, hide in the shadows, wait for her to pass and hope they wouldn't be seen. He turned the *Lanark* sharply, picked up speed, and headed for the shore, panicking.

When they hit the deadhead, the boat was at full throttle. It hit portside, skewing the boat's angle as it rose in the air like a duck taking flight. But instead of lifting off, it flipped over in mid-flight, performing an arc graceful in its deadliness. The bow hit Frank sharply across the temple as he fell into the cold of the lake.

They were good swimmers, and they were not far from shore. Harold's first thought was for the boat, and for the trouble they would get into if there was damage, for it was certain now they would be discovered. The motor was wet; they would not be motoring quietly back anytime soon. Once his ears cleared he noticed, as he sputtered on the surface, the silence. Above the distant approach of the *Minto*, the shoreside birdsong, the lap of disturbed waves and the final crank of the upturned propeller as the motor flooded with water, the absence of Frank's voice boomed.

Harold dove under the boat. He dove again and again, a circle of frantic plunges around the craft, unsure, now, of where they'd first hit, the deadhead out of sight, the boat drifting. His heart pounded, his ears roared, and when he rose for air, he cried out in panic the name of his best friend.

At the funeral, Richard North, at his strongest and most assured in the presence of grief, felt a duty as the boys' teacher to offer words of comfort to Frank's family. Harold stood apart from the gathering beneath the big pine. North watched as Harold shook off his mother's touch, turned away from his father's words, and watched his parents leave, herding Harold's younger brothers before them. Frank's own young brother and sister had stared unabashedly throughout the service while Frank's parents glanced at Harold, then away. They did not resent him; neither could they speak to him, not yet.

When they left the graveside, Harold stared at the space they had occupied for several minutes, then sank beneath the tree, sobbing. The approach of Mr. North in that moment was an unconscionable intrusion, and North recoiled at the naked hatred turned upon him by this boy in the worn, black, borrowed suit.

"Go *away*." Harold spit the words through tears, snot and gritted teeth.

Richard North squatted beside him and picked up a tasselled grass stem, twirling it. There must be something, he thought, that he could say.

"It's always h-hard to lose a friend," he ventured, feeling the smallness of his words. Harold turned his face away.

"My best friend was killed," North tried again, but could not think of what, next, to say. Harold didn't move, putting all of his energy into willing this intruder away.

"My best friend," began North again. What was important about Roger? When he tried to see his childhood friend's smile, his eyes, hear his quick jokes, there was nothing but the sight of blood and intestine and the noise. North used all of his willpower to bring himself back to this moment, this tree, the threadbare cuff of what was his best suit. This blade of grass, turned around and around by long, white fingers.

"My best friend was killed in the trenches in Germany. B-beside me. He never knew I held him."

Harold got up abruptly and walked away, his back to his teacher, who did not look up. North stayed crouched for some time on the edge of the cemetery. Around him, daisies bobbed like children playing.

Richard North did not resent the German spoken by half the village residents. He understood that these people were pacifists, that they were as far as anyone could be from the battleground. He never even hated the German soldiers, not really; they were just young men, doing what they were told. Fear, now that was another thing. He feared them, because what these boys had been told was to kill him.

And so the enemy became the thing he could not control, and the banishment of fear became dependent on surrounding himself with things he could control: by living alone, he could control the emotional demands on his life, and he took pleasure in the obedience of inanimate objects. He knew if he left a newspaper on a table, his slippers under his bed, his cap on its hook, it would be exactly there when he went to look for it. He liked this precision, this assurance. Training as a teacher after his release from the hospital at Craiglockhart, encouraged by his doctor, he set upon this new work with a sudden, surprising optimism. He hadn't thought he would be optimistic again in this life. When he heard of a job in a remote community in British Columbia, he was pleased. The teacher was leaving; he could start mid-year, with lesson plans in place. He had no ties; he could no longer talk to his sister, whose husband's medals for bravery rebuked him; his parents were dead. Here was redemption. Here was a new start.

Here, he could maintain the control he knew he needed in his working life as he controlled his students, his classroom, the lessons taught, his day. At 9 a.m. they arrived. At 3 p.m. they were dismissed. It was punctual. It was safe. There was nothing unexpected, at least most of the time, and if, occasionally, he lost his train of thought, there was no real damage done.

He was quite prepared to put the incident on the day of the stump blasting out of his mind, to carry on as if nothing had happened. That it was also not the first such occurrence did not greatly concern him; he had become adept at dismissing these incidents as smaller than they were, or forgetting them altogether. His students obeyed him, even seemed to like him a little. They were good children, for the most part. It would all be forgotten quickly enough.

George Hartmann and Jack Armstrong did not blast

any more stumps. Out of concern for the nervous teacher, they pulled the last three stumps out with the friendly, steamy efforts of the two big horses, Ace and Gabi. But if George and Jack and a handful of well-wishers were sympathetic, others were not. North sensed the talk in the village but determinedly showed no outward sign, touching his hat and nodding amiably, if with his customary shyness, at the people he passed in the street. But in the classroom he was rattled. One slip, he felt, would be another nail in the coffin. He could not afford to lose this job; he had not the heart to leave, to start again. Yet he was finding, increasingly, odd lapses in the chronology of his day, as if he had left for a moment, taken a short walk outside, and returned to find twenty-seven pairs of eyes staring at him expectantly. When he looked at them, he felt such a surge of love and responsibility he had to still his quaking hands against the rough wood of his desk, and mask his fear of failure in gruff instructions.

He was helping young Dorothy Shannon understand the complexities of long division when a sharp sound made him jump.

"Dropped my book, sir," said Harold, eyes rounded in a parody of innocence. He leaned and picked it up off the floor. There was snickering, all eyes on the teacher. He nodded sternly, returned to Dorothy and her open scribbler. He could not concentrate, couldn't think of where he was, what to tell her.

A sharp crack sounded a moment later, and North whirled around to see two books on the floor. More snorts of suppressed hilarity, and then Ursula said softly into the silence that followed, "I'll help her, Mr. North."

North returned to his desk and took stock. All of the children had been assigned work dependent on their level, and now all were working diligently at their desks, model pupils. Even Josephine Epp, a flirt at fourteen and more likely to be passing notes than passing tests, was hard at work, hair in disarray as it tried to escape from two careful braids, but tongue protruding industriously from her mouth as she lined up columns of numbers. A quarter-hour more, he decided, and we will begin a new lesson in geography. He turned to pull the big map of Canada, the one ordered especially from Calgary for this school year, in order to buy time to consider his approach.

Immediately, the room exploded. He turned to see fall the last of a dozen text books that had, in unison, been jettisoned to the floor. His hands were shaking. There was no sudden retreat to the trenches at the sound, he knew what this was, and yet he did not know how to respond to such contempt. And he did not know which was worse: his indecision, or the fact that Ursula Hartmann took charge, adeptly usurping any control he might have mustered.

"Stop it!"

They stopped. Indeed, those responsible had already stopped, for the plan did not extend past the dropping of the books. There was a prolonged silence.

"Thank you, Miss Hartmann, you may sit down," said North curtly, and, chastened, she sat, tossing a glance over her shoulder at Harold before she did. North thought she actually hissed at Harold, like a cat. He could not look at the sixteen-year-old girl who had come to his rescue.

That night as he slept, North was again at Passchendaele, this time sitting against a sandbagged wall, Roger beside him. He turned to his friend to offer him a cigarette, saw Roger smile through the grime, nod in acceptance and reach out his hand. But before his fingers reached the cigarette they were gone, and what reached towards North was a bloody stump. Looking up in alarm, he saw that his friend's head was now a mass of blood and bone, and that on his head was a German helmet. The skeletal teeth grinned redly. Somebody was screaming.

The next day he arrived at school and immediately assigned work to each level. The smaller children were set to practising the alphabet in broad strokes; the older children were to work on their essay: what makes a good citizen? With a little time freed, North took pen and paper and began to draft a letter of resignation. He thought a job someplace quiet, a library perhaps, would suit him. He closed his eyes to better coax the words, and saw the blood, the strips of flesh, the shattered bone.

When the noise came he was quite unprepared for it, so engrossed was he in the wording of his letter. He was on his feet at once, hands gripping the table edge, eyes wild. There was no movement in the room. On the floor two dozen books wafted little puffs of dust that caught in the morning sunlight streaming through the windows.

"Back. To. Work." He said through clenched teeth. "Tomorrow, we will h-have a test."

In fact, the plan had been to enjoy the last days out of doors before serious frost, to examine the ways in which the animals prepared for winter. They would look at squirrel middens, pine cone husks littering the ground beneath a cache; they would find cocoons, examine the last of the spawning trout, see the coats thickening on the horses. It was an outing he remembered from his own school days, a wonderful day of scientific discovery, and he had long planned this day with his students. Their scribblers were full of drawings, lists of things they would investigate. In truth, it was hard to say who was the more enthusiastic about a break from classroom lesson: the children, or their teacher.

Ursula, Dorothy Shannon. Dorothy's brother, Peter. North looked at them, not blinking. These were the three whose books still lay on their desks. Ursula looked at him with shock and sadness. A lover of all things outside, she, above all, should not be punished for this.

"We will reschedule our outing," said North, stuttering, horribly regretful, "when we can all b-behave." His ears buzzed; he felt a hot, rising panic.

He then turned around and left the schoolroom, striding only as far as the nearest pine where he leaned heavily, breathing hard, trying to find composure among a whirlwind of thoughts. He held his hands before him. They would not stop shaking. Behind him in the classroom a cacophony had erupted. From the corner of his eye he could see Jack Armstrong approaching, curious. He had been about to arrange delivery of a cord of wood for the stove when the noise within alerted him that something was wrong. He did not see the figure beneath the tree.

Talk that night at the store was, again, about the teacher and his fitness to teach the children of Bear Creek. Harold was not there, but the regulars: John Fischer, Frederick Schroeder, Jack Armstrong and Jacob Weider stood in the doorway or leaned against the railing. They were joined by George Hartmann.

"I feel sorry for the fellow," said Jacob, "but he can't

stay if he can't teach. He's got to get a handle on himself. Jack, you were there, what did you say? A whole classroom in chaos and North nowhere to be found."

"My Ursula told her mother it is the Weber boy's fault." George looked around with his knife-sharp gaze. "She says he should not be in school."

"He's been a handful since the Klaussen boy drowned." John looked uncomfortable. He changed the subject: "You were good about that boat, Jack."

"Well, it still floats." Jack looked at the men standing around him. "Look, I think we should just let things be, maybe each of us check in once a day for now. No point in flying off the handle. He's a quiet fellow, Richard North, and sure, he's nervous, but he's not a bad fellow. Let's give him some time."

They watched as Roy Weber strode up the road, a piece of paper in his hand. When he reached the porch he looked at each of them.

"Wife's been gathering names," he told them. "North ain't fit to teach. Who wants to sign?"

That evening, North took a walk on the upper trails, heading towards an outcropping of rock on the north end of a scoop of bay that had become a thinking spot for him. Hands behind his back, head down, hat low over his eyes, he strode along, refining in his head his letter of resignation and planning his departure from Bear Creek. Better to resign than be let go; perhaps this remote settlement had simply not been the right choice. He felt the weight of failure, a fog descending, and with it a confusing mixture of despair and anger. His feet fell softly on a carpet of pine needles as he left the path and turned towards the lake.

He almost stepped on Harold Weber, chucking stones into the water from the top of the precipice. The splashes of the rocks as they hit the surface were timed with the footfalls of North's approach, and so Harold did not hear or see North until he was right there. North stopped, felt a rising anger for this surly, aggressive boy who, he was now absolutely sure, was solely responsible for his urge to flee Bear Creek like the coward he was.

Harold was ready to bolt, but held back; he was here first, after all. Ursula had given him a talking-to after school, had even pulled Josephine on side, who now wouldn't return his smile or even look at him. He hated Ursula, an only child, spoiled, stuck-up, too damn smart for her own good. But he hated the teacher more, a ridiculous, pathetic yellow chicken-livered coward. He'd heard of soldiers who got out of service because of nerves, nothing more than an excuse for cowardice; his own father said so. And he hated that his father had made him go back to school, hated him for the lecture he got for being late for chores that day, hated North for keeping him back to chop wood so he had to catch hell from his old man and *still* had to do all of his chores, until when he finally came in the house his dinner sat waiting on the table, sausages cold in puddles of congealed fat.

Harold drew his arm back, pulled the anger from his boots and out into the cocked arm and into the stone that sailed, propelled by fury, into the slate surface of water below. For a time he kept his gaze averted from North, mechanically bending, grasping, rocks spiralling outwards towards the lake. He was cold, his breath hung in clouds, and his hands were numb. North watched him for a full minute before looking away.

Harold ignored him, kept pitching. North focused on the opposite shore and spoke with quiet anger.

"I should throw you out of school."

Harold said nothing, thought: *Yes*; then thought, again: *Pa*. He didn't know which was worse, school, or the anger of his father. *I could leave,* he thought. *I could sleep here, sneak aboard the* Minto *when it comes, find work in Trail. To hell with all of them.* He heaved another rock into the air, heard it splash in the distance.

"I don't care," he said after a minute. But it was not said with the sneer North had come to expect. It was uttered with such despair that North felt his anger seep away from him and into the rock. He eased himself down into a squat, hung his hand between his knees, and watched Harold's arm draw, back, pitch, release. So much time passed that Harold almost forgot North's presence.

When the voice came from Harold's right in the gathering dusk, it was as if it came from far away.

"Roger could pitch a rock farther than anyone I ever knew."

Harold, squatting, angled himself away from his teacher. The voice was spooky; he'd heard it before in the classroom, and it scared him, made him angry. It was like a voice under water. It was like drowning.

North picked up a rock, pulled his arm back and tried to remember his cricket pitch. The rock fell well short of the water, disappearing silently into the brush below them. Harold barked a derisive laugh. North picked up a second rock, hefted it, and then returned it gently to its place. He began to laugh softly.

"He was a funny guy, Roger. He once ran a brassiere up the flagpole at training camp. There we all were at reveille, it was Roger's job to raise the Union Jack, but what came up the pole was the biggest brassiere you ever saw, he must have got it off a clothesline or something. And there we were, all trying to keep a straight face, and Roger, looking wide-eyed and innocent like he'd never seen a brassiere before in his life and had no idea what one was, or how it got there. Of course, he was on KP for a month."

North had never spoken so much to Harold, to anyone, almost, never so long without a stutter, and certainly never about Roger. He crouched, sensing memories of his friend in the air around him, almost tangible.

After a time, Harold spoke. He could not find another rock to pitch without moving, and did not want to move. He knew if he did, he would leave, and then where would he go? He eased himself down, stretching his legs against the cramp from his squatting position. Beside him North shifted, staring fixedly across the lake.

"One time," Harold ventured, "Frank and I moved Jake Epp's outhouse four feet, and he fell in the hole in the middle of the night."

North passed a rock from hand to hand, left, right, left. He held Harold's story like he held the rock, feeling it, and through it reached back, smiling to himself as he did. "There was the time we short-sheeted the sergeant-major's bed," he said softly, remembering Roger's horse-laugh at the triumph of the joke.

Harold looked out across the lake. "He always hated cleaning the chicken shed. Hated it, the smell of chicken shit made him want to puke. I went to find him there once, he had a shovel to scrape, a bucket of water, and he was standing there, his stomach heaving. Afraid to go outside, afraid his dad would see him. Afraid, and sick, he couldn't say anything to me, even, just stood there, sort of choking." Harold squinted at the low mountain across the lake, backlit in the fading light. "So I looked out, saw his father had gone around the side of the barn, and I grabbed the shovel and pushed Frank outside and did the coop for him. Later, he paid his little brother to do it, in secret. I gave him some of my money from the cows. His dad never even knew."

North spoke again, softly, as if to himself: "The time he got the letter from his sister, she was getting married, and you know, he was happy for her and sort of jealous all at once, because he had a special friendship with Marjorie, and he thought, once she was married, they wouldn't be friends the same way. But he was happy because she was happy. And then when he got the letter that her fiancé had been killed—he was a naval officer and they were torpedoed—he cried for her. We were camped in a farmhouse, there was shelling all around, and he cried there, in the corner, while the others looked away."

Harold shifted in the silence that followed, listening to the trees rub their spines together. Minutes passed.

"Frank could imitate a crow just like the real thing. He could talk to them; they'd talk back, all those crazy noises they make."

"He laughed louder than anyone I ever knew. In a room full of people, you could hear Roger's laugh above everyone else's."

Harold had stopped throwing stones at the lake; North had settled into stillness, felt rooted to the rock, calm.

North said, "When my own father died, of a stroke, and I got the letter, Roger yelled at our commanding officer for insisting I go to mess, obey orders. The officer backed down. Roger should have caught hell for that, but then Roger could get away with anything. I don't believe I ever thanked him."

"If Frank heard of a job, of work for money, he would tell me, we would go together. He would never go on his own. I have dreams about him," said Harold, looking over at North for the first time. "All the time."

"So do I," said North. They sat in silence for a while. It was dark, now. North could hear a small choking sound. He said quietly, "It was me who talked him into joining up, so we could go together. Roger was a year younger. He could have waited."

North felt tears coursing down his cheeks. He was grateful for the darkness, and, strangely, grateful for the salty warmth he felt on his face against the cold October air. He heard the choking sound again, reached out his arm, and touched the rough weave of a hand-me-down jacket, pulled the shaking shoulders close.

"All the time," said Harold. "All the time."

North sat on a cold rock under a dark sky on a lake in the mountains, the head of a teenaged boy against his chest. He could barely see, now, but could feel the living warmth of this boy, feel the heaves subside. After a while Harold straightened himself, suddenly aware, embarrassed, and wiped his nose on the back of his hand.

"I better be getting home," he said, looking away.

"Yes," said North. He stayed, unmoving, feeling the warmth, still, against his chest. He listened while Harold's feet found the path in the blind dark under the trees, until the sound of footfalls and cracking of branches had faded. He stayed there until he could hardly tell the rise of mountain against the sky, or the shift in tone from the land to the gentle lap of the water at its feet. His hand closed around a rock, and he felt its coolness, its solidness in his palm. He heard the splash as the stone struck the water.

1932

To this day I can't explain why the sight of the group trudging on snowshoes across the flat towards the Hartmann's orchard, pulling the sledge and talking in low voices, made me pull deeper into the hollow. There I crouched, mittens frozen around the rope of my toboggan. A normal boy would have rushed forward, curiosity pushing him headlong into the group, to ask: What? Who?

But I was not a normal boy. Everyone said so. I stuttered in the face of the simplest phrase; Ds and Bs twisted my tongue into knots. Consequently, I spoke seldom, and avoided any human interaction that could lead to the need for conversation. And so at nine years old, in the winter of 1932, I was a watcher, and a listener.

It was the winter of the Big Snow. The blizzard that began just after Christmas started with a howl that shook the frame of our two-storey plank-sided house and ended with drifts against the doorframe so large that my father had to crawl through the living-room window to wrestle the shovel from the shed and dig us out. Although the weather calmed after a few days, it didn't stop snowing. Now, already the end of February, it looked as if it never would.

The only telephone in our village hung on the wall in the corner of the Bear Creek store. There, it kept us in touch with the rest of the world until the middle of January, when the weight of snow became too great for a single line in a vast forest.

Without the cares of the adult world, I loved the feeling of snowbound isolation and the heady possibility of adventure. I was reminded of the *Boy's Own* and *Girl's Own* annuals my teacher, Mr. North, kept in his desk for students who finished their assignments early, and I could see myself clearly in the pages of *Boy's Own*. Me! Thomas James Klaussen, marooned in a snow-covered mountain wilderness, left to my wits and bravery to survive!

I dreamed about snow houses like the Eskimos had. When the snow covered our house, we would have to build an igloo. I worked out every detail: how my parents would be beside themselves with worry, but I, who had seen pictures in books, would tell them exactly how to cut the blocks from the snow, and how to stack them into a dome that filtered light through its seams while inside my family sat, warm, around me, grateful for my help and amazed at my knowledge. Even my fourteen-year-old sister Ellie would say: "Kid, we never knew," and would ruffle my hair affectionately.

As the snow piled up Dad carved deep paths through the banks: to the shed, to the barn, to the root cellar. I ran through them, crouching, fighting the Jerries from my trench in France, my gun rat-at-tat-tatting over the edge and killing one after another. At school, the trenches made way for a different sort of war. Billy Weber, who liked to make me stutter, could now corner me by the outhouse and wash my face with snow, crowing, "Does it t-t-t-taste g-g-good, T-t-tommy-boy?"

As I lay on my back in the snow that evening, my toboggan angled below me where it had finally come to rest against the bushes, I watched the swirling flakes and thought about snow, and heaven. My mother called it sugar snow, flakes as big as my wool mittens, as light as the cotton candy Dad bought me at the Chautauqua last summer in Nelson. They came from heaven, which at that moment was a dusty grey with the glow of the moon behind it. They began small, and as they danced towards me became as big as the moon before they landed on my cheeks and my eyelashes. It was a peaceful moment, and I drew it around me like a cloak, shutting out the evening's earlier argument.

"Jack at the store said they're going to send planes in to drop food if it goes on much longer," said my mother, standing at the sink after supper with her hands in the dishwater. She turned to look at my father, seated at the table with a two-week-old newspaper, and pushed the hair out of her eyes with the back of a damp hand.

"I'm still going," he answered, snapping the broadsheet to attention by way of punctuation.

"Frank, you are *not* going! You are not going to trek down the lake and risk going through some weak spot in the ice, leaving me and the kids to bury you, meanwhile pretending you are some kind of hero for doing it." She spit out the end of the sentence like a bad apple.

From my vantage point in the far corner of our L-shaped kitchen and living room, where I sat as close as I could get to the warmth of the woodstove and still be out of sight behind a chair, I could see my father set the paper down with a precision that seemed altogether too careful.

It reminded me of the way he would lay out his tools, one by one, placed just so, before embarking on a repair job in the shed, something he did for extra cash: a rusted hinge or a car manifold, it all meant a chicken in the pot or a box of apples. For Dad, what with the box and shake factory shutdown early in the season and the promised job on the *Minto* halted by weather and small-town politics, the repair shop was meaningful work that kept him close to his family; for Mum, it just wasn't enough. He should go to the City, get himself a job as a mechanic, she told him, the better to snag that job in the *Minto*'s engine room come spring. But Dad said it was about who you know, not what you can do, and he set his chin the way he does and went out to the shed where he spent more and more time, now.

The way he set the paper down that night had nothing to do with the paper itself or the fact that he had read it front to back more times than he could count for want of a more current issue, although that, and the snow that still fell steadily outside, was certainly a part of it. It was because my mother, who after telling him for weeks he should leave us to find some work, was now telling him not to go, now he'd made his mind up to do it. It was because of too much snow, and not enough space or money, and all of it piling up all at once like the drift outside the window. One moment you can see, the next, you can't. In that deliberate movement was a month of whispered late-night arguments and accusations about being the provider, about taking action.

"You wanted me to go! What the hell have you been saying to me for weeks?" My father's voice was barely contained; it pushed at the edges into a shout, but held itself.

"Not *now*, Frank. *Then*, when it would have made a difference. Now you're going to leave me in a snowstorm to wrestle with food drops and kids and go crazy shut in this house while the snow comes down and buries us all.

You are *not* going to leave me in this house now."

She turned, then, and slammed a spoon against the enamelled edge of the iron sink. I flinched in my corner. Dad did not.

"I'm just never good enough, am I?" His voice was quiet, like the still of the yard before the first crack of thunder. "I'm just never any damn good."

The cutlery, entering the dishwater in a sharp clatter, was the only sound. I wasn't breathing, and I realized I had not been for several moments. I took a slow breath as quietly as I could.

"Never the right timing, don't know the right people, not like your father, who greased the right palms, didn't he, got his precious girls everything they wanted."

"Don't bring my father into this!"

"That's right, Dora, I'm not your father, I'm the man you married, and I'll do things my way. You want things a guy who fixes odds and ends can't afford in a month of Sundays; fine then: I'll send you my paycheques. You can run the house whatever way you damn well want to, because I won't be here for you to tell me what's wrong with me every damn five minutes."

"Do you think our neighbours actually need those things fixed?" Her voice was low, and biting.

"Bloody hell. You have no idea."

There was a blur of movement, the red-brown of my mother's dress colouring the air as she turned. The handful of wet cutlery coursed in a graceful arc, beginning as one and separating in mid-flight, so that it hit my father across the head and chest. One fork missed him entirely, and skidded to a stop a few inches from my left hand. It lay there, quivering on the floor.

"Get out, then," she hissed. "And go to hell."

With that, my father rose. A fork had glanced off his forehead, and the bead of blood there was like the period at the end of a sentence. Final. He jammed his feet into his boots, grabbed the heavy wool coat and reached a gloved hand for the doorknob. My sister Ellie, poised on the opposite side, almost fell into the room, barely registering my father as he pushed past her into the snow. She had eaten dinner with her friend Mavis, and so entered with fresh-faced excitement into an altogether different kind of chill, oblivious.

"Everyone's sledding. Chores are done and I don't have any homework. Can I go?"

Mum had turned back to the sink, where she leaned her full weight on its edge. "Take Tom," she said to the dishwater. "He's there, behind the chair."

There is sledding, and then there is sledding in the dark. The snow had lightened, and the full moon illuminated the sky behind the clouds. The toboggan run stretched a ghostly white in front of the dozen kids who, after a running start and precision-timed leap, sailed down the hill and into the thrill of the slide. Dark patches through the snowfall were our warnings; here were brambles, look out! Whatever we used—the curved side of an old barrel, or a real toboggan like the one my father had built—we were experts at steering, and rose to the challenge. If we wound up in the brush, it was on purpose.

I had veered off down a side hill, missing scrubby pines and bushes, and had come to a stop in the hollow, out of the wind. It was a peaceful place to rest a moment, and I stayed there for a little while before voices shook me upright.

The first sound I heard were the low voices of men,

five of them, and I recognized the voices of Mr. Armstrong, Mr. Schroeder, old Bill Wylie and Charlie Strautman, and Mr. North, who I considered a kind of kindred spirit since sometimes in the classroom he stuttered just like me. They were all wearing snowshoes.

"What a fool," I heard Mr. Armstrong say. I could see him shaking his head as he passed not far from me.

"Well, his wife told him to go, I heard. You know how that is," replied Mr. Strautman. It sounded like a joke, but nobody laughed. I saw then that they were pulling a sledge, which skated across the top of the snow.

The second sound I heard was Ellie's laugh, a high, girlish giggle. Peering around a Syringa bush, I could just make out the bulk of her blue wool coat, short in the sleeves, frayed in the lining. Another shape, and a deeper laugh, then a push. There were two shapes on the snow, now, my sister at the bottom, Billy Weber's older brother Gerold on top, the bulk of their winter jackets pressed tightly together. I thought he must be tickling Ellie, and I thought that was horrible, because I hated all the Weber brothers with a passion. She was laughing in a muffled sort of way, and then they both grew very quiet, their faces pushed together.

As the men drew past, out of sight of my sister and Gerold Weber, I must have made some sound, because in the next moment there was a blow from behind me and I tasted snow in my teeth, felt it push into my eyes and ears. I struggled, gasping, thinking: *Billy*. But it was Ellie's voice that hissed in my ear. "Don't you *dare* tell."

I sat up to see the retreating back of my sister. Gerold was nowhere in sight, and the men with the sledge had passed. I realized, then, that the other sledders had gone home; no noise came from the toboggan run above me.

The snow had stopped, for a moment, but its memory muffled the passage of air and I felt stranded in a cold, white cloud.

All at once, I knew who the sled was for. They were going out on a rescue. Last winter, they had found a man who had hurt himself bucking trees at the top of his property. A limb had fallen on his head, knocking him unconscious. He had frozen to death.

And it became clear to me, then, that my sister knew that my mother and father had fought; she must have been listening at the door. *Don't you dare tell.* Of course, Ellie knew about the fight, and knew, as I did, that some horrible accident had befallen my father. An accident caused by my mother who had said those words: *go to hell.* It was a terrible thing to say those words, and in their wake my father, no doubt shocked, had run out the door and straight into the snowstorm. That put my mother at fault; she would be a murderer and would be taken to jail. With our father dead and my mother in jail, who would take us, and where would we go? It was best to remain silent. I sat on my toboggan, shaking, my mother's words echoing in my head: *go to hell.*

I could not go home. I could not face my mother, the murderer, or the wrath of my sister, for surely someone would weasel out of me the awful truth. Across the sled run I could see the white hump of snow piled as a bank against the curve of the run. I left my toboggan where it lay and scrambled across, digging into the snow with a sharp stick until I had created a round hollow just a little bigger than my curled body. My igloo. A place to hide, to wait until the men came back.

If my dad was still alive, I would go home. I imagined my dad unconscious, my mother and sister at his side,

Mr. North and the others gathered in the doorway, concerned. I would explain: he heard an animal, went outside to investigate, must have gotten lost. They would all believe me because I was so earnest, and my sister would be proud of the ingenuity of my lie.

If my father was dead, I would live in my igloo until I had a chance to escape. I could run away by dogsled, I thought, just like the Eskimos. I could sneak into our yard and catch Arrow, our big black dog, and harness him to my toboggan. In cover of darkness, I would whisk down the frozen lake, being sure not to yell "mush!" until I was too far from Bear Creek to be heard. I would start a new life.

Would I take Ellie? Yes, because she would be so grateful to me, her hero in the storm.

Time passed, and I waited, my thoughts coursing through my head like runaway trains. I was not cold, and although I could not feel my feet, this didn't bother me unless I moved, when they felt like dead blocks of wood, like someone else's feet altogether. Then I tucked them further under my body like a hen on a laying bench, imagined the snow above me a soft wool blanket, me nestled deep under the covers. My thoughts quieted, and I began to feel sleepy.

To keep myself awake while I waited for the return of the men and their sledge, I sang the song I loved most, the one I heard my father sing when he was fixing something, a song he remembered from the war. It was a song my tongue rejoiced in, because it sounded just like me:

"K-k-k-Katy, beautiful Katy, you're the only g-g-g-girl that I adore…"

My voice sounded thin against the night, which squatted above me like some huge animal, waiting. The snow, which had fallen steadily for an interval, had stopped again, and the full moon pushed through the clouds, turning the snow to a million tiny diamonds. There was no wind. Against that massive stillness, I tried again.

"When the m-m-moon shines,
Over the c-c-c-cowshed,
I'll be waiting at the k-k-k-kitchen door…"

My voice trailed off, and I listened to the silence for a time, equally scared to leave my little nest as I was to stay. I looked up at the moon, just like the one in my song, a friendly presence that seemed to return my gaze. Again, I sang, this time in a whisper:

"When the m-m-moon shines,
Over the c-c-c-cowshed,
I'll be waiting at the k-k-k-kitchen door."

I must have dozed for a bit, because the next thing I heard were the voices coming back, drifting down through the trees above the toboggan run. I heard Mr. Wylie say: "Send 'im down the hill, it'll be faster."

"That's no way to treat the dead," Jack Armstrong grunted, but Mr. North's voice followed, all reason and common sense: "We should have been back an hour ago, Jack, if it weren't for the sledge being heavy, and sticking like it is on the snow. We'll save t-ten minutes sending it down the hill. I can't feel my feet, Jack. We're all frozen."

"He's dead anyway, he ain't gonna know," said Mr. Strautman, and then I heard a shifting high above me, and grunts as the men manoeuvred the sledge into position.

"Bomb's away!" yelled Mr. Wylie, and Mr. Armstrong warned: "Bill," because everyone knew Mr. North had been shell-shocked during the war.

With a sound that began as a whistle and ended in a wail, the body of my father tore down the hill, screaming across the hard-packed snow. When it hit the bank I must have wailed too, because a moment later I was lifted out, sobbing, staring at the bottom of the overturned sledge. A blue hand extended from beneath it, freed of its bindings by the impact. Mr. Schroeder let go of me for a moment at the sight, and my legs, frozen into chunks of ice themselves, collapsed beneath me.

"Stupid thing to do," said Mr. Armstrong angrily, helping me back up. I could not tell if he meant me, hiding in the snowbank, or my mother, sending my father to his death, the sledge and the body beneath it, or the fact that my legs were too stupid, it seemed, to hold me up.

"I'm s-s-sorry," I sputtered. "Ellie t-t-t-told me not to tell! I'm s-sorry."

"Tom!" came my father's anguished voice directly behind me. Mr. Armstrong relaxed his grip, and I landed on my bum in a circle of men beside an overturned sledge on which lay a dead man who was not my father.

He had been looking for me, my father told me later, everywhere. In the barn, in the summer kitchen, in the chicken coop. He was sure I was just hiding out, at first, but as time wore on he became desperate, pounding on doors up and down Bear Creek's main road, and soon enough the town was buzzing with the news: a man and a boy, both missing.

Earlier that evening Bill Wylie, who ran the store, Jack Armstrong, Frederick Schroeder, Charlie Strautman and Richard North were playing cards in the back of the display area, their wet overcoats steaming by the stove.

Around them were shelves, sparsely stocked—here a tin of sardines, there a jar of pickles—and, behind the door in the corner, Bear Creek's sole telephone. When it rang for the first time in weeks, five hands of cards hit the table and five heads turned as one. Bill Wylie lunged towards the wall, then, and caught the heavy cylindrical handset on the second ring. Heavy static meant for a loud conversation, but the four remaining card players understood little except that the card game was over.

"Yes?"

"What?"

"Alice? When? No, what day?"

"What?"

Alice Epp's brother-in-law, who lived up the lake, planned to hike down from the rail line above Bear Creek to check on his sister-in-law and her family at the behest of his wife. He should have arrived two days ago, having taken the cleared rail line as close as he could get, then setting out on snowshoes. It was a five-mile walk, but Anthony was a seasoned outdoorsman, Alice told the assembled search party, sobbing. He should have no trouble making the trip down the mountain, even in the snow.

Then, perhaps an hour after the men left to rescue what they'd hoped would be a live, possibly injured man, Frank Klaussen's boy went missing, and soon, everyone who could was getting into boots and coats preparing to go out, calling into the dark for young Tommy Klaussen.

I heard all this bundled up in my old, soft quilt, with a hot-water bottle tucked against my belly, as close to the woodstove as I could get. I cried when my feet began to thaw, sending a million tiny needles through my legs and feeling as if they must be as icy and blue as the hand of the man on the sledge.

"Tommy, Tommy," my mother crooned, while my dad paced and my sister leaned in the doorway, watching. "What were you doing out there?"

Suddenly, my father looked up at Ellie, and then at me. "*What* did you promise Ellie not to tell?" he asked. Somehow, my first frozen words had been forgotten in the rush of bundling me into the warmth of the house, while the rescue party, much subdued, resumed their solemn task of respectfully delivering the body of Alice Epp's brother-in-law to an anxiously waiting household.

And suddenly, I could not remember what the secret was. Had I really thought my mother had sent my father to his death in a snowstorm, that Ellie and I would be orphans when my mother was taken away in handcuffs, and that we would live forever as Eskimos because it would be winter, forever, here in Bear Creek? It all seemed so ridiculous, now, as I held my mug of warm milk and felt the needles subside to tingles, with three sets of eyes watching for my answer.

And then I remembered Ellie pushing me into the snow, and all at once this seemed a monstrous thing, the thing that started it all, and I began to cry again, in great, shaking sobs.

"It w-was Ellie!" I blurted, snot running. My mother wiped my nose, as if I was a baby, and I turned my head away. I could feel my sister's eyes like augers, and I stared at my hands.

"She was on the snow with Gerold Weber."

There was absolute silence in the room, and I did not look up and so did not know what looks were exchanged between my mother, my father, my sister. I heard the slamming of a door, and the double sigh of my mother and father as the moment passed and now they must decide what should come next.

Of course, because I never got to fully explain in the confusion that followed, it did not immediately become clear my sister and Gerold Weber were simply kissing, and while it was certainly a sin to be fourteen years old and kissing a boy in a snowbank, it was not so bad if you had so many clothes on it was almost impossible to do anything particularly sinful, never mind struggle to your feet with any kind of grace once you had been spotted by your baby brother.

Gerold had run home without a backward glance, and I believe that it was this that stung Ellie more than Mum and Dad finding out. My parents, for their part, believed Ellie's teary confessions about her lapse in judgment and felt assured, eventually, that she was not heading straight to hell for her actions. Dad went over to the Weber's the next day and had a long, private talk with Mr. Weber that resulted in an incident between Gerold and his father in the barn that, later, made my parents speak in guilty whispers after Gerold showed up at the store with a black eye and a story about a sledding accident.

I was in my spot behind the chair a few days later, listening. It had not snowed since the night I almost froze like Mrs. Epp's poor brother-in-law. In fact, the temperature had lifted abruptly, the lake ice breaking up with great pops and cracks. The body had been sent home on the first boat to get through, a tug with an ice cutter that pushed up the lake, checking on settlements, distributing food and news. With the release of winter came a shift in Bear Creek, as if a long-held breath was suddenly expelled.

In the sudden thaw, everything dripped, and my mother stood again at the sink, this time looking out the window at the water running in rivers off the roof. My dad came up behind her, and put his arms around her. He had no promise of a job, yet, but with the shift in weather had come hope, and a new playfulness that emerged between them.

"*How* old were you the first time I kissed you?" he said into her neck.

She tilted her head to one side, brought her arms around in front of his.

"Mmmm. Sixteen, at least," she said. "It's an entirely different thing."

"Of course it is," said my father. My mother turned around then, and they kissed. Then she grabbed each side of his suspenders and gave them a good, hard snap.

"But I always knew how to keep you in line," she said.

Ellie came out from her bedroom at that moment, and my parents pulled apart.

"I haven't been out for a week. Could I please go to Mavis's? Just to do homework. Please?"

"Take Tommy with you, then," said my mother. "He's behind the chair."

As a chaperone, I was not appreciated. My sister didn't speak to me the whole way, and, in fact, wouldn't speak to me that spring until the snow was almost entirely gone and Bear Creek was a raging torrent that caused new worry for creekside properties and the parents of small children. On top of that, I was slow; I limped on one bandaged foot that remained a curious shade of blue, with a toe that turned purple, then black. In two weeks, when the *Minto* made its first stop at Bear Creek since December, I would be bundled on board and taken to the hospital in Trail, where my baby toe would be removed, leaving me with an odd gait I carry to this day. But at that moment, I was left to stumble along behind my sister's angry, quick pace, dreading the thought of passing the Weber house. I needn't have worried; my sister gave the house a wide berth, crossing to the other side of the roadway, then crossing back again, while I followed, the dutiful brother.

When we were almost at our destination, Ellie stopped, then whirled around in the slushy road to face me. She loomed large against the grey sky, and she scowled at me.

"B-b-b-baby!" she sneered, and left me standing there in the road, afraid to go on, afraid to go home without her.

I climbed up through the rotting snow to the top of the sledding hill. There I sat, my foot throbbing and my bum wet, watching people come and go, and listening to the voices calling greetings below me until dusk told me suppertime was near. I saw my sister begin walking home on the road below and listened to her calling for me, her voice small and pale against the sweep of the darkening sky.

1936

To: Mr. Duncan P. Wylie
Bear Creek General Store and Post Office
Bear Creek, British Columbia

May 21, 1936

Dear Mr. Wylie,

*This letter is to confirm your appointment as
Wharfinger for the Village of Bear Creek, British
Columbia, effective June 1. As discussed, you will be
responsible for the collection of Tolls for use of the
Government Wharf, including docking by vessel or
other commercial or non-commercial use. Financial
Reports and Remittances will be made on the first day
of each month, and payment for your services will
follow these reports.*

> *Yours very sincerely,*
> *Charles Fyfe*
> *Department of Transportation*
> *Province of British Columbia*

Duncan

When I bought this store and post office from my cousin
Bill Wylie, way out in some godforsaken place called
Bear Creek—what kind of a name is that anyway?—
Duncan, he told me, it's a trade: you get peace and quiet,

I get civilization. And sure enough, I wanted the peace and quiet as it had been a hell of a year in Toronto. First, I lost my job on the construction site, and this is after Lillian left me, by the way, walking out like she did for some streetcar driver—a streetcar driver!—and then that very day, Lil gone a week and then me getting the speech, you know the one: I'm sorry, you're a good worker, Duncan, but times are tough, and I walk out across Bloor and what happens but doesn't a car come tearing around the corner and I leap with both my boots right off the payment and into an oncoming streetcar, my face right smack into the windshield. The irony of being hit twice by a streetcar driver—once stealing my Lillian, once on Bloor Street, was not lost on me, let me tell you, when I woke up later at Toronto General, all stitches like a goddamn quilting bee.

Anyway, once things started to heal up and the big red train tracks across my face began to fade, it was no real surprise to find I couldn't smile on half my face, all those muscles and nerves having been sliced like a side of pork in a butcher shop. No real surprise because it was obvious to me that this was the way things were going to go for yours truly, now, one goddamn thing after another, and I suppose that's just fate. But who was going to hire an ugly man who could only talk out of half his face?

Bill, he'd been in this Bear Creek for a couple of years after following some romantic notion he got from the back of a magazine about New Opportunities in the West. He went out to buy land from this guy Stoddart, son of some other guy Stoddart, had been wheeling and dealing out that way for years but when he got there he decided maybe farming life wasn't half for him and here was the store for sale and he had some money saved and bought the place for a song.

But it wasn't for Bill, this country life, and while he liked the town well enough it soured for him when he got jilted by a girl for some other fellow whose family had been there forever. I'll always be a stranger here, he said, there's no point, and he thought that Toronto, ugly as sin as it is, was the place to be after all.

Me, I liked the idea of going away—far away—and thought that in a town that small, people'll get to know you for who you are, given a little time. There's a poet's heart inside me, although Lil never saw it, and that was even when I was half good looking. I wrote her things, verses and such. I found one folded into a wedge, holding up the short leg of the kitchen table, the day I came home to an empty apartment.

Anyway, the thought of going way out to British Columbia struck me as attractive, truth be told, and there was nothing for me in Toronto, that's for sure. So now I pay by the month, send off the cheque to Bill, who's got a job selling government bonds door to door, and you know, Bill was always a charmer anyway.

Bill stayed just long enough to show me around, introduce me to Jack Armstrong and George Hartmann and a few others and then tossed me the keys and left on the next boat. I guess I was quiet, didn't really know what to say when people came around for the mail and whatnot. And God's truth, when I look in the mirror in that little room in the back where I sleep, all Bill's collected this-and-that crowding every corner, *I* don't even know what the hell I'm thinking, my face all twisted like that. So the folks of Bear Creek, not knowing me and not being able to get a good reading, eh, they're cautious-like. Used to

ANNE DeGRACE

be, Bill told me, this was the place people came to pass the time of day. If it weren't for folks needing their mail and consumables, I wouldn't see a soul.

Those Epp twins, one comes to get the mail, no idea which one, and he looks at me when I hand 'im a letter and clutches it to his bony little chest and runs headlong out the door like he's seen a ghost, grabs the other one offa the porch, whichever one *that* is, and they go tearing off up the road home. I should make a horror movie, one of those Bela Lugosi films. Wouldn't need no makeup.

A poet's heart. Hah. But in the evenings, I still turn a rhyme or two, just to keep it up. It can't hurt any.

Then there's Ursula Hartmann, daughter of one of those here-forever families but sweet as all get out, comes swishing in here with those ankles, that hair, always has a kind word, voice like an angel, but deep, like. Grew up here but then went off to the prairie somewhere, heard she got arrested in that big riot in Regina, shook her up. So she came back to teach school here. Not married, not ever, and you got to wonder why, now she's 30 if she's a day, but then, she's got a head on her, I figure that's gonna scare 'em off. She's always talking politics and such with that wife of Armstrong's, Isobel her name is. Suffragette. Not stuff I pay attention to. But you know, I wait every day for Ursula Hartmann to come through my door, and she smiles at me and it's suddenly a sunny day, no matter if it's raining cats and dogs outside.

Ursula

Sometimes I wonder what I was thinking, coming home after all those years away. The first day, home with Mama

160

and Papa, in the old kitchen, the smells, Mama stirring a big pot of borscht, I traced my finger along the thin blue line around our old plates and it was just like sinking into a warm bathtub. But then I remember there is no big clawfoot bathtub to sink into here. Mama and Papa still use the steel tub and Mama still heats up water on the stove, but at least the water comes in through wooden pipes from upper Bear Creek and now flows straight out of the tap and into the kettle.

Some days, I think, Regina could be on the other side of the world.

It was Mr. North who urged me to become a teacher in the first place, and then my dear friend Isobel, who knew how much I wanted to see the world, said I could board with her friend Lisbet in Winnipeg if I wanted to study there. The house was always full of Lisbet's friends and they'd stay up all night drinking cheap brandy and talking about politics, and after a while, I knew enough to join in. "Up the Revolution!" they'd shout at 4 or 5 a.m., and if I wasn't asleep, exhausted from studying all day, I'd be shouting too. There was a man there. James. I didn't know he was married; he didn't tell me.

I don't know how I passed, but I did. Lisbet said I had the brains of ten women, which, she said, is the same as saying I had the brains of twenty men. But pass I did, and my first job was at a one-room schoolhouse in Prince Albert, the oldest boy in the class not two years younger than me. It was a tough school, and those students got the better of me in the first hour and held onto it for the whole year. When Lisbet wrote in June to say she was moving to Regina to start a chapter there, I could think of no reason not to join her.

That's how I wound up in Regina, and, unable to find

a teaching job, I started working for a printer. It was the only job I could get. And then Lisbet wanted me to make arrangements to print pamphlets at night, and the boss was fine with it all, as long as we left him the cash and he didn't know in any official way what was going on after hours. Harvey the pressman was in on it; moonlighting was going to earn him enough money to go to Toronto, and that's all he wanted.

Lisbet and I rented a two-room apartment over a milliner's shop, the smell of steam and wet felt drifting up in the daytime, except on Sunday. That was the day Lisbet's new friends would come over, and Harvey too. Harvey was sweet on me but I wasn't having any of that, knowing he was practically on the next train out.

There was a movement, we learned, a protest that had left Vancouver that spring. Hundreds of relief camp workers had boarded the freight trains and were going to Ottawa, going to make their case to Prime Minister Bennett himself, right there on Parliament Hill. They were picking up more men all the time, we heard, the numbers swelling. They would be in Regina sometime in June, who knew how many, hundreds and hundreds for sure.

On June 14th I was handing out leaflets on the corner of 12th and McIntyre that said:

> *On to Ottawa.*
> *The Relief Camp Strikers will*
> *leave Regina via C.P.R. Freight*
> *Monday, June 17 at approx. 10 p.m.*

Of course, they didn't leave then. They'd arrived, all right, but the government had made a deal with the railway that they couldn't board the trains, and so they were milling about the train yards, setting up camp in the weeds, seething.

On July 1st I went down with Lisbet to see the protest. There had to be 1,500 workers, mostly men, and then the police came. Somebody threw a rock, and then another, and then somebody hit a policeman with a big piece of cordwood and he went down, and then we could hear the guns being fired, but we couldn't see anything else. Everyone was running. I turned to watch a woman screaming for her baby, lost somewhere in all that, and then turned back and Lisbet was gone. Someone put a rock in my hand and I looked at it, not sure how it got there or what to do with it. When I looked up, there was a policeman, and he wrenched the rock out of my hand and twisted my hair and pulled me into the paddy wagon. There was a woman there, her dress torn, and she looked at me through her hair and spat and said, "Bunch of bloody pigs."

I was in the holding cell three days. At the beginning, I sat with my back straight, trying to look defiant. By the second day, I was tired, and dirty, so dirty, I just curled into a corner with my hands over my greasy hair and thought of Bear Creek. I walked up the roads; I threw rocks into the lake off the dock. I watched the mountains coloured by sunset light. I smelled Mama's cooking, felt her hand on my head. And then there was a pressure on my arm, and when I looked up it was a policeman and he was pulling me to my feet and out the cell door and there, on the other side of the counter, was Lisbet. And she took me in her arms and smoothed my matted hair and said, "My brave, brave girl," and then murmured, "We are all just cogs in the wheel, sweetheart."

Lisbet must have written to Isobel about me. By then I had no interest in being a cog in any wheel, thank you very much, I had had enough. I just didn't know what to do next. After two weeks of staying inside our apartment, shades drawn, lights out, Lisbet came to me with a letter.

Ursula, it said, *we're going to need a teacher here in Bear Creek. Richard North is getting married—can you imagine?— to the sister of a friend of his, someone who died in battle. Apparently he'd been writing to her since the War, if you can believe that. It's all very romantic. He kept it quite a secret until he just announced out of the blue that he is moving back east. And of course, we all say good for him, with all his troubles, even though it means finding a replacement on short notice. When Lisbet wrote that you are between teaching posts, well, we all thought who could be more perfect? And so the post is yours in September if you want it.*

And so began the first slivers of light into our dark apartment, curtains opening slowly, followed by tentative forays out into the street, the shops. New clothes, a train ticket. Lisbet raised the money; I had lost my job. She has her ways.

And now I am here, and the nostalgic thrill of Mama's bread and the warm safety of my old room has worn away, and we are into the spring, the end of my first year, with only a month left of school, and I am tired, tired, tired of this life all over again. If it weren't for dear Isobel and, of course, Eddie, I'd be going crazy.

Duncan

When the advertisement for the Bear Creek Wharfinger job came to me as Postmaster, to put up in the store for anyone to apply, I kept it to myself. Who better for the job than the Storekeeper and Postmaster, situated close to the wharf as the store is, knowing the comings and goings of everyone. And with things going the way they are, the store and postmaster money don't pay near enough, not near enough to get out of Bill's smelly old shack in the back and get something comfortable. Bad enough there's no electricity here and just the one phone. I don't think anybody figured when the government took down the old wharf and built the fancy new one they'd be charging tolls. It'll come as a surprise, when the tolls come into effect, sure enough, but if somebody's gonna do it, might as well be me. And here's a notice, come today, with orders to put it up "in a public place," and as there's no more public place than this, I've put it up right beside the big black phone by the door. And it's time for Ursula Hartmann to come for the mail like she does after school. She'll be the first to see it, and when she asks, I can tell her, the government gave me, Duncan Wylie, the job of wharfinger, an important job, that's for damn sure. And what will she think of me then?

Ursula

Eddie caught me up on the path I take as a shortcut down from the schoolhouse to the store where I pick up our mail. It was the bushy part of the path, and so I'm quite sure nobody saw us as he caught me about the waist and bit my earlobe. He ran his tongue inside, and that always sends shivers down my spine, so I laughed and pushed him away.

"Will I see you tonight?" he asked, and I thought of the narrow daybed in the mill where he works for his father, where they make boxes for the fruit, and I said no, not tonight, Mama and Papa will think something's up. He doesn't understand why I want to keep it a secret, but I know if I bring Eddie into our home like a proper suitor and Papa pins him with that glare it will poison something, truly. I can hear Papa now: he is too young for you, Ursula. What will people say, the school-teacher carrying on with someone only a handful of years out of school himself? And of course Mr. Strautman and Papa have never been the best of friends anyway. The box factory is right next door to our orchard, and there is a dispute about the property line that has been going on forever.

I pushed Eddie away and he carried on up the hill, laughing and whistling. He was off to make a deal with Jack Armstrong to clear the top of his land, I knew. They're short of lumber for the boxes, and cherry season isn't far away.

When the screen door slammed behind me and I adjusted my eyes to the light in the store, I saw Duncan Wylie looking at me the way he does, that half-smile on his face. He is a sight, but then I think, he is not so different from the rest of us. We are all people, just people, that's what Lisbet taught me. We all have rights, she said.

"Good afternoon, Mr. Wylie," I said. "I've come for the mail," and he ducked behind the counter and emerged like a troll from behind a rock with a letter from Lisbet, which I would keep in my pocket until I could be alone with it.

"Best to yer folks," Mr. Wylie said, like he always does. And then he looked at me curiously, and I wondered why but thanked him and turned. That's when I saw the notice tacked to the door beside the phone. And I knew he was watching me read it.

Treading Water

Duncan

She didn't say a word. Not a word. I waited for her to look back at me, but she didn't look back, not for a moment, and I am left, here, with the echo of the door closing and the outside screen banging on its spring. Damn, why didn't I say something? I could have said something.

Ursula

Of course, I went straight to Jack and Isobel's house. Isobel wanted to march right down there and read the notice herself, but I convinced her to make me a cup of tea and wait for Jack to come home, so we can all talk about it together. There's nothing there I haven't told you, I said. But Isobel leapt into one of her rants about the working farmer, barely enough to survive the winter once you pay for the picking and the crating and shipping and those prairie brokers, who knows how honest they are, and there's precious little left as it is. "And now," Isobel told me, "there's this new Natural Products Marketing Act—" and she can see right through that, she said, our profits will end up in somebody else's pocket. She's a great believer in the worker, Isobel is, and although Jack is president of the Bear Creek Fruit Growers' Co-operative, we all know Isobel's the real push behind it all. "These wharf tolls," she said, and made a face. "We pay our taxes and they build roads. How is a wharf any different from a road? We're paying twice, we are. And the worst thing is, we don't even have a damn road."

When Isobel starts to swear, things are getting hot. I sipped my tea, nodding, letting the rant run its course, relieved when Jack came in the door, dirty from the orchard. "We're going to have a bumper crop of cherries," he said. "We're going to make some money this year."

And then we told him about the wharf tolls, and his first question was: Who around here would even collect them?

Duncan

Doesn't take long for word to get around this place. They haven't stopped buying from the store, there being no competition, and they have to get their mail, but they're not spending a minute more than they have to, not that they would anyway. And then Ursula came in this morning, and she smiled at me the way she does, and she asked me right out: "Is it true you'll be the wharfinger, Mr. Wylie?" And when I nodded, she said, "I think you should know that there is a meeting tonight at the schoolhouse about how we should respond to the tolls. Perhaps you should come, Mr. Wylie," she said. And I told her yes, I would come, but I know when I swing the sign closed I'll go back into Bill's old rat's nest in the back and cook myself an egg and work on the books, balancing the numbers, trying to make it come out even.

Ursula

Papa had been blustering the way he does since I came home from Isobel and Jack's and told him about the

wharf tolls. He said he'd heard that Charlie Strautman
will have to up the price on boxes because now his nails
and sawblades will cost him more and that means the
co-op's going to pay twice, more for the boxes and more
to ship the fruit out. And who's going to buy Bear Creek
Co-op fruit if it's cheaper coming out of Robson, where
they can just load it right on the train, no tolls? It does-
n't matter how good our cherries are. I could see a future
argument between Papa and Eddie's father about the cost
of fruit boxes. But for the moment we talked about the
meeting at the schoolhouse tonight, and what's to be
done. "Wylie better be there," he said.

After dinner, Mama said she'd stay home, and I could
tell she was looking for a quiet evening with Papa out of
the house and blustering somewhere else. Papa wanted
to walk with me, but I'd promised Eddie I'd meet him at
the lookout first, and so I told him instead that I promised Birthe today I'd drop off some of Mama's mustard
for a plaster, Frederick being so sick, and that was true
enough, but perhaps I was in more of a hurry than I
needed to be for that.

So I went on ahead, stopping at Birthe's with the
mustard and then cutting up behind her house. And as
I came up the path to the lookout I could see Eddie
standing, smoking, back to me, looking out over the
water. In the spring evening the lake looked so beautiful, dancing light on a slate and cobalt tabletop. I never
cease to wonder at its moods, this body of water that so
defines us. And Eddie, with the sun's reflection casting
a glow across his face, looked so handsome at that
moment I felt a little punch at my heart, a weakening of
my knees, and I stood for a moment, looking. When he
turned, his ears were sticking out the way they do and

his eyes, a little too close together, reminded me that he's just a man, after all. But then he kissed me, on each eye, behind my ear, and then, finally, on my mouth, and I felt like soft, melted butter. "It's only a meeting," he said. "They'll be fine without us." And he pulled me towards the bushes, but I mustered my good sense and said: "Later." We spent a few moments, then, tucked into the trees before I pulled away and ran ahead back down the path, knowing he would follow a few minutes behind me, whistling.

The meeting was the usual for meetings in Bear Creek. There were as many women out as men, and Jack, of course, presided. The women sat at the small desks, while the men stood, arms crossed, at the back. Birthe was home with Frederick, but Albert, who is working the orchard these days, was there. Eddie leaned in the corner, not looking at me. There was much discussion as the situation was explained and rumours shared. Adeline Strautman stood up and said she'd heard it will cost ten cents just to *walk* on the wharf, and that had everyone shouting angrily. I looked around: Duncan Wylie was notably absent, and I thought of him, alone at the back of the store, while all this went on.

In the end, it was decided: we would simply not use the wharf. It was such a simple plan that Isobel laughed out loud and clapped her hands. The forestry boat and the Signet, owned by the Bear Creek Co-op, could easily pull onto the beach to load people and fruit. Even the *Minto*, with her shallow keel, could pull up close, although it would take a little more work and some ingenuity to load her. "But will the boats comply?" asked Charlie Strautman. I knew he wanted to get a word in, look like he was on our side, but I know from Eddie he was also counting up the increase on the box prices, something that has already set Papa muttering.

"They'll have to," said Jack. "They need us as much as we need them. I'll get the word out."

Duncan

So now the word is out: Duncan Wylie is the new wharfinger, and if folks were not exactly friendly before, they're sure not passing the time of day with me now. In three days my job begins. I have the government ledger book, the fee schedule. I've put the sign up in the window.

Ursula

After Jack went in to talk Duncan Wylie out of the job, and got nowhere, I went in to get the mail with a resolve to be kind. In truth, my main goal was to try another tactic, because the easiest thing for all of us would be if the job could not be filled because nobody in the community was willing to do it. Of course, the government might just send someone out, then, one of their own boys, but non-compliance would be a start, and buy us time. As it is, the boats still have to be convinced to load from the beach before the first cherries are ready to ship, or we'll lose the crop.

You catch more flies with honey, my Mama tells me, and I think she must have been cultivating that saying since the first time she met Papa in Manitoba. If Mama is honey then Papa is flypaper: the end result may be the same, but the flies aren't as happy about it all. I took the honey approach.

"Mr. Wylie," I said. "How are you today?" I put on my most charming smile.

"Been better," he began gruffly, but then looked up and saw me smiling and stopped talking altogether. He smiled back out of the good side of his mouth, and blushed. "You want your mail."

"Actually, yes, I did come for that, but I also wanted to talk to you."

"About the wharf tolls." He said this sounding beaten, like a dog. I felt sorry for him, then. "I have a contract," he said, mustering himself. "Somebody's going to collect the tolls, Miss Hartmann. It may as well be me. You folks think you can stop the government, but you can't. They own this province. They own that wharf."

"They don't own the lake, Mr. Wylie." I didn't know if he knew about our plan.

"Look, the government built the wharf, how do you think it's gonna get paid for? It won't be forever. You folks just need to accept that this is the way it's gonna be and stop griping."

"I wouldn't count on that. We had a perfectly good wharf that didn't cost us a penny to use, and if you think the tolls will stop when the wharf's paid for, I think you're mistaken. We are all cogs in a wheel, Mr. Wylie. It just depends on which wheel you want to push."

Duncan

She left, then, and for the next five minutes I thought of the things I should have said, my mouth working though no words were coming out. I was still talking to myself that way when Eddie Strautman came in and caught me with my hands in the air making my point to an empty store.

"Looks like you're conducting an orchestra, Duncan," he said. He's one of the few who calls me by my first name, and I never know whether to be insulted because it's not respectful coming from such a young sap, or to take it as friendly when there's not so much friendliness directed at yours truly. I put my hands down flat on the counter, and then collected myself and reached for the Strautman mail.

"Has the schoolteacher been in yet? I wanted to ask if she needs some more wood for the stove up there," he asked me.

"She left, oh, five minutes ago," I said. "She didn't say where she was going."

He looked at me, and I thought he was going to launch into a speech about the wharf tolls and to tell you the truth, I had no patience for it. That Ursula had left me rattled, all that nonsense about cogs and wheels, and with the tone of her voice, all gentle, like. What the hell was she talking about? You do your job, you get your paycheque, that's all there is to it. It's not a popularity contest. I was steeling myself for whatever Eddie was going to say next, but he gave me a grin and tucked the mail in his jacket pocket.

"Later, Duncan," he said. "I'll see you later."

Ursula

When Eddie caught up with me I was just rounding the bend towards our house, and I felt annoyed because Mama might be watching from the window, or Papa from the orchard. But he tipped his cap to me very formally, then hooked his hands behind his back and rocked on his heels, looking for all the world like a labourer politely asking if he could be of service. When I tried to suppress my laughter it came out as a kind of snort, and I wiped my nose with the back of my hand in a very unladylike manner.

"Miss Hartmann!" he said, "How lovely you look when you come over all pig-like. Perhaps we might wallow together?"

"Eddie…"

"Pretend we're talking about wood for the schoolhouse."

"Are we? It's getting awfully warm for woodfires."

"There are leftover odds and ends from the mill I could deliver. For next year."

"We *are* talking about firewood, then."

"I could deliver them, say, this evening, at about, say, midnight? When do your folks turn in for the night?"

"Ah, we are *not* talking about firewood."

"Of course we are. We're just arranging delivery," he said, tipped his hat again, and turned away.

Later that night, I did slip out, and made my way in the dark to the schoolhouse. Eddie was there, on the porch, so still that at first I thought he was part of the woodpile stacked against the outer wall. He had not brought kindling, of course, just an utterly charming grin as he caught me up in his arms and I smelled the wood and cigarette smoke on his jacket, in his hair. Mama and Papa would never forgive me, but they don't know how the world is changing, do they? And I love him, this boy who would go anywhere with me.

Duncan

It's the end of a long day in which nothing happened, and I'm sitting now in Bill's godawful clutter thinking they gotta come around, how long can they hold out?

Today was the first day of the wharf tolls. The boats came and went, and the people of Bear Creek stayed off the wharf. I pushed the wheelbarrow up the dock to pick up the mailbags as usual, and the store supplies. They should all be grateful that as wharfinger I don't have to pay the tolls for the store supplies or I'd have to raise the prices. They should be *grateful*, goddamn it. Instead, custom has dropped off, hardly anyone in the store today.

I watched that young Shannon boy row out to each boat in turn, have a conversation, row back. Something's up, smells to high heaven around here, but what?

Ursula Hartmann came by after school to get the mail. She is the only one who's really friendly, and I tried to make conversation, to keep her in the store longer. You know, little things, like about the weather and such. And as she spoke I didn't even hear what the heck she said, just watched her mouth move over those teeth. When she smiles there are little extra creases at the corners, like her face isn't big enough to contain all that smile, and her eyes disappear into these little half-moons, and I wait for them to come out again like stars.

I have been writing poetry, secret-like, since I was a young lad. The poems I wrote to Lil, she'd just laugh that laugh of hers, like icicles falling. Even when she was running with that streetcar driver and I knew—I must have known—something was up, I'd still leave a poem on the pillow, in her handbag, by her compact in the bathroom. I never knew what she did with half of 'em. I think if I wrote a poem to Ursula, she wouldn't stick it under some table leg.

Ursula

When I heard the *Minto's* whistle this morning I left the children where they worked away at their lessons and went out onto the schoolhouse porch. From there, I could see the sternwheeler pulling in, and I waited to see if it would pull up to the wharf, where Duncan Wylie waited, or the beach, where my father, Jack Armstrong, young Albert Schroeder and a half dozen others waited to load the first shipment of cherries. The sternwheeler bypassed the wharf and angled up to the beach where the men leapt forward, pushing the floating dock, anchored at the shore side, into position to meet the loading plank as it was lowered from the cargo hold. Then, hand over hand, the boxes disappeared into the belly of the boat while, on the wharf, Mr. Wylie raised and lowered his arms, paced in circles, picked up the handles of his wheelbarrow, and set them down again. You could almost see the steam rising from his ears, but I didn't laugh. I felt sorry for him, truthfully. Then I felt a gentle pressure at my elbow and looked around to see Annie Weider looking up at me. "Back inside," I said, and laid my hand for a moment on the top of her brown curls.

Duncan

No mail today, thanks to that trick they pulled. Three boats in today, including a barge bringing supplies for the box factory and for the store, but I was not about to go down there and haul supplies off the beach the way they are doing. But while the store is my own—and they can starve, I surely don't give a damn—I am hired by the Canadian Postal Service to pick up and sort the mail, and if the boat won't dock at the wharf tomorrow, I'll have some hard deciding to do.

Ursula

When I stopped at Isobel's after school before heading down for the mail, she told me the whole story: how poor Duncan Wylie tried to push his wheelbarrow down to the beach to get the mailbags, and, when it wouldn't go through the sand, had to haul the bags up the beach to where the barrow stood waiting at the road. It took him three trips, and not one of the men on the beach lifted a finger to help. She said it gleefully, and clapped her hands together and threw herself back into the over-stuffed armchair and laughed, and I joined in, I'll admit that. But now I feel a little sorry, for all that, because he is such a sad man, is Duncan Wylie.

ANNE DeGRACE

Duncan

They all stood there, smirking, while I hauled those bags up the beach. They wouldn't be smirking if they didn't get their mail, though, would they?

Ursula

I tried to talk to Duncan Wylie again today. It has been two weeks and he is still hauling the mailbags up from the beach.

"You could resign from the job as Government Wharfinger, and you could tell them that the tolls just won't work here," I told him. "Nobody else will take the job, and with nobody to collect the tolls, the boats will dock and the fruit will load and all will be just as it was before. After all, as it is you're not collecting any tolls, and having everyone against you can't be very pleasant.

"You would be a hero," I told him, then thought: that's laying it on a bit thick, Ursula, don't you think? But a look was already coming across his face, an expression I couldn't read. "Think on it, Mr. Wylie," I said. I tried to sound firm, tried to muster up a bit of Papa, who I believe, along with almost everyone else, had had a few words already with Duncan Wylie. But what he did was smile, if you could call it that. Half a smile, one side of his face wrinkling up like an old man. When I left the store, I could feel him watching me.

There are two weeks left of school and I am preparing examinations for the students. I have still not said a thing to Mama and Papa and Eddie remains a secret to all but Isobel—and probably Jack as well, since she tells

178

him everything. But those two can keep a secret, and so it really is up to me. And now I have a secret of my own, one I haven't told a soul, even Eddie. It has been three weeks since my monthly time was due to come, and did not.

Duncan

Soft of cheek and bright of eye,
Comes Ursula into my day,
A grace of limb, a toss of hair,
And then she stands, a breath away.

She does not come for me alone,
And yet I wait, each day anew,
For my love to stand again,
Before me with those eyes of blue.

Which of course makes no sense at all because her eyes are grey and anyway, the mail doesn't come every day, and she's not my love, she's as good as a million miles away. She comes for the goddamn mail three times a week and not for yours truly, and if anyone saw these verses I'd be a laughing stock. Least of all if *she* saw them.

But what if she did see them? What if she did?

Ursula

I left for the schoolhouse early this morning. I wanted some time to think, without Mama clucking over me. She knows something is wrong, she just doesn't know what, and so her best solution is to feed me, which is absolutely not what I want, especially in the morning.

When I arrived at the door there was a piece of paper wedged in there. Eddie, I thought, melting a little as I read the poem. I didn't think he could write such a thing; he has never written to me before. My eyes aren't blue, of course, but they can look a little that way in the right light. The way I meet with him, so often, about wood for the schoolhouse or some such pretext. How carefully he's written in our little games.

I stood for a while in the morning sun on the porch, enjoying the quiet before the children arrived, thinking: we must go, as soon as school is finished. We'll have to elope, there's no other way for it now. When I tell him, he'll agree, I'm that sure of him. I tucked the poem into my pocket and fingered it over the course of the day, drawing courage for this evening's conversation. There are only three days left of school, and I don't want to wait a moment longer.

I watched the men stacking today's cherry shipment on the beach, ready for the boat. It is a beautiful day, and I will feel sorry to leave this place.

Duncan

Ursula said nothing about the poem when she came in today for the mail, but then, of course, I didn't sign it. But it was all there, the clues, because where else would she go every day for something and stand across the counter from a fellow? I looked for a new softness in her features, some telltale sign. Poetry can change a person. Well, it didn't change Lillian, but Ursula is nothing like Lil.

Could a woman like that love a man like me? She looks as if she sees inside a fella, that's what. Perhaps she could.

Ursula

I saw Eddie ahead of me on the walk as I was coming up from the store. I had just had the most unsettling conversation with Mr. Wylie, and I was going to stop in at Isobel's and tell her everything. I had come to the conclusion I needed a good heart-to-heart talk with my best friend, even before Eddie. I don't know what it was about the conversation with Duncan Wylie, but something snapped inside, all the bottled up worry, when he opened that twisted mouth of his and spoke.

"You said something before about wheels, Miss Hartmann," he had blurted. "About cogs." It took me a minute to grasp what he was referring to, and I stared at his mouth without meaning to as I tried to catch up.

"Well, yes," I said, finally. "Yes, we all play a part in something much bigger."

"And the wheel," he said, and he was looking down, now, at his stubby fingers as they gripped the countertop. "The wheel you talk about. Is that... is that like...fate?"

I didn't know what to say. What would a man like Duncan Wylie be doing thinking about fate? But as he uttered the word, I thought of Lisbet. *We are all cogs in the wheel, sweetheart.* I thought of the labour movement, of women's rights, of the things we can change, and about the wheel that is that change, all of us pushing. And all of a sudden I was thinking of the changes in my own life, and how they seemed to be rolling right over me. And the image came to me suddenly of the paddle wheel churning all that water as the *Minto* chugged down the lake, so much power in the movement of water. Down the lake that would be carrying me away, and all at once I felt like I was drowning.

"Like fate," I said, but I'm not at all sure what I meant by my answer, with the blood roaring in my ears. And then I ran out, the door slamming shut behind me, without the mail I had come for in the first place. As I hurried away up the hill, I looked ahead, and there was Eddie.

I called after him then, in broad daylight, on the main street of Bear Creek. What was I thinking? But he was far ahead of me, out of earshot, his broad stride carrying him quickly as he cut up the hill, and he was gone before I could call again.

Duncan

Fate. Is fate something that happens to you, or can you shape it? I sat down and wrote the letter. I wrote it out twice, once for the Government, once for Ursula.

> *To: Mr. Charles Fyfe*
> *Department of Transportation*
> *Province of British Columbia*
> *June 27th, 1936*
>
> *Dear Mr. Fyfe,*
>
> *I wish to inform you that I am resigning from my job as Wharfinger for the Village of Bear Creek. I don't*

*think you will find a replacement here, Sir, as the
people have found a way around the dock and are
working together to avoid the need for it. Enclosed is
my Remittance Form, which you will see is empty as
no tolls have been collected.*

> *I remain, yours respectfully,*
> *Duncan P. Wylie*
> *Bear Creek General Store and Post Office*

I put one copy in the mailbag, and the other I left at
the schoolhouse, stuck in the door where I had left the
poem. It was the last day of school. Then I went home
to wait. To wait for her to come for the mail. So I could
say to her, when she came, *we are all cogs in the wheel.* So
she will know that I understand.

Ursula

Only Isobel saw us off.

I arrived at school on that last day, but I was not the
first to arrive. The children had come early, with cakes
their mothers had baked, and they had decorated the
classroom with flowers. Tommy Klaussen, who was
always so good with the younger ones, had everyone sitting at their desks, beaming at me. On the desk was a
pile of cards they had made, folded bits of paper. I saw
among them a long white envelope with my name in
block letters, and I thought it must be one of the parents
thanking me. Perhaps Mr. and Mrs. Epp. Their twins are
such a handful.

I handed out their marks, and then we had a little

party. I felt so bad, knowing I wouldn't see them in the fall, to be their teacher as they expected. I was close to tears the whole day, as if I was walking on eggshells. And when Isobel came up the path when the last child had waved goodbye, I wept.

Leave it all here, she told me. I'll clean up. Go home and spend some time with your parents. And so I left it all there, the flowers, the crumbs, the pictures tacked to the wall. The pile of handmade cards. I never even looked at their cards. I would have so liked to have taken them away with me as a keepsake.

Later, I said goodnight to Mama and Papa, knowing I would be up and away before they woke. Mama's kiss lingered on my cheek.

I harboured just a tiny fear that my Eddie would not be there, in the morning dark, on the beach. But as I came down the path with my suitcase, my pounding heart choking my breath away, there he was, a dark figure, smoking nervously as he paced the sand. The glow of his cigarette as it lit his face disguised, for a moment, the man I knew, and I felt a sudden terror for that which fate had cast my way. I thought of Duncan Wylie and his question.

But then Eddie smiled at me, tossing his cigarette into the sand, and took my hand. "All ready?" And I placed my hand in the hand of this boy and thought: I don't know him. I don't really know him. How can you really know someone? And then there was that wheel again, rolling over me as if I was nothing more than a daisy in the road.

And then Isobel was there, and the boat Jack had arranged was pulling up to take us to the train station at Nelson. We loaded our bags and waved goodbye. And now the sun is coming up and Mama and Papa will read my letter and I think of how that will be, and what they will say. I spent so long over those words.

The lake is so beautiful in the morning light, and my heart is full, and my heart is breaking.

Duncan

She's gone, and the boats dock on the wharf and there is nobody collecting tolls and I believe that they will just leave it alone, now. She's gone and it never mattered what I did or didn't do. She's gone, but now the Epp twins come in, together, and sometimes I give them a licorice whip and they smile at me, and they don't run away. And sometimes folks meet up on the porch when they come for the mail and they stay and chat with one another. Of course, they don't talk much to yours truly, but they stay all the same. She's gone with her smile and those ankles but I suppose that's just fate.

The lake looks damn pretty these days, like a poem.

1946

A shadow falls across the bench, and I look up into the gentle eyes of the woman from the Red Cross. She has brought me tea, and a sandwich. The bread is white; it still looks so strange, white bread. Inside, eggs. So much food, after so little for so long! She mimes to me, holds a telephone, shakes her head. That she has not been able to reach Peter, who is not here to meet me, or that there is no phone where he is, I cannot tell. She is speaking to me now, but I can't understand her words, as I only have a few, and they are almost all names of places. Canada. Halifax. Pier 21. Montreal. Winnipeg. British Columbia. Nelson. Bear Creek. The city girls I met on the *Mauritania*, they could speak so much more, calling to the returning soldiers on the deck below, but we had less need to learn such a language where I lived. I can say Hello, I come from Holland. My name is Aliesje Beijer. But it's not anymore. Now, my name is Aliesje Milner, but Peter, he calls me Alice.

I try to conjure Peter's face, the way he looked as he held me in his arms when he said goodbye. Saying my name over and over, Alice, and in his voice it sounded exotic, and thrilled me. Now, it just sounds foreign, not me at all, and here I am: somebody called Alice in a body not at all like my own in a country that is endless eating a white bread and egg sandwich beside a stranger who is telling me something I cannot understand while I wait for a man whose face I can't remember.

I am a day early, though, I know this. But I sent a telegram from the Red Cross office in Halifax, and surely he received it and knows to come a day earlier than what I cabled before. And now the Red Cross lady has gone away, and there is just me, and this bench, the man in the ticket booth and a fly that buzzes noisily at the window.

Along the second slat from the top of the bench there are four initials carved, encircled in a heart. It says: W.M. above, and S.L. below. I think about W.M. and S.L. and wonder where they are now. Are they married? Are they happy? Or was this just a passing fancy, perhaps a sudden romance after a dance. A chance encounter, or a life changed?

I look out the window, at the blue of the lake, the green of the mountain that looms above me. My eyes rest on a little outcropping of rock halfway up. I can see two people up there, a picnic, perhaps. It must make them dizzy to be so high, as it makes me dizzy just to be in this odd, lumpy landscape after my own country, with its flatland and gentle hills. It is early summer, and the leaves on the trees are a vivid green, sunlit. It is very beautiful, and yet it feels like my whole life is centred in this train station, on this bench. Inside me, the baby shifts, then rolls, a somersault. They would never have let me on the boat if they had known I was so far along.

The Red Cross woman, who has told me her name is Bunny—when she told me this she held her fingers above her head like rabbit ears, honestly, I have no idea what she's doing half the time—is back. She is asking me to go with her, and I know this because it's not the first time she's mimed our departure. She doesn't think that my husband is going to come for me, and she wants me to leave the station, get some rest, she says, placing her palms together under her head, tilting it, her round face looking peaceful in feigned sleep. I run my hands over hair, which I tried to clean in the tiny cubicle on the train so as to look as good as possible for my husband, and I shake my head, no. He could come at any moment, and what if he couldn't find me when he came? But I have been here, now, since morning, watching the hands on the big clock above the ticket window move like soldiers in slow motion.

She leaves me, here, with my bags around me, my hand folded over my large belly. She smiles her moon-faced smile, and I smile back, nodding my head. I am terrified, but I won't let anyone see. But when she is gone, and the ticket master has moved away from the window, and the waiting room is empty, I let the tears come, sliding down my face, salty pools in the corners of my lips.

❋

In the spring of 1945, as the liberating armies arrived, the Dutch people emerged like mice: fear of the cat made every step tentative, and yet each wanted to believe that these handsome Canadian allies, smart in their uniforms, kind in their manner, were not only real, but had treed the cat for good. Some, the courageous resistance hiding Jews or guns, hid a little longer; so much was at stake. The starved were fed crackers and lard until shrunken stomachs could tolerate richer food. Some fared better than others. For the young, the strong, jubilations could not begin soon enough, and the young women, painfully thin but with a new blush to their cheeks, were quick to accept a dance with the liberators as musical instruments were dusted off and dance floors swept.

Aliesje Beijer, nineteen years old, had been required to

work in a German barracks kitchen in her village. All of
the girls had to work in some way, but of the duties
assigned, kitchen work was among the safest, and for this
she was lucky. Some girls, sent to clean officer's quarters,
did not fare so well. And while she grew weary of peeling
potatoes and sick of the smell of onions she managed at
times to hide small amounts of food in her coat lining,
and in this way her family remained healthier than some.
The day she arrived at work in the pre-dawn dark,
clutching the pass that allowed her to move through the
streets during curfew hours, to find no soldier standing
surly by the door, she knew, with a small jolt, that something had changed. Afraid to open the door and begin
work, afraid of the silence, she hurried back home
through the first grey morning light and told her mother,
who locked and bolted the door and put out the lights.
Together, they waited.

The hum began slowly, separate sounds that merged
into a single note they had never heard before nor would
hear again. Along with the sound of footfalls and vehicles and tanks came the buzz of talk, first whispered
from room to room, house to house, then raising into
calls across alleyways, from doorway to doorway. The
Canadians were coming!

They met at a dance, like so many did. Standing there
at the side of the cavernous room, she smoothed the
front of her dress as the dark-eyed soldier approached.
Aliesje, she said. Peter, he smiled, and that was that.
They married before he shipped home, with a promise.

She knew of girls whose husbands or fiancés turned
out to be married or engaged back home, or whose families discouraged a union with a stranger half a world
away. She knew of babies who had no fathers to claim
them at all.

❄

Many of the brides on our boat, mostly English and Dutch war brides, were already managing babies. I don't know which would be worse: trying to wash diapers and feed these babies, or trying to sleep on narrow bunks with all the aches of pregnancy. And, of course, the fear we pregnant women felt that we might lose our babies during the rough crossing, so many of us seasick and throwing up constantly. I was lucky that the motion didn't make me sick. One evening I stood at the railing beside another bride, both of us escaping the stench and noise of the cabins. Below us were Canadian soldiers returning home, and we were not allowed to talk to them. They could see us if we leaned over the railing, and one called up to us in English, and although we didn't know what he said we certainly knew what he meant! This girl, Anneke, laughed and blew them a kiss, and I pulled her back from the railing.

"They say if we are caught fraternizing with the men, we'll be sent back," I told her. Anneke had beautiful blonde hair and pretty grey eyes that turned up at the corners. She laughed at me.

"Why would they do such a thing? Send us all the way over here only to send us back for a little flirting? That would be crazy!"

We became friends, Anneke and I, and I think that if we had not spent so much time together, single women without babies to care for, something might have happened she'd have regretted later. Or, maybe not. But when we arrived at Pier 21, a list of names was called and we heard later that these women had been caught kissing the soldiers in the lifeboats, under the canvas tarpaulins, and they were being held on board and sent back. I wonder, what did they think then? What did their husbands think, waiting on the dock, or at a train station somewhere across this enormous country? Would these husbands have forgiven their errant wives had they had the chance? So many of us, like me, could hardly remember what our husbands looked like, so much time had passed since we'd seen them. We really didn't know the men we married.

Did Peter get a message that maybe I had been sent back? Perhaps I was confused with another woman, and so her husband waited in vain while mine, who got a message that should have gone to another man, had given up on me, decided he was better off without me, was even now having the divorce papers drawn up so he could marry another girl?

As some girls disembarked during the long journey, Anneke and I had wondered aloud if being sent back would have been so bad. So often we stopped at a siding in the wilderness, and a girl would get off with her bags in all that vast forest, to be swallowed by trees and a life none of us could imagine.

We travelled to Winnipeg, where Anneka stepped off the train and into the arms of her waiting Canadian soldier. She had wondered if she would recognize him in civilian clothes, if she would like her in-laws, but I watched her embrace her young man on the platform as if she hadn't harboured the slightest doubt all along, while a little niece stood by, waiting for the moment when she could give her new aunt the bouquet of flowers she held. I still had such a long way to go. I cried for Anneke like I'd known her all my life.

❋

While the train that carried his wife chugged across the prairies, Peter Milner got up early Monday morning to help load the crates of cherries onto the Bear Creek Fruit Co-op boat that was heading to Nelson. It was a day early, but he wanted to be sure to meet his bride; the cable had said Wednesday. When he got to the wharf, Tom Klaussen had the boat hauled up on shore and was pushing pitch into a seam.

"It'll be tomorrow Peter," he said through the knife he held in his teeth. "Sorry, I should have sent John up to tell you."

For Peter, already nervous about meeting Alice, this was the worst possible news.

"I can't be late, Tom. You know that."

"You won't be," he said, taking the knife from his mouth. "You've got time. You'll still get there a day ahead. Phone down to Nelson, tell them at the station if you're worried."

But when Peter picked up the heavy black receiver at the Bear Creek Store, Duncan Wylie turned from where he was sorting mail into boxes and told him: "Sorry, Peter, it's been out since yesterday. I've sent word. I don't know when she'll be working, though."

It was not a boat day for the *Minto*. There were other boats heading down the lake towards Castlegar, but he'd have to find someone going to Nelson from there, and anyway, Tom was right, there was time. And he'd agreed to load the cherries, he didn't want to back out of that, it was part of his duty as a co-op member. It would be fine, he told himself.

And it was, he reflected the next day, as, cherries loaded, they struck out into the centre of the lake. He looked back at the figures on the Bear Creek wharf, looking like dolls, the scattering of buildings like a toy village. It was pretty; it was perfect. He hoped she'd like it. He tried to remember what she looked like, and he could see her then, eyes shining in the gaslight, illuminating the street corner after years of blackouts. Pregnant! He could not imagine her body other than as it had been, so small under his touch. He had counted every rib.

After a time, smoking with Tom and Bob Epp in the cabin, drinking moonshine and talking about this and that, the boys ribbing him a little about his new bride, Bob leaned forward and said:

"Aren't we riding a little lower than we should?"

"Nah," said Tom. "She's just loaded up is all."

Much later, when questions of sobriety or accuracy or safety or any other matter came up in conversation, "Ah, she's just loaded up is all" would be the refrain, meaning, "don't trust it, it's worse than it looks." Because within an hour, the cherry boat was under water, and three men stood on the roof of the cabin, which remained, in the shallows, about an inch under the surface. Don Kroeger, who ran the lumber barge, picked them up, but not before taking a photograph with the camera he'd bought in Spokane with his savings. The photograph was later posted in the store, where it became a standing joke; under it, Don had written: *Ladies take note: Bear Creek Men Walk on Water*.

Most of the cherry boxes were rounded up and made it to market none the worse for wear. Some said the chill of the lake water probably delayed spoilage. Some drifted downstream and became an unexpected windfall that resulted in a batch of preserves and several pies.

❄

Last evening I stayed at the house of the Red Cross lady, Bunny. She is very nice to me, and her family was very warm and smiled and did their best to make me comfortable, the little girl giving up her bed to me and sleeping with her mother and father. The houses here are big! Everyone has his own room, even. She wanted me to stay here today, too, while they worked to find my Peter. I know they will send me back, they will think I am an abandoned war bride if Peter doesn't come today, but I will not stay at the house, I insisted I would wait at the station. He will come. He must not have received the second cable, he'll be here today.

So I am back on this bench, with the clock tick-tocking and my old friends W.M. and S.L. And the baby moves and rolls and I think of Anneke and wonder what she is doing at this moment. And my shoes are pinching because my feet have swelled, and I would like to stretch out my legs on the bench but I am in a strange country. I don't know what the customs are.

In our schoolbooks we learned little about Canada. I understood that there were wild Indians here, and snow. When the train pulled into that tiny station in Manitoba, poor Mariette sobbed when she saw her husband there, with his family. Many of the brides, looking through the train windows as the trains pulled into the stations, barely recognized their husbands in civilian clothes. But Mariette's new family were all Red Indians, dressed in hides and beads and feathers! Mariette, crying, some of us holding her, was sure she would be living in a tepee. A Red Cross lady hurried on board. "Come," she said, "your new family has dressed up in their traditional clothing in honour of your arrival." And what could she do?

❄

The day the cherry boat sank, Peter had gone home, wrung out the suit he'd put on in order to be presentable at the station, and then gone over to the Schroeder household, where he figured there were enough boys and men that someone should have a suit that would fit him. He then spent some time trying to arrange passage before deciding the best bet was to hike the five miles up to the closest siding and flag down the afternoon train. Foolish, he thought as the pushed up the path, to wear the suit. He couldn't figure out how to carry the thing and figured he might as well just wear it, but now, carrying the jacket and sweating small lakes into the armpits of the shirt, he felt ridiculous, but more than that he felt nervous, panicky. He had not been thinking straight for days, he realized, and at that moment became aware that he had left behind an item of some consequence.

The trick was to signal the train, due just before 3 p.m., with enough time so the thing could reasonably stop, and he had forgotten to bring the white cloth that was commonly used to let the train know in advance that there was a pickup. It was now close to 3 p.m. There was nothing to be done, therefore, but take off the trousers and remove his white Stanfields, and it was in this state, wearing only a damp shirt and socks, one foot in the leg of his pants, that he heard a rustle on the path below him and froze, thinking: bear. There were always bears about, mostly black bears, and Peter was seldom too alarmed by the prospect of meeting one. But there was something altogether too vulnerable about confronting a bear when not wearing any pants. The rustle became a crashing.

What emerged from the brush, as Peter swivelled on the one foot not entangled in a pant leg, was his brother Earl, a tea towel on his shoulder.

It was some time before either of them could speak. Laughter is a fine thing for nerves, Peter thought five minutes later, sitting on the bank beside the tracks,

"Jesus, Peter," said Earl, "I almost pissed myself, there."

"What are you *doing* here?"

"I thought a family welcome was in order. I thought you could use a little brotherly support. And I figured you might have forgotten this," he held up the towel. "Do you want me to come or not?"

❋

I don't know if Peter is to come by train or boat or motorcar. I don't know how far he lives from Nelson, where I'm sitting, but I showed his address to Bunny and she nodded and waved her hand several times northward, so I think it is a long way from here.

If I were not so pregnant I would find a boat and go there. If he's abandoned me, then I want to see him. If I have come this far, I at least have to have the satisfaction of slapping his face. I'll make him pay for me, for the baby. I'll tell the Canadian army about him. I'll find his family. An hour ago, I was frightened, but now I can feel an anger building in me. Even if he didn't get the second cable, he should still be here by now.

How dare he? How dare he?

If I could talk to S.L. I would tell her: don't trust men. That German cook, he tried to put his hands on me, promised me food, we can all speak some German in my town, it is so close to the border, so I understood what he promised. And I kissed him, because I needed food, needed to be strong, and I thought of my parents and my sisters. But then he laughed at me when I held out my

hand. When he tried to touch me again I began cough-
ing, so he would think I was sick. Then, I coughed
whenever he could hear me, so he would leave me alone.
He did leave me alone, and I peeled their potatoes and
cut their onions and could not eat a bite myself because
he was always watching. I would have choked on their
food anyway.

All men are cowards, I tell the initials on the bench.
They are bullies, and they are cowards. And I didn't
know my husband when I married him, this man who
could not even say my real name. How well do you
know this W.M. anyway? Do you know what you're getting into?

And now I am crying, because I have been here all
yesterday afternoon, and today since I came back this
morning, and it is evening and here is Bunny, telling me
to come. And we go to the wicket and she arranges for
my ticket east, on the train tomorrow afternoon. And I
sob and sob and sit down, again, on the bench and it is
some time before I can trust my legs, my swollen ankles,
enough to be lead away.

❋

At 4:30 p.m. Peter and Earl Milner knew the train was
not coming.

"Derailed? Delayed? Broken down?" Peter looked at
his brother, his forehead a washboard of anguish.

"Jack's Walton. We'll take the old Walton. Come on,"
said Earl, tucking the towel in his pocket and standing
up, offering Peter a hand up.

"That old thing?"

"Or Don's barge. He should be back by the time we
get there. Anyone will help who can, Pete. The train's not

coming. It's an hour back. Maybe we can get a ride before dark."

There was not a boat available until morning, and in any case, it was not a trip to be made in the dark. By now, Peter figured, she'd been waiting a day and a night. The phone at the store, when he picked it up, was silent. He looked, again, at her picture, and Earl gently took the small, creased photograph from his hand and tucked it carefully in his brother's breast pocket, put his arm around him and took him off to Jake's place, where there was a bit of a kitchen party starting and some potato moonshine. There was nothing to be done 'til morning, anyway.

"They'll keep her. The Red Cross is there, they looked after Jake's sister-in-law when she came over and married his brother, what's his name? Henry. When she came over to meet Henry, he was an hour late coming in to meet the train and they just stayed there with her, looked after her."

"I'm a day late, Earl."

"It's okay, Pete. There's nothing more to be done now. C'mon."

Later, the musicians well beyond playing, they sat around Jake's kitchen table and passed around the photograph of a thin, dark-haired girl, making appreciative sounds.

"Good thing," said Peter, gesturing at the photo as it passed from hand to hand. "If it wasn't for that, I wouldn't have a clue what the hell she looks like. It's been six months already." He slurred slightly, rose from his chair, fingers reaching for the photograph, then sat down heavily, empty-handed. The room swayed.

Earl retrieved the photograph and placed it gently in his brother's hand.

"Better get you to bed, old fella," he said. "The boat leaves early."

The barge smelled like bark but all Peter could smell was moonshine, which saturated the early morning air as it emanated from his pores. Earl slapped him on the back.

"All set?" he said, and then looked at his brother more closely. "A little rough today, buddy?"

Peter winced and spit into the water. He had not eaten and, in fact, couldn't imagine when he would be able to eat again. He held onto the frame of the small cabin for support and squinted into the sparkle of sunshine on the surface of the lake. Don, owner of the barge, was nowhere to be seen, feeling, he imagined, as rough as he did himself.

"He won't mind I took his keys," said Earl, reading his brother's thoughts. "Hell, he won't even know 'til this afternoon."

"Let's go, okay?"

Peter was quiet during the morning, letting Earl ramble about plans to increase the water line from upper Bear Creek, about the disputes over water usage, about the lack of rain so far this season. Water was always a source of discussion, but for now all Peter wanted was a tall glass of the stuff and a bit of shade. His mouth felt like something had died in it, some small verminous creature. He leaned over the side, cupping his hand to catch the lake water, and drank what he could as it slipped through his fingers.

"Here," said Earl, handing him a chipped mug. He filled it four times, then rolled onto his back and watched a herd of high cirrus clouds band together for the next hour or so.

"Mare's tails," Earl said after a while. "Could be rain. Or maybe not. Where's that picture?"

Without taking his eyes off the sky, Peter extracted the creased photograph from his pocket and waved it in the direction of his brother, who reached for it, steadying the wheel with one hand.

"I can't really remember her, Earl. When I look at the picture she's there, sure enough, but when I look away, she's gone again. Six months is not so long as all that. Why can't I remember her?"

"It's going to be like riding a bicycle, baby brother. Soon as you lay eyes on her, it'll be like no time has passed. Don't you worry, it'll be fine."

❋

My train does not leave until 1 p.m., and yet I cannot stay in Bunny's house and I insist, through words she doesn't understand and gestures that she does, that I go back to the station in the morning. The bench has become a sort of home to me; in my misery, W.M. and S.L. are like family. We have become friends, that bench and I, and there is comfort as I lower myself onto it. I feel more and more like some massive sea creature every day.

And I feel numb, because the very worst thing has happened, and that is that I am an abandoned war bride. What will happen now? They will not send me back on the boat, with only two months to go before my poor baby is born. "Red Cross. Toronto." Bunny said to me. I am not the first, I'm sure. Perhaps they have some place for us. I cannot imagine telling my parents. I trace my fingers over the initials, think of these lovers who left their mark behind, and then trace, very gently, my own initials over the wood's surface. I trace the letters A.B. I am not Aliesje Milner after all. And I am not Alice to anybody.

❈

Peter Milner, motoring into the dock at Nelson, looked towards the train station. It appeared to be a very long way from the dock, although in truth it would be a sprint of a few minutes at most. Would she still be there? He took out her photograph, creased and finger-marked, and hoped she looked the same. Before the boat was tied, he scrambled onto the dock and broke into a run.

❈

Bunny is talking to the man in the ticket booth. There has been a telephone call, there is some excitement, and for a moment the dog turns tail and my heart quickens. Then I hear words and glean their meanings, it is unmistakable: accident. Boat. And I don't know what is worse, to be abandoned or to be a widow, for what else could it be but death by drowning? It is 12:30 p.m. and the train will soon be here, and I need to know, and I grasp at the words I learned at war's end that I so quickly forgot once my Peter left for Canada.

"What," I say, rising from my bench. "What?"

And Bunny turns and her look is one of pity because she has come to the same conclusion as I have, that there has been a drowning in this huge, wild lake, this enormous, dangerous country, and I want to go home, I just want to go home, now. I am a little girl and I am maybe five years old and I am choking on my sobs and I want my mother, but instead I am in the arms of this Red Cross lady. In my anguish, and with the pressure of the baby, I have wet myself. I sob harder, in shame and despair.

We are standing like this, and in that funny way when something terrible or alarming happens. I am thinking only of my clean knickers in my suitcase and how I must find a way to go and change as soon as I can, and then I hear Bunny say: "Oh!" a small, girlish gasp.

And this is how my husband finds me, choking tears, a huge walrus in the middle of the station house. He stands there, breathing hard, turning a small white square around in his fingers, staring. There is a man behind him, and he is smiling, standing back. Bunny has stepped away from me now, and as this man approaches, I am suddenly furious.

I hit him, a small, ineffectual hit with my balled up fist, on his chest. Then another, harder. Bunny, the man in the background, and the man in the ticket booth are all watching, I can feel them.

"You smell like a still," I tell him in Dutch.

"Let's go home," he says, for just me to hear, and I understand the words.

1950

The day Ace died was a sad one for us, but for Jack especially. If Ace was responsible for our happiness together, he was equally responsible for keeping Jack happy. I have never seen a man and beast so close; when things were bad between us, as things can be in any marriage—things that would send another man off drinking with the boys—Jack would go and find the horse. I often imagined the conversation between them.

"It's about Isobel," Jack would begin.

"So, what else is new?" Ace would respond in horse-language, and the two would raise eyebrows at one another. That is, if horses had eyebrows, which they don't. But Jack always had wonderful eyebrows, which became, as he aged, great bushy caterpillars with lives of their own. If Ace had had eyebrows, they'd have rivalled Jack's for sheer expressiveness. "That horse has more personality than a lot of humans," Jack would always say, and he was right.

Ace and Jack had similar attributes: Ace would be bound by no fence, no gate, no tether of any kind; if you wanted Ace to stay put, he wouldn't, but if you wanted him to move, well, he might not do that, either. Jack, too, forged his own path, and wouldn't be swayed to do a thing a certain way because that's the way it had always been done. Stubborn, Jack was, and more than once I was angry at that man enough to spit.

But both were gently circumspect: nobody ever saw Ace in the act of escaping from the yard, and folks never realized that they were doing something they hadn't intended to do, but that Jack wanted them to do, until after it was all over. I was the exception, of course. I always knew exactly what both were up to.

It's not easy to bury a horse. The thing to do, if you can, is dig a grave as close as possible to where the body of the horse is.

The loss of Ace was the beginning of the loss of Jack, really, even though ten years passed between their deaths. When Ace died I wrote to Ursula, who by then had moved from B.C. and was living in Calgary, Eddie having found a good job. They were raising their girls there, lovely children. It's hard to imagine they are grown, now. Jack and I never had children, and I suppose that's why the death of a pet—part of the family, really—hit us so hard. Ursula wrote back at once, and I remember reading her letter that day, sitting on the porch with the lake sparkling in the afternoon sun and the mountains looking soft like moss, a day that felt good to be alive in. I still have the letter dated June 27, 1940:

> *Dearest Isobel,*
>
> *I am so sorry about dear old Ace, and I know you must be feeling the loss deeply. I remember when you both came to Bear Creek. You probably never knew, but everyone was talking, first about the horse, then about you, and then about you and Jack. There were a lot of kitchen table conversations about the whole affair, let me tell you. Did I ever tell you about hiding Ace in the orchard so Mama wouldn't get angry that he'd trampled the garden? He was a great horse, a true friend, and I know you will both miss him very much. But the funeral sounded lovely, I must say, with Scotty hauling out those moth-eaten old bagpipes, and*

fitting that good old Ace should be sent off in grand style.

I will write a long letter soon, but wanted to send my condolences right away. Please pass them on to Jack, with my love.

Ursula

Ace was no small beast, and if he'd drawn his last breath in the barn, that would have been quite a challenge indeed. But Ace never could stay in a barn, and so when he died he was in the yard by the house under the Spanish Cherry tree, which he had been methodically stripping. He was not sick, although he was certainly old for a horse; we figured he had to be over 30. I was watching him through the kitchen window, and was just about to take up the broom from beside the back door and go after him when something stopped me. I could see Jack come around the side of the barn, probably looking for Ace, and he stopped in his tracks also. Ace crumpled, almost in slow motion. He swung his big head around towards Jack as he went down, first onto his knees at the front, the rest following, a gentle lowering. By the time Jack reached him Ace had rolled onto his side and was sucking air in small gasps.

"He looked at me, before he fell, as if he was full of questions," Jack told me later as we held one another in bed, both of us acutely aware of the big grey tarpaulin that covered the body of our friend out in the yard. "I could see it from where I stood, he didn't understand what was happening. I think he was ready to bolt, the way he does when he's caught, but he couldn't."

We dug the grave right beside where Ace had laid down, under the Spanish Cherry tree. We had to chop through some roots, but by God that tree lived, and the cherries were bigger for the influence of Ace, I swear. It took four men—Albert Schroeder, Joe Arndt, Buddy Walter and Peter Milner—and a fair bit of planking to lever Ace into the grave, and even then we had to chop away some more at the ground afterwards because of course he didn't fall squarely in. Ace was never one to make things easy for anyone. A fair bit of beer had been consumed by the time the horse was underground, and that horse was well and truly toasted.

We were just going to have a little memorial, Jack and I: some flowers, maybe a picnic beside the grave in memory of our old friend. But the spectacle of burying Ace, the shouts and grunts to get him into the hole, and the fact that the old beast was so beloved despite his transgressions, brought most of Bear Creek out to watch. Before we knew it we had Scotty and the pipes, some choice words spoken with great emotion, and a tribute of green apples left by children. That night, our house was full of people.

"A grand old wake for a grand old horse," said Charlie Strautman afterwards as he and Jack sat drinking whisky together on the porch. The evening air was still cool.

"I hope my own wake will be half as good," agreed Jack.

It is ten years later less three months, and Jack is buried under the cherry tree, next to Ace. It's not easy to bury a husband, either. There were a whole new set of challenges, different from those of the horse, but challenges nonetheless. For one thing, we have a graveyard in Bear Creek, and there was some discussion about whether a burial on private property should be allowed. But this is Bear Creek, after all. We do things our own way, not in any small part because of Jack's influence.

"We're on our own here," he'd say. "We've got no road, no police, and those government folks are only interested in us when it comes to taxes. We can write our own rules."

And we do. Young folks in Bear Creek will drive anything they can get their hands on as soon as they can reach the pedals. There's no point in having a licence unless you're going to drive on the other side of the lake, and no point in insurance, either. When Joe Arndt rolled his '28 Studebaker over the bank in upper Bear Creek, he just left it there and let the woods grow in over it. When Buddy Walter did the same thing, but landed on top of the Schroeder henhouse, there was quite a bit more said about it but the matter was resolved with a new henhouse and six new chickens and a rooster, plus a fair bit of additional manual labour for the inconvenience. We generally work things out in Bear Creek.

Laws don't apply here unless there is something serious like murder, which hasn't ever happened, although the accidental shooting death of Joe Arndt's Uncle Simon, mistaken for a bear, shot by that hunter down from Edgewood, did bring the police out on that one occasion. So it was with Jack's final resting place: while convention dictates burial in the graveyard, there was only the slightest objection to putting Jack in beside Ace, and nobody much wanted to have words with me about it at the time.

Ace loved green apples and cherries, and was known to eat pretty much anything in his path, but his first love was the asparagus shoots that came up in May, crisp and green and sweet. I gave up any notion of growing asparagus with that horse around, but an occasional off-spring of the original patch would still poke its green head up and Ace and I were generally in competition for them. Jack never had a chance between the two of us, so when Ace died, he ordered a new set of asparagus roots to plant on Ace's grave, and they took off like wildfire. We never ate asparagus after that without a few words for the horse.

When it came to digging Jack's grave it was late March in an unusually early spring. The ground was soft enough, but I had to warn the young men who came to dig: don't hurt those roots, and put them right back where you found them. That's Jack's asparagus patch, and he'll want to share them with the horse, now. The boys looked at me like I'd gone strange, and I suppose I had.

I am a little crazy, on my own, here, with the ghost of Jack in every corner of this house and that horse back again, I swear. Yesterday the gate latch was open, and I know I firmly closed it. This was not the first time.

The rain began twenty-seven days after Jack's funeral. From my kitchen window I could see past the cherry tree and the barn to the banks of Bear Creek, which does a dogleg through our property on its way to the lake. It had swollen considerably, and before long one of my nephew Joe's boys was up asking after my welfare, sent by his parents no doubt, and to tell me there was talk of a flood.

"Ma says come over. She said whenever you want," he told me.

I told him I was fine, but by the next morning there

was a new joint to the dogleg, coursing through by the front gate and nudging at the corner of the barn. There was nothing in that old barn by then, but just the same I didn't want to see it damaged. So I went out after breakfast, pulling on Jack's green raincoat with the hood and shoving my feet into his boots because they are higher than mine, and sloshed on over to the barn. By the time I got there I had to wrestle open the door against the current, even though the water where I stood was only a few inches deep.

Inside the barn the light was grey with bright shafts poking through cracks in the wall like leaking seams in a boat. Old hay bales were stacked up against the far wall, well away from the water, but the smell of mildew was in the air from the general damp. One of Ace's harnesses, too old to sell and too dear to part with, still hung by the door. I ran my hands along the cracked leather.

Jack had aged very fast, and very suddenly in his last years. He was sixty-five when he went, and that was only three weeks after seeing the doctor in Trail. Cancer, he told me. Both lungs.

My hands against the old leather: both have seen smoother days, I thought, and yet fifty-five is not old. Odd, I don't feel a day past twenty-five except for all the living I've done, but that has gone by so quickly. How can that be? Ursula is awaiting her first grandchild; she could not come for the funeral, but promises to come in the summer for a visit. How can little Ursula be a grandmother? I held the harness to my cheek, felt the rasp of the leather, the cold of the metal, and stood there dry eyed while the rain poured outside.

After a little while I turned to push the big door

open, and found I could barely move it against the force of the water. When I finally did open it enough to squeeze outside, the creek was a roiling grey snake full of branches and leaves, and I held the side of the barn for support as I pushed through and onto the crumbling earth at the water's edge. I stood for a moment watching it, then hurried back past the cherry tree on the rise—and the fresh mound that is Jack—to the house. I was grateful for the sweat-smelling oilskin hood of my husband's raincoat and inhaled its man-smell, wishing for Jack's good, common sense. He would know what to do.

"What?" I asked as I turned to look at the creek again before going inside. My voice sounded thin against the rush of water.

I put the kettle on the stove and banked the fire. When in doubt, I always told Ursula, a cup of tea. It's what my mother always told me. That's a woman's solution, Jack would say, but he'd say it smiling, crinkles gathering at the corners of his eyes. I was the talker, Jack the doer. We fit well together, that way.

Just as I removed the kettle from the heat there was a knock at the door, a pounding, really, that made me jump. The door swung open immediately—Bear Creek people seldom wait for an invitation—and there was Joe, who had apparently come to make sure young Perry had delivered the message properly.

"How're you holdin' up?" he asked me, to which I replied: "Tea?"

"Nah. I have to be getting back. Cellar's flooding, cow's getting trenchfoot," he laughed, but continued to stand in my doorway, puddles gathering at his feet.

"Worried about the creek," he said. "Higher up, it took out the irrigation pipes, now there's whole trees coming down. You're closest to the creek of all of us."

"We always did have the prettiest view," I said, nodding. He regarded me for a long moment before speaking again.

"Ada says you should come back with me. We'll double up the boys, spare up some room for you. It'll all go down in a few days, meanwhile we don't have to worry about you getting marooned over here."

"I'm just fine, Joe," I told him. "Jack and I are just fine."

He looked at me strangely.

"Oh, don't worry, I know he's gone." I was still holding the steaming kettle, I realized, and I put it down. "I just don't like the idea of him being here and me being there. You know."

"Just the same…"

"No, I really mean it, Joe, I'm fine. It's not going to come up much more. The house is well away from the banks now, I can't see a problem. And I have dry firewood, and lots of food. I'm fine," I said again.

When he left, I sat with my tea looking out the window at the cherry tree. The house will be fine, I thought, but Jack and Ace must be getting a little damp out there.

Jack's wake rivalled Ace's for sure. The funeral was a more sombre affair, however, with more than a few tears shed. There will be a proper service when one of the travelling ministers comes through, but for now we fashioned the Bear Creek variety, as we do, with one of the church elders officiating at the graveside. It was March 27th, a sunny spring morning, and I was sure I could see, as I stood with my stiff black shoes in the new grass, the first tips of asparagus poking up through the moist earth. But then I looked again, and realized I was mistaken. It was far too early for asparagus.

Afterwards, my kitchen overflowing with plates and casseroles and pies, there was much talk of the generous nature of Jack, of his cleverness, of the good times. Jack always told me he wanted a good party, so I left them to their spoons and their fiddles and walked down along the creek, so meek then with the snowpack up above just starting to melt. I sat by the beach at our spot and looked down the lake. There was a sliver of moon, and it illuminated the white sands of the shoreline into ghostly ribbons that described the contours of the water.

"A lovely night, isn't it, Jack?" I said, and there was no answer, none at all.

I have always had a practical attitude towards death. I was taught by my oh-so-practical father that it is just another part of life. I have helped to arrange funerals in Bear Creek, and been a pillar, I've been told, to those bereaved. A pillar. It makes me think of a great Roman column, unmoveable, unemotional, stalwart. Stoic. I felt very small, sitting there on the beach, and soft, like butter, as if the slightest touch would leave an impression on my skin. Death is part of life, I thought, words my father used. There is Jack and there is Ace, lying side by side under the cherry tree, and there is me, here, on the beach, in the dark, with the sounds of the party going on behind me, travelling across the still night air. How can there be so much distance?

I went out to check the creek one more time this evening, before dark fell altogether. It would not be possible to open the barn door, now. I couldn't get that close, in any case, without the water coming over the tops of Jack's rubber boots. I walked instead up to the cherry tree slightly above and to the west of the barn, and stood looking at the crushed dead flowers on Jack's grave. I should have removed them a long time ago, and as I bent to pick them up my hand brushed a firm shoot of asparagus, and I pushed them out of the way to touch its waxy tip. It will be perfect in a couple of days, I thought, and marvelled at its presence: it was still so early for asparagus. Perhaps it was the rain. I turned and looked back at the creek, more a river, now.

When I woke up the next morning, the barn was gone.

The wall that the hay bales were stacked against was still there, or at least, part of it. The rest was just gone, and in its place was far more light than there should have been, making the yard look completely different, the cherry tree and the ground beneath exposed, vulnerable.

By noon I had received no less than six visitors expressing concern about my barn and my welfare. The rain had lightened somewhat, but the torrent that was once Bear Creek, irrigator of orchards, benefactor of drinking water, preferred hike of picnickers, had grown. I'm fine, I told them all above the roar of the water. Look, the water is still a long way from the house. The first sign of any danger, I'll come straight over, not to worry.

When I wrote Ursula to tell her that Jack had died, I had so hoped she would come. She wrote back right away:

Darling Iz,

Of course I would be there for you, if only I could. I remember how I felt when Mama died, then Papa so soon after. It was hard to come back when Mama was ill; I wasn't sure either of them ever forgave me for leaving like that, but in the end, of course, they did. I believe it was Jack's words, then, that made all the difference. Life's too short to hold a grudge, he said, and Papa always listened to Jack.

We will all miss Jack. I can't imagine Bear Creek without him. I hope you are holding up, and I am glad you are where you are instead of in some big city where nobody knows you. Jack was right to want to die at home, hard as it must have been. You were right to hold your ground as long as you could, but as you say, when he needed more help than you could give, what was there to do? I think of you in that hospital, and I wish I had been there.

I will be there soon, Iz. Once Edwina has the baby, and all is settled, I will come, I promise. Just hold on for me, and keep your chin up.

Love always,
Ursula

A week later, she wrote:

I'm a grandmother, Isobel! So much joy in little Sarah, and yet I want so much to be with you, my friend. Edwina had a difficult time, and she needs me for a few weeks more, she's still very weak. I'll be there before the cherry tree blooms, Iz, and we'll walk on the beach and talk it all out.

My dear friend, ten years my junior. I met her when she was just fourteen years old, saw her grow into a lovely young woman full of spunk, brimming with opinions and ideas. Even as a teenager she was beyond the giggling of adolescence, and yet held that sense of humour I so long for right now. When she comes back to visit, she illuminates the darker corners of this old home, smiles the tarnish from the memories. We had a good life, Jack and I. I know that if only my friend could be here with me, I could stay up all night remembering, and then lay him to rest in the morning. I want to share her joy, but my heart is dark. As it is, I cannot cry, and yet it seems the sky is doing it for me as it rains, and rains, and rains.

The creek is subsiding now. It's terrible that so much has been lost, orchards flooded, chickens coops swept away, all that work on the irrigation pipeline to be reconstructed. But it's almost over. Already the creek has shrunk, and by tomorrow we'll be planning repairs. I'm fine, I told my neighbours. Really.

Sometime towards morning, the sky still dark, I awoke to a roar as if the whole mountain was raging at the sky. A landslide, I thought at once, and threw Jack's raincoat over my nightgown, pushed my bare feet into his boots and, with grey hair streaming behind me, ran into the deluge. Pausing at the bottom step, it was as if sky and water and earth had all forgotten their rightful places and had joined to rampage through my yard. I covered my ears against the sound. Small trees were passing only feet from me.

My eyes swept the rise above where the barn had been, the cherry tree barely visible in the darkness on its little hill. In a moment, I was sure, the torrent would wash away the tree, my Jack, the bones of poor old Ace. The wind crushed the raincoat to my body as I pushed against it, and as I stepped off the porch I slipped in the mud and the tear of water pulled at my legs and in a panic my hands flailed at the slippery wood of the step. I cried out then, an old woman's impotent wail against the storm, and with all the strength in my bones pulled myself up and stood, holding onto the porch railing, and against the onslaught of wind and rain I dragged myself to higher ground.

Turning my back on the creek I climbed the rise, slipping, getting up, slipping again, drenched in mud and water and my own tears. When I reached the cherry tree I wrapped my arms around it and then sank to the ground above my husband. I leaned my back against its bark and dug my nails into the earth, turning my face to the storm. The howl that came from inside me joined pitch with the howl of the water and I thought: if I die here, so be it. This is where life becomes a part of death.

I stayed there until dawn broke, a slow, grey lightening, low clouds draping the lake. I was drenched, muddy, cold to my bones and utterly spent from crying. Empty. Bear Creek had pulled back, frightening still but pushing into no new territory, a controlled violence. It had taken what remained of the barn, all of the garden tools I had stacked against the side of the house, and the rain barrel. A wash of mud had flattened bushes, uprooted small trees, and swept across my front steps.

It had not reached me or Jack or Ace or our Spanish cherry tree, and I thought, as I sat there, that it had to be sheer stubbornness on the part of those two that kept the water back. That horse wouldn't move for God himself unless he felt like it. Jack would have engaged God in a friendly conversation and by the end of it, God would think it was his idea in the first place to leave them both there and let me get on with things. And I began to laugh.

I leaned against the cherry tree for some time, knees drawn up under Jack's raincoat, watching the clouds lift. After a while I looked down, and there, not far from where my right hand clutched at the grass, was the asparagus shoot I had noticed the day before. I reached for it and snapped it off, inhaled its earthy scent. It smelled like life.

It's not easy to bury the love you have felt, and in truth, one should not try to. Better that it flows through you and if, occasionally, it overflows in loss and grief, then all there is to do is wait it out.

Ursula came two weeks later and now we sit on the porch together, talking. It is evening. The creek is its regular self again, and by the house the new grass is pushing through the mud, all the greener for the disturbance. The cherry tree is in full bloom and the scent wafts across to us as we sit on the step, elbows on knees, like children.

"What now?" asks Ursula, chin resting on knuckles, looking straight ahead. Before us, clouds collect like bunching sheep, their undersides turned pink by the setting sun. She means: what will I do now, with life so changed, alone in this old house. How will I live?

"We always did have the prettiest view," I say after a while, and she looks at me sideways, the way she does when she doesn't know what to make of me. It's not the answer she wants, but then, it's not a question I want to answer.

"But," presses Ursula. I purse my lips and shake my head.

"We always had the prettiest view," I say again. "Don't you think?" The rosy sky is reflected in the lake below, two sides of heaven. I hear her characteristic grunt.

"Yes," I answer for her.

1954

Tom Klaussen leans against a piling, smoking. Beside him on the wharf sits his dog, a lanky mud-brown mongrel who shadows his master, seldom barks, but will smile and wag for the people Tom likes; for the rest, he is watchful. Tom calls him Dog, and this works for both of them.

When one of the people assembling on the wharf passes him and waves, he responds with a sideways grin and a small salute with his cigarette. He likes the flow of people before him, likes that he knows every name, every history, the small details of resident life: whose aunt just died, who's expecting relatives to visit, who's arguing over water rights. It is April 17, 1954, and the *Minto* will dock at Bear Creek for almost the last time. Many assembled at the wharf are taking a final trip, while others are there to drink in the sight of the great white sternwheeler, knowing her days are numbered.

"Afternoon, Tom. Not bad for April, warm, eh? Hello, Dog." Charlie Strautman, Sr., here with his wife Adeline, has aged considerably, Tom thinks, as he nods hello and raises his cigarette, then looks at its remaining length and grinds it under his boot against the dock. One of the Epp grandchildren runs headlong into Tom's leg, and Tom catches him by the shirt before he can topple over the dockside into the shallow water at the shoreline. The dog wags his tail and positions himself firmly between the boy and the dock edge.

"Whoah, Sid," Tom says, but the boy barely takes a breath before barrelling off to join the rest of the kids at the end of the dock.

From his vantage point at one end, Tom takes inventory of the people on the wharf. Although he's thought of leaving, these are his people, his community. There's Isobel Gray, dressed in Jack's old jacket, looking down the lake. With her is Ursula, moved back here and into her folks' old place with Ed, their kids all grown up and gone. Peggy Shannon greets them, her oldest daughter smiling shyly alongside.

Marty Weber approaches, youngest of the extended Weber clan, and Dog wags his tail and whines. Marty is considered slow, and lives with his aging parents. A large man, he beams at the folks gathered on the wharf, waving his hand enthusiastically. Tom wonders what will happen to Marty when his folks die. Of course, he'll always have his job at the mill, but he sure can't count on Gerold and Ellie to take him in. Tom always tries to be kind to Marty, who is, after all, his brother-in-law. He gives Marty a friendly grin.

"Mornin', Tom," Horst Schroeder leans into the piling Tom is propped against and scratches the dog with a dangling left hand. Tom passes him a cigarette and puts one in his own mouth, then cups his hands around the match flame to light them both. "Don't see your sister here," says Horst. "Where's Gerry?"

"Coming in on the boat. Don't know where Ellie is. You'd think she'd be here."

"The whole town heard that fight a couple of days ago. Good thing those two never had kids, eh? Maybe she's giving him the cold shoulder, still."

Tom stares down the lake, avoiding the gaze of the older man, watching for the sternwheeler. After a few moments Horst moves off to join the waiting crowd.

Ellie Weber sits at the kitchen table smoking a cigarette. She flicks the ashes into a heavy glass ashtray, its picture of Niagara Falls obscured by the butts of cigarettes smoked in the last forty-five minutes. The air is blue with smoke.

"You better go," she says to the man in the dress pants and undershirt who sits opposite her, his good shirt and jacket lying across the living room couch like pelts. She tosses her head towards them. "Now," she says.

When her brother Tom appears in the doorway several minutes later, squinting through the blue air, she's alone at the table. She watches him lean against the doorframe, a tall man who, she thinks, has always needed to be propped up one way or another. She holds the cigarette package out to him, a peace offering. He shakes his head, no.

"Why aren't you waiting for the *Minto*?" she asks, tossing the package back onto the table.

"Why aren't you?" he counters.

"It's no big deal. It's just a boat. No use getting all sentimental about it."

"I don't mean about the boat. I mean about Gerry."

Ellie blows smoke through her nose. "Those big shots up from Seattle," she says, ignoring the question. "It's all going to change, Tom, none of this is going to matter one bit."

"What do you know about it?"

Tom has seen the engineers, the speculators, whatever you call them. They've been around the area since early March, a half dozen of them, boarding in homes up and down the lake. They've been seen taking photographs, standing in groups, clipboards in hand, pointing, gesturing. Calculating. One fellow was so complimentary about the community of Bear Creek that Bernie Schroeder, charmed, gave him her last jar of home-canned cherries to take home to his wife. He expressed amazement at the size of the fruit in the jar, making Bernie beam.

It was not the first time the lake had been the subject of hydroelectric speculation. In '46 a corps of engineers from the U.S. Army had been up, nosing around. Most folks saw the strangers as guests, or as revenue: they spent money at the store, offered generous compensation to board with local families, were cause for a little excitement.

"I know that they're talking about a dam, Tom," Ellie says now. "They're just figuring out where. Things are gonna change. There'll be a lot of work around here, for a lot of years."

"That's good, then."

"For you, maybe. I'm going." Ellie grinds her cigarette into the base of Niagara Falls and looks at her brother appraisingly. "You should go, too. Should have gone a long time ago. You can spend your life working in a sawmill, but you're never going to meet a wife in Bear Creek, and before you know it you'll be too old to buck boards and then where will you be?"

Tom shakes his head. All he wanted to do was talk his sister into coming to meet the boat, docking this minute. He had not expected this.

"Mum and Dad have the farm, and, yeah, I suppose you'll have that too, eventually," Ellie goes on, "but I just have this place, and Gerry. Not even any kids. What's to stay for?"

"Going? You and Gerry are going?"

The whistle blows, then, and Ellie rises, waves her hand through the air to clear the smoke, smoothes her slacks, and joins her brother in the doorway. "I don't know about Gerry," she says as they step off the sill. Dog, lying in the shade of the porch, shuffles to his feet and follows.

It's not far from the Weber house to the dock, but Ellie walks briskly, dark hair tossed behind her, and Tom has trouble keeping up despite his long legs. When they arrive, Ellie pushes through the knot of people while Tom takes up his post against the piling some distance away. He watches while his sister approaches her husband, who throws a meaty, proprietorial arm around her neck. He's been gone a couple of days, picking up supplies for the mill's operations.

Tom regards the sternwheeler in the sharp morning light, her white paint glowing. The sky is an intense blue; there's something about the light in spring, Tom thinks. It's deeper, somehow. By the time he pushes himself away from the piling, most of the crowd has disbursed, and his sister and her husband are gone. Saturday or not, there is work to be done, and Tom heads back towards the cabin he built on his parent's property. He'd promised to help his father today.

"Ellie say anything to you about wanting to move?" Tom asks his father before he is fully in the yard. Frank Klaussen, standing by the tailgate of his old pickup, ignores his son and his scruffy dog and continues to draw the file across the chainsaw teeth for a moment before pausing. He brushes his gloved hands against his pants and straightens.

"What that girl does is of no interest to me."

"Dad, you can't keep this up. What do you do when she comes for dinner? Mum talks, I talk, you just keep your mouth shut and eat. That's no way to go on."

"She made her bed."

"Right, Dad, years ago. You don't have to like Gerry—hell, none of us likes Gerry, or most of the Webers for that matter—but she's your daughter for God sakes."

"She's a hard girl, Tom. She hasn't had a kind word to say to me for years. You couldn't melt butter in that girl's mouth, and I don't see why I should stand for her guff."

Tom looks up the slope to the tree they will take down today.

"We'd better get at it," Frank follows his son's gaze, and then hauls the heavy chainsaw off the tailgate. "Anyway, what's this about her moving?"

"Nothing. Probably nothing," Tom says. "You should just talk to her is all."

"Get your mother to say something."

The two work through the morning, and as dinnertime approaches a well-dressed man appears on the drive, walking. From beside the steps, Dog is silent, watchful.

"Left my car down at the store," he says conversationally when Frank shuts off the chainsaw. "Nice day for a walk."

Frank sets down the saw and looks at Tom for a clue, thinking he's perhaps missed something about this man and why he's standing in the drive with his hand outstretched. Frank has been forgetting things lately, something that bothers him but is better left unmentioned, as if putting a name to it would give it some sort of power over him. Tom knows this, and comes to his father's rescue.

"Tom Klaussen," he says, holding out his hand, barely stumbling over his own name; a childhood stutterer, T had always been difficult, and he often had to take a breath before attempting it. He let the breath out now. "I don't think we've met."

"Jim Porter. Your wife kindly asked me to dinner."

Dora Klaussen is setting the last dish on the table when the three men enter. The house smells of chicken and apples. Tom looks at his round mother—all that weight in so few years—and feels suddenly protective as she beams at the stranger.

"Mr. Porter! Welcome. I see you've met the boys. Come, come on in. Sit down. No, here. There you go." She pulls out a seat at the table. He pauses, hands her his coat and hat, and smiles at all of them, but does not sit down. Instead, he looks from one Klaussen to another, waiting for a further cue.

"You didn't tell me, Dora," Frank says amiably, but Tom senses an underlying tension. His father has never liked surprises, likes to know what to expect. Today was to be a working day, not a social day.

"Didn't I? I met Mr. Porter at the store, didn't I, Mr. Porter. Alice had him over for supper last week, and I thought we'd continue the Bear Creek welcome." Dora makes forward swooping motions with her hands, and the men sit down. She sits and folds her hands at the edge of the table. "Mr. Porter works with those engineers studying the river."

"Yes, I do." Porter affirms, his voice warming. "This place is going to see a real boom if this dam goes through."

"Boom, how?" asks Frank, digging in although Grace has not been said. Tom catches his mother's eye and she shakes her head, uncharacteristically dismissing the tradition because Mr. Porter, taking his cue from Frank, has also started eating.

"Construction! There will be jobs, and good paying jobs, too. This whole area will see a big influx of dollars, and not a moment too soon, looks like property values are at rock bottom all along here. This will be a great opportunity."

Tom swallows. The table is silent.

"First I've heard of it," says Frank finally, although Tom knows it isn't. "Where is this dam supposed to go?"

"South of here," Porter gestures with his fork. "It's going to bring a lot of money into this region. But it's just speculation, now. I wouldn't be worrying about it if I were you. Good chicken, by the way."

Tom watches the American dig in. When he looks around the table, he can see that they're all watching their guest eat, while he chews, intent on his food, oblivious.

Gerry Weber suspects something is not right. He has felt this for some time, but he can't put his finger on it. When Dora Klaussen and Bernie Schroeder visit the Weber household with the petition, Ellie is uncharacteristically quiet, and this bothers him. It surprises him that it bothers him, because he's usually telling her to shut up with her opinions.

"They're collecting names all up the lake. If this dam goes in, we'll lose all the homes along the waterfront. That means yours, too, Gerry. They'll buy us out," says Dora, clipboard in hand.

"I heard you had one of them Americans for dinner or supper or some such. That one's been boarding with the Milners. I heard you gave him a jar of cherries, Bernie." Gerry eyed the two ladies on his doorstep. "Now you want to kick 'em out?"

"We were just finding out about the situation,"

explains Bernie, looking at Dora. They both look at Ellie, who emerges from the inside dark towards the sunlight that slants across the doorway, but hangs back, her face in shadow. She says nothing, but folds her arms.

"We're here on behalf of Bear Creek Women's Institute," begins Dora, but Gerry cuts her off.

"If someone offers us enough cash, why not just take the money and run? Been thinking about leaving. Haven't we, Ellie?"

"Yes. Maybe. I don't know. I don't care."

"Ellie, these are our *homes*!" Bernie is aghast. Ellie grew up here, after all, as did Gerry. Say what you will about the Webers, she thinks, they've been here almost since day one.

"...could start fresh somewhere," Gerry is saying. Ellie stands behind her husband with her arms crossed, looking sideways at nothing. "Whaddaya think, El?"

Ellie looks surprised at the question, then comes back to herself and looks past Gerry at the two women with the clipboard standing expectantly on the step. "I don't care," she says again and turns back into the dark of the house.

"What's up, El?" Gerry asks when the door is shut and the ladies are gone.

"It's a backwards place, Gerry. They think they can fight a bunch of American bigwigs, there's no way. Them and their women's institute and their clipboards, like a little club. It's all going to change, and we won't have a thing to say about it, and Dora and Bernie and all the rest will just be left in the dust. In the damn dust," she raises her hands in the air in a gesture of hopelessness, and then lets them fall again.

"What do you know about it?" says Gerry, more

quizzically than angrily, but he says it to empty air, because Ellie has brushed past him, plunged her feet into the green rubber boots that stand by the door, and is halfway to the chicken coop by the time he gets the last word out.

There are two days before the *Minto*'s final sailing, and Tom sits and smokes at the end of the dock, watching the empty lake. He has his boots off and the air washes over his sweaty feet where they dangle above the water. He feels like a kid when he does this, like the kid he was, mostly alone, content to hang back and mull things over in his mind. He has a few things to think about.

Nobody really knows what a dam will mean, and Porter wasn't saying much at dinner, being vague and using big words to avoid saying anything at all. Tom, whose knowledge of the world comes from books and week-old newspapers, could gauge that much. But some folks were saying things like "flooding," and "expropriation," with alarm, while others did not believe such things could happen without the approval of the people who would be affected. They owned the land fair and square, didn't they? You can't just take it away. If there was even a hint of that, the government would have been holding town hall meetings by now. So a dam could surely not affect Bear Creek except for the jobs it would provide for the young people, so they'd stay in the community. Property values would go up with all the work, and the town would grow. Progress, people said, was a good thing.

There are two camps, Tom thinks as he exhales, blowing smoke straight ahead into a cross-breeze that lifts it, carrying it southward. There's the Weber camp, folks who'll milk it for whatever cash they can get out of it, and there's the Schroeder camp, folks who will defend their way of life whatever the cost. And then there's all the folks who don't have a clue, and won't until it's too late. Tom doesn't know what camp to believe, but he knows that Porter fellow made him uneasy. He usually trusts his guts.

After a while Tom stands and picks up his boots and begins unrolling his socks from where he'd stuffed them inside. They smell like sweat, like wet dogs. He pulls them over his feet, shoves feet into boots, and looks at his own wet dog, who looks back.

"C'mon, Dog," he says.

When the two reach the cabin at the edge of the Klaussen land, Tom is thinking of tomorrow's work at the mill, another day working alongside his brother-in-law. He'd like to find Ellie, like to have a good heart-to-heart with her. As if she'd let him.

Ellie sits in the woods up behind the house wearing Gerry's plaid flannel jacket and a pair of jeans. She's sitting on a stump, on the lower plane of the flat surface where the two approaches of the cross-cut saw did not quite meet twenty years ago. She has a cigarette burning, its glow a firefly signal in the darkening sky. Supper is past, the dishes are done, and she's told Gerry she's out for a walk, not something she could dress up for. But she's brushed her hair, and it falls about her shoulders in a dark frame. Her best attribute, she thinks. She is on her third cigarette when Porter comes up behind her, puts his hands over her eyes and then slips them down to her breasts.

"Heard you coming," says Ellie, leaning forward to

grind her cigarette beneath her boot, which dislodges Porter's hands. "A mile away." She sounds cold, but already she can feel the warmth spreading upwards from her thighs. Porter, still behind her, gathers her hair into a ponytail and gently pulls her head backwards until he can kiss her on the lips, nose to chin, tongues reaching.

It's much later when Ellie stands up and begins pulling on clothing. "Help me," she says, and turns her back so he can brush off earth and pine needles. He does her back, brushing from the top down, then turns her around to do the front, but instead kisses her again, and she laughs, clasps her hands behind his neck and holds him there until he begins to pull away against them.

"Friday," she says, disengaging her mouth.

"What about Friday?"

"What's the plan, Jim? How are we going to do this?"

"Do what?" he says, and she thinks: he's teasing me. As if on cue, he gives her nose a little flick with the back of an index finger and winks at her. "Don't you worry about it, Lady Ellen." As she walks back home, picking her way down the darkness of the path, she turns the name over and over, like a lucky pebble.

When Gerry awakes the next morning his wife is already up and in the kitchen. On her pillow he sees a brown pine needle, and when he moves the pillow, notices several more nesting in the folds of the sheet.

At the sawmill, Gerry is surly, brushing off his brother Marty's cheerful Hallo over the top of the push broom. "Get to work, Mar," he tells him, and catches Tom's eye over the buzz of the saw blade. On his way to the out-house mid-morning he almost trips over Dog, lying in the doorway. "Leave your damn mutt at home," he tells Tom, who calls the dog and points to a new spot well away from the door, watching until the dog is settled and unlikely to move again. Earl Milner, stacking boards, looks at Tom, grins, and shakes his head. Some days, you just steer clear of Gerold Weber, that's all.

But at noon when Gerry heads home for dinner, he asks Tom along, and Tom, surprised, accepts, even though he knows Ellie won't have made food for three. As the two walk the dirt road to the Weber house, Dog ambling behind them, Gerold talks while Tom listens, and this is no surprise to Tom. Gerold has never asked him for an opinion about anything, but is happy to provide one any time.

"This dam thing," he says, and Tom hears: 'this damn thing.' "El figures we should be the first in line to sell, says there'll be a budget for land, we should negotiate high while there's still money. Those folks who wanna hold out, there won't be much left. On th'other hand, I figure they'll offer low at first to kinda set a standard, so we'd be best somewheres in the middle of things."

"There's no offers on the table, Ger," Tom says. "There might not even be any offers. We don't even know if there's gonna be a dam."

"You don't send a whole damn bunch of experts up here if you don't mean business," Gerry stops and faces his brother-in-law. "Folks who think it's not gonna happen have their heads in the mud. It's gonna happen, it's just a matter of time. And you've seen what the beavers do up the creek. Think of that across the whole width of the river, and think how big a lake that's gonna make. You," he pokes a finger into Tom's sawdust-covered jacket, "are dreaming if you think things are gonna go on just as they've always been. Besides," he adds, walking on, "s'time for a change."

At the Weber table, Ellie is laying out food, humming. When she sees Tom, she reaches for another plate.

"Didn't know you were coming, Tom. There's enough, I guess. Sit down."

There is a smell in the air Tom can't place, and he thinks it must be something about the meal. Dog stands in the doorway wagging until Tom tells him to go lay down outside. He spends some time sniffing the ground around the front door before settling down.

"Give him a bone or something, El," says Gerry, and Tom and Ellie both look up. Ellie can't figure why her husband, so surly this morning, is suddenly being kind, especially to her brother's dog. The dog, as if having heard and understood the remark, returns to the doorway smiling. Tom looks at him, shakes his head, and the dog disappears. Gerry picks up the conversation where he and Tom had left off, ignoring his wife and immediately forgetting his own suggestion.

"El and I, we think a new start'll be good, don't we, El?" Gerry asks, and Ellie shrugs, looking down at the ham she's slicing. Gerry's been wearing her down, so unpredictable lately, up and down, like a seesaw. "Hell, get a good price on this place, we could start our own operation, get some machines, get a timber licence, supply the big mill at Edgewood." He speaks with his mouth full. "Mind you, plenty of folks don't like it. But ya can't stop progress, can you, Tom?"

Tom, unused to being included, hesitates before opening his mouth to speak, and Gerry goes on before a word is formed.

"It's the way things are gonna go, that's all. Th'Americans have all the power. Or at least, will have," he laughs at his joke, then grows serious. "Your folks can get set up somewheres else, a little retirement home, Ellie and I can live close by, can't we, El? That's what we need, a new start. Been thinking about it all morning. You and I, we could log together, Tom."

It takes Tom several moments to follow, then a few more to formulate a response.

"I don't know, Ger," he says finally. "I'll think about it. Nothing's going to happen for a long time, these things take years. Good ham, El," Tom smiles at his sister, waiting for the opinion he knows is coming. It doesn't. A surly silence has again descended on the table, a weight like the air before a storm.

When they rise to return to work, the weight lifts suddenly, and Gerry is again talking about the future, the things they will do, as if deciding for Tom his course of action. Ellie smiles weakly at Tom and raises her eyebrows. She gives her brother a ham bone wrapped in wax paper, which Tom tucks in his pocket, thinking: this'll make for a quiet mutt this afternoon. All the way back, he swats Dog's big nose away from his pocket, while Gerry walks on ahead, lips working, calculating.

The next morning Tom walks from his mother's house to his sister's, annoyed. He'll be late for work, not that anyone will have all that much to say. He doesn't know why his mother was so insistent he take a pan of brownies over to El's place first thing, calling over to him as soon as he emerged from the cabin. She could walk over herself, for that matter.

"I have a lot to do today, that's why," she told him. "I want Ellie to have these for Gerry's lunch. They've been going through a bad patch."

"Ma, brownies aren't going to fix a marriage. You take them over if it's so important. Besides, she'll talk to you."

"Not these days. Go," she told him. "Go on. You have time."

Tom has to hold the pan high above Dog's salivating jaws, and he feels foolish like this, walking down the road in the opposite direction from the sawmill with one arm over his head. Gerry, always an early starter, will already be working away, thinks Tom, and here I am delivering brownies.

At the step he can hear voices, but he can't hear what they're saying. Dog whines, and he shushes, a low hiss. The dog pushes against his leg and whines again, louder, and Tom digs into the pan, extracts a wedge of brownie, and holds it behind him, not looking. As the dog earnestly licks at his master's fingers with single-minded intensity, Tom hears a male voice, not Gerry's, then Ellie's unmistakable laugh. Try as he might he can't hear any words, and after a while he leaves the pan on the porch railing and backs out of the yard. Down the road, away from the house, a black '52 Chev is parked like a crow near a roadside kill.

Later, Ellie cuts up the brownies she presumes her mother has left for her, arranging them on a plate. She wonders when they were left, if it was when she was down at the store, and if so why they were left outside instead of inside on the kitchen table. Her stomach contracts in a sudden fear. She cuts around the hole in the corner, thinking some animal must have got at them. She puts her fingers in her mouth, tastes chocolate, and then licks her fingers one by one.

When she goes for her walk after dinner, Ellie finds Tom where he can be found most evenings, on the wharf, the dog sniffing among the rocks at the shoreline.

"Was by your place this morning," he says as she sits down beside him. She was going to reach for the cigarette package in his breast pocket, a gesture of sisterly familiarity, but this stops her and she holds her breath, waiting for the next sentence. She can hear the dog dislodging rocks as he moves about behind them, and the sound of water against the pilings. They wait, listening.

"You got something going on with that American?" he says after a time, looking straight ahead. A moment passes, and then Ellie takes a deep breath, composing herself.

"Can I have cigarette?"

He hands her the pack, still not looking at her. The matches are tucked inside. There is the strike of the match end, the rush of the flare, the brief smell of sulfur, the sharp inhale.

"'Course not," she says finally, exhaling. "He wanted to ask about the petition is all. He wanted to know what's going on."

"So he came to you?"

"He knows we're not against the dam, I guess," she shrugged.

"Why didn't he talk to Ger?"

"Guess he thought he'd still be home. Didn't think he'd start work so early."

Tom makes a sound in his nose and continues to look down the lake. Ellie watches him. She waits longer than most would wait for a response, then longer while she turns over the things she might say. They had grown up together here, after all. They had not been exactly close, and Ellie always resented they way her mother protected her brother, a favouritism that still irks her, never mind the rift that occurred with her marriage to Gerry. But he's her brother. She knows that if she is to speak, this is the time: now, into the silence they have created like a wall in the last several minutes. She draws a breath.

"Dog," calls Tom then, and the animal looks up and begins trotting back towards the dock. "Look, I gotta go, El. If you want to talk, you know how to find me."

I do, thinks Ellie as she watches his frame recede down the length of the dock to meet his dog, waiting at the shore end. I do want to talk, but I don't know where to begin.

Ellie rises early, before Gerry is awake. She feels sticky, and gives herself a sponge bath from the warm water on the stove. Last night they had clung together like rutting animals, the first passionate sex she's had with her husband for months. For Ellie, it was an apology; for Gerry, a beginning. He felt the way he did the first time with El, but better. New plans always made him feel this way, and chewing on the prospect all day had made him buoyant, his excitement spilling over into a new enthusiasm for his wife, for her body.

She has packed the things Gerry won't notice are missing at first, things she doesn't wear every day. Now, she adds a few personal items: a brassiere, some underwear. She fluffs the remaining garments in their shared drawer to fill the extra space. When he finally wakes up she has his breakfast ready. As he pushes his plate away, he reaches for his coat and then hesitates, moving towards her where she stands beside the kitchen table, hands gripping the back of her chair, and kisses her on the cheek. In the breeze of the closing door she lifts her hand to her cheek and rests it there.

When the whistle blows to signal the arrival of the *Minto* on her last run, almost everyone is at the wharf. Tom, leaning against the piling, Dog at his side, thinks that Gerry must have been the only one to show up for work today. Marty, Wilf, young Charlie and the others; everyone is here instead. Some things are just more important than work, or school. Bear Creek's kids are here, too, all of them, running around like little whirlwinds, the teens hanging in packs. There is a buzz in the air, the babble of voices, and this merges with the noise of the engines while the great sternwheeler docks, the wood of the wharf groaning against the pressure of the hull as it pulls alongside.

There is a group of passengers waiting with bags at their sides. They're off to visit friends and relatives in the towns to the south, to take a historic last ride on a beloved boat, a victim of progress. There are roads, now, to almost everywhere except for Bear Creek. The new ferry waits in her berth, due to start her runs across the lake when the *Minto*'s wake recedes. It will hook up with the new road pushed through from Robson. The *Minto*'s passengers will ride back on this road or they'll take the train and hike down from the siding. The age of sternwheelers is over.

Looking at the gathering of folks waiting for the ropes to be tied and the unloading to begin, he sees, suddenly, his sister standing among them. As he approaches, she is tossing her hair and laughing, explaining to Peggy Shannon that she's got a friend down at Trail, left a phone message at the store inviting her down just last night, Gerry thought she could use the break, told her:

go on, I'll be fine without you, and what a fine husband is that? Peggy listens, curious: Ellen hasn't spoken this much to any of them in months. Tom stands outside the circle, watching Ellie's back, straining to hear what she's saying. He's still there when Horst comes up beside him.

"Did you hear?" He says to Tom.

"Hear what?" says Tom, not looking at Horst but staring intently at the group, trying to listen.

"Those Americans pulled out. Booked Fred's boat this morning, left at seven, all of 'em."

Tom pulls his eyes from his sister. "Why?"

"Ottawa backed out. Bennett doesn't have the clout everyone thought, I guess. Everything's on hold, and the company pulled all their guys. Guess they've known for a few days, didn't say nothing."

Tom watches his sister, who has stopped talking and is looking around. Looking for someone.

"Excuse me," he says to Horst, and pushes his way into the group standing beside suitcases and bags. He takes Ellie's arm and pulls her out of the group, leaving her suitcase where it stands at the dock.

"He's gone," he tells her. She looks at him, her face blank.

"Who's gone?" She says, but at that moment she sees Gerry striding down the dock towards them, hands in pockets, looking cheerful. She freezes.

"Buncha lazy idiots," he says as he draws up, punching Tom in the arm. Gerry is glad for the holiday, Tom can tell, and playful as a result. Tom has difficulty shifting gears. Beside his master sits Dog, watching.

Tom clears his throat and speaks to both of them, but looks directly at Ellie.

"Heard the Americans have pulled out," he says.

"Heard they all left on Fred's boat this morning. Ottawa's pulled out of the deal."

"No deal?" Gerry's voice is disappointed, surprised. "No deal?"

"No deal," says Tom, and looks at Ellie, who is staring at him, face blank. Behind them her bag sits, orphaned in a throng of people. There is commotion all around them, yet to Ellie it's as if she stands in a vacuum. The sound has blurred into a roaring in her ears. She can't breathe.

Gerry does not look at his wife, but turns and spits, disgusted. "Figures," he says. "I'm going back to work. Don't care about the stupid boat. Coming?"

"In a minute," says Tom, and stands there until Gerry has turned away. Then: "Come on," he says to his sister. He turns, picks up her bag and hands it to her, folding her fingers around the handle, announcing "change of plans" to nobody in particular.

"No, I'm going," says Ellie suddenly. "I gotta go, Tom."

"Jesus, El. Where? Where are you gonna go?"

The passengers are boarding, and there is no time. Tom looks at his sister, searching her face, and then nods. Beside him, the dog whines. The sun is shining, the sky an impossible blue in an April morning when the great white boat blows its final departure whistle.

Her face is a round moon looking down at him from the deck, expressionless. She does not look like his sister, but he waves just the same.

1965

When Stanley Cheevers knocked on our door earlier that morning I was working on a crossword puzzle. I had been struggling over a twelve-letter word for "dishonourable."

"Unscrupulous," I said out loud when he poked his head in, hat in hand.

"But I haven't even said anything yet," he protested, smiling slightly.

I pointed vaguely to the crossword. "I know who you are."

"I suppose you must," he said sympathetically. "You're Ursula Strautman? Should we wait until your husband is home?"

"No. Yes. I don't know. I usually deal with these sorts of things."

Cheevers stood, his briefcase held before him like a shield. "I could come back," he said, looking uncomfortable. Perhaps he thought he was wasting his time with me.

"No. Sit," I told him, pulling out a chair.

For the next half hour he explained the process: he talked about assessment, appraisal, fair market value and compensation, and each time he looked at me to make sure I fully comprehended the words. I'm Queen of the Crosswords, I wanted to tell him: throw all the big words you've got at me.

He was not an unlikeable fellow, this Mr. Cheevers, with his round face and the thin spot on his crown, a man just doing his job. But I didn't want to like him, and I certainly didn't want to let him off easy.

"I don't see how you can talk to me about compensation, Mr. Cheevers," I said. "I was born in this house. My parents died here. We don't *want* to move."

"The government is prepared to be more than fair in ensuring that displaced residents realize market value for their properties and are compensated generously for moving and inconvenience."

"We've been under threat of dam development for years, Mr. Cheevers," I told him. "There *is* no market value in Bear Creek, so I don't see how you're going to apply one."

"Part of the formula involves assessing current purchase price of similar properties in the region in areas that will not be flooded."

He sounded altogether too comfortable with his answer. "We don't want to move," I said again, but my words sounded small.

After Cheevers left, I walked through the house that was once my mother's and father's, touching things: the neat hem of the kitchen curtains, sewed by my mother's hand; the bottle my mother always kept on the kitchen windowsill that cast a watery blue glow across my hand as I reached for it. I sniffed at its rim, but there was only the scent of dust. What had it held? I picked up a framed photograph, inscribed on the back in my father's formal script almost twenty years ago: *Ursula & Edward with the girls, Summer '46, Bear Creek, B.C.* It was a slow odyssey undertaken in smoky late-morning light, dust motes swirling around me as I held a needlepoint pillow to my breast.

It wasn't that I hadn't expected the visit: the land negotiators had been working their way through communities up and down the lake, one house at a time. It was inevitable that one would eventually reach our property, a small holding that touched the lake on one side, and then rose with the landscape, gently settling onto the bench nestled at the base of the mountain. The change had been coming for years. Now, it was here at last. The realization that our time was up came to me suddenly in the way I imagine we finally come face to face with death, which was why, once the negotiator had gone, instead of making lunch for Ed and Sarah I was walking from room to room, remembering.

In the bedroom I shared with my husband, Ed, I curled my hands around the curve of the iron bed frame. I imagined standing there as I had as a small girl, waiting quietly for my parents to waken. I moved from our bedroom and stepped across the floorboards, every creak a familiar whisper: *here*. At the doorway to my granddaughter's room I smiled at the poster Sarah had brought from Calgary: four boys with mops of hair and an insect name. Life does go on.

"What are you doing?" Sarah came through the front door, the screen door banging behind her, feet like the trampling of small elephants: a girl with a presence. She stopped at the sight of me staring off into her bedroom.

"Hi there, hon. Thinking, I guess."

Sarah looked at me sideways and turned to the kitchen where she pulled a bottle of milk from the icebox. Her friends at home could not believe she existed for two whole months without electricity, but she didn't seem to miss it. There were things to do here: fishing from the wharf; swimming in the chill of the lake; driving around on the dirt roads in one of the junkpile cars some of the boys had cobbled together, thinking I didn't know. Sarah poured herself a glass of milk and leaned back against the sink, the uncapped bottle dripping condensation onto the counter beside her.

"Are you going to put that away?"

Sarah shrugged again and recapped the bottle, then pushed it back into the icebox, while I watched, considering. It had been two years since Win, Hugh and Sarah moved away. In those two years she had become an adolescent, applying all the shrugging and eye-rolling she could to any situation. If it wasn't for my daughter Edwina—Win, we call her—calling with a plea for one last summer for her girl who seemed to be at odds with everything, I would have said: we're getting too old, Win. I don't know if I can handle a teenager at my age.

"I'm going to Barb's for lunch," Sarah said, setting her glass beside the sink. "I just came back to change." She had been at the Kroekers' for dinner the night before as well. I kept my mouth shut. It was going to be her last summer here, after all. I felt a small, warm wind as my granddaughter brushed past, then a cross-breeze as she shut her bedroom door.

When Ed came home at lunchtime I had been sitting at the kitchen table for several minutes, hand pressed to my breastbone. There was a weight in my chest, as if something large was sitting on it.

"I told him we aren't moving," I said after describing the visit. "I know it's ridiculous, but it's what I said. There isn't any hope, is there?"

Ed ran his hands through his greying hair, and then pressed them to his eyelids for a moment as if his eyes were weary. "Isobel says she's not leaving. She won't leave Jack's grave. Stubborn old thing, they'd have to drag her out," he said. "And Tom Klaussen. He's sunk everything he's got into that place; he told me the other day at the store he's refused their offer."

"The Milners, Gerry Weber, old Helen, they've all settled," I drew on the border of the unfinished crossword puzzle as I spoke: a box, then doors and windows. Home. "Gerry Weber says he got the best deal, and now Peter's spitting nails because he thinks Gerry talked down about the other properties to Cheevers. They're all mad at Tom for holding out, like he'll get a better deal when he does settle." I drew a chimney, a plume of smoke. Behind the house, an M described the flanks of mountains.

"We might as well settle, Urs," Ed pulled my hand away from my drawing and held it gently. "We're getting older, and this place is a lot to keep. Besides, even if we won, even if they moved the house to higher ground, what's the point in being here if nobody else is?"

"You may be right, but I'll tell you what," I said, pulling back my hand. "We're not going to take their word for it. We'll get our own appraiser in. I heard some are doing that up the lake. I'm not going without a fight, Ed. We'll get the best damn deal we can."

A week later I hauled Cheevers around the property as I pointed out its attributes. Waterfront. Mature fruit trees in neat rows. A sturdy two storey frame house with not so much as a crack in the old foundation. I had him on his knees to prove it. When the tour was complete, I looked at him.

"I'm not saying I'll move, Mr. Cheevers, but I'm curious to see what sort of price tag you and your government will put on all this." I swept my arm to indicate the house, the barn, the chicken coop and the orchard. I was bluffing, and we both knew that. Moving was a given; only the details remained.

Cheevers had been nervously polite all day. Yes, Mrs. Strautman, No, Mrs. Strautman. "We'll see, Mrs. Strautman," he told me then.

"Ursula," I said, a small gesture. "I think we might be seeing quite a bit of one another through this whole mess."

"Stanley," he offered, looking relieved.

"Just the same," I told him, "even though you and I are on a first-name basis doesn't mean we're moving."

He smiled weakly. "We'll begin the assessment and put an offer together as soon as possible."

After Cheevers left I called around until I found a private appraiser who could begin right away, fairly bullying him on the phone that it couldn't wait. Ed steered clear.

"I'll leave it up to you, Urs. It's not like I could tell you anything anyway," he said, and went off to play cards at the store, where they have a table set up in the back. Sarah had been staying out of the way, off with that pack of teenagers all the time, mostly with Barb Kroeker. I'm not easy to be around at times like this. A bulldog, Ed calls me.

The appraiser's name was Howard Sprate, and he'd been doing a fair bit of work in these parts, apparently. Money from misfortune. We tromped around the property just as I had with Cheevers, me in my rubber boots, jeans and an old flannel shirt, a kerchief over my grey hair, him in his business suit. He looked about balefully, sweating in the heat, which caused the strands of hair he had combed across his bald head to sag over his forehead. When we had finished, I asked him inside for iced tea.

"I'll have the appraisal ready in about two weeks," he said, swallowing his drink in several noisy gulps, and then wiping his mouth with the back of his hand. "Sorry for the delay; it's been pretty busy lately."

"I need it in a week," I told him, and then fixed him with what I hoped was my father's steely gaze, one I had been cultivating in my later years. He looked away.

"I'll do my best. Is there more iced tea?" I drained the pitcher into his glass.

I fretted after that, wondering which would arrive first, the government contract or the private appraisal. No matter, really: if Cheevers showed up first, I'd send him packing until I was ready to see him. Hydro could wait; it was me going crazy with the uncertainty of it all. Late in the afternoon Ed was still not back, and I remembered he'd agreed to do some work for Isobel that afternoon. I found them both at Isobel's kitchen table drinking moonshine.

"Who made that?" I asked, sniffing the air. It smelled like sandpaper feels: abrasive.

"Gerry Weber," said Isobel, grinning. "I know, I'm bad. But Ed and I were talking over all this garbage and it just seemed the best solution for the moment. Get yourself a glass."

Isobel herded me towards a chair, bottle in hand, and there I was, four o'clock in the afternoon, drinking moonshine. It felt good.

"I got Sprate to commit to a week," I said after the first glass.

"What's the rush?" Isobel, sitting there in Jack's old jeans and one of his shirts, gathered up her loose grey curls into an elastic band. She looked like a backwoods mountain woman, and I remembered her arrival in Bear Creek forty-five years ago. She came to help her sister Helen, whose twin babies had died, then met Jack and never left. She has become Bear Creek, I thought. Leaving would kill her.

"I want his appraisal before I see Cheevers. What are you going to do, Iz?"

"I won't leave Jack," she said, nodding towards the Spanish cherry tree where her husband is buried alongside Ace, his beloved horse.

"Well, you might have to drown, then" I said. Flippant. It appeared the moonshine was taking effect, and I put my hand over my mouth, then looked at my glass in what I hoped was an accusatory manner. "Sorry," I said.

"No, you're right," Isobel sighed. "I'm just not ready to settle, I guess. Make 'em sweat, that's what I say."

"At the card game today," began Ed, and something in his voice made us both turn to look at him. "Gerry Weber accused us of holding up the process, trying the negotiator's patience so that Hydro's offers will be lower. Acting like we were better than the rest of them. Roy Epp said we'd always acted stuck-up. Said he was sick of us."

Ed had set the cards back on the table mid-hand and left.

"These are our neighbours," he said, looking into his empty glass. It felt as if the day got a little darker then.

We walked home together, Ed and I, holding hands. Sarah joined us on the road, coming back from the Kroekers'. It was a lovely evening, the kind I loved best, and it was easy to pretend that everything was okay. The ghost of the sunset crouched on the horizon in a pale glow, while above the evening star hung like a jewel, impossibly bright. The dark shoulders of mountains appeared to be rolling over to sleep; the lake lay like glass. For the moment, the smell of smoke was absent.

The leaflet was in the mailbox when I went to get the mail. *The New Outlook for the Arrow Lakes* it said optimistically, and I thought: Outlook indeed. Look out! I said out loud.

I was still waiting for both Sprate and Cheevers. With one telephone in Bear Creek, they were unlikely to make an appointment; land negotiators and other undesirables appeared unannounced, generally, a knock on the screen door interrupting your quiet moment with your cup of tea and your crossword puzzle.

I spent the better part of the morning reading, biding my time, thinking either man might show up at any moment. Land would be purchased to the elevation of 1,453 feet, the leaflet told me, and I had difficulty imagining what that meant in terms of the water's rise. As I looked about the kitchen I could see the house, for a chilling moment, under water: small trout swimming by, my hair loose, floating about me as I sat at my table.

Sites were suggested for new communities of 150 families. A nice, round number, I thought; how convenient. The new community, the leaflet explained, would be efficiently planned. I could see it would bear no resemblance to the hodgepodge that is Bear Creek, its roads curving around property disputes, its buildings a bit of this, a bit of that, renovations that told of births and deaths and the passages of lives. I was still reading when Ed came in.

"Look at this!" I told him, poking my finger at the paper in front of me.

"It looks nice," he suggested, looking at me to see if he'd said something wrong.

"It's not *home*," I said, looking up, and then the tears started. Ed sat and put his arm around me.

At that moment Sarah came in, a little breathless. "There's a reporter here from the *Vancouver Sun*," she said. "He wants to talk to people. He was over at the Kroekers'. I told him to come and see you."

I was weeding the kitchen garden when the young man approached, and I rubbed my hands against my jeans before holding one out, and then withdrew it again sheepishly.

"Sorry. A bit muddy," I said. "You're the fellow from the *Sun*?"

"Bill Androsoff," he said, smiling. "I'm doing a story…"

"So I've heard. I guess whether I talk to you depends on whether you're sympathetic," I told him.

"We try to be balanced," he said, "but I'm not working for Hydro if that's what you mean."

I sized him up, and then tipped my head to indicate the porch. We sat, and over the space of the next half-hour I told him a great deal more than I'd intended. It just came rolling out: about my parents, my childhood, and summers here with the children, the grandchildren. How Ed, too, was raised here, his parents both buried in the cemetery as were mine. How the community worked together—most of the time, anyway—where it had come from and the improvements we had made.

"It's a peaceful life," I told him. "Hydro can give us money to buy property somewhere else, but how can they guarantee a good life? How can we be expected to gamble what is perfect for something that may not be?"

"I don't see you have much choice," Androsoff said sympathetically.

"Not the first time I've heard *that*," I said. "I'm going to hold out for the best deal I can get, though."

"You're not the only one," Androsoff flipped open his notebook pages. "That fellow Bob Smyth up the lake, owns the Grizzly Bear Hotel. He's holding out, wants Hydro to move his hotel to higher ground. They say it's an engineering impossibility; too big, too expensive. They want to buy him out. It's getting ugly up there, let me tell you. They've offered him a lot more than it's worth, too. He says the same thing as you: you can't put a price on all that work he's put into it, and all the dreams he had for the place."

I waited, while Androsoff almost visibly picked through what he knew for what he was willing to tell me.

"There have been threats," he said, finally. I waited, my eyebrows raised.

"I tried to interview Stanley Cheevers, the land negotiator, but he wouldn't talk to me, said I have to go through proper Hydro channels. He's a mess, that guy."

There was another pause while Androsoff, cub reporter, eager beaver, tried, in a last bid at journalistic professionalism, to hold back the gossip he was dying to spread. I gave him my most encouraging grandmotherly smile.

"Seems like there's a lot of pressure on the guy, a lot of people angry," he offered at last. "He was seen falling-down drunk last Tuesday—in the daytime, mind you—but he denied it afterwards." Androsoff looked out over the lake, paused, and then continued on. "He wasn't drinking at the Grizz, that's for sure, because Bob wouldn't have him in there. Folks think he's got it stashed in that briefcase of his. Bob complained to Hydro about him, wants to see him off the job, but Cheevers, I think he has a wife and kids somewhere. Probably needs the work."

"Where's he staying?"

"Hotel in Edgewood."

After the reporter left I sat on the porch, thinking. The smell of smoke was back. As Hydro acquired properties they burned the buildings to discourage vandalism. Some communities further up the lake were almost cleared but for a few intact houses, people still negotiating or holding out altogether. While they waited, the homes around them settled to ash, and the air stank.

"I have photographs," Androsoff told me before he left, "of old people crying in front of their homes as the buildings went up in flames. Sure, they had the cheque in their pocket, but it's the end of a life for them."

When Cheevers came back the next time, Isobel's bottle of moonshine was sitting on the kitchen table. She'd brought it over the night before.

"Take this," she'd said. "Ed can drink it. It makes my stomach hurt, and anyway, it's not seemly for a woman my age to be drinking moonshine."

"Since when have you been seemly?" I asked my friend, but took the bottle all the same, placing it in the middle of the table beside the salt and pepper shakers.

Cheevers tapped on the door frame the following afternoon, looking apologetic.

"I haven't got our appraisal back yet," I said in the general direction of the door.

"Maybe I could just come in," he said through the

screen. "Talk about your concerns." His voice sounded smaller than it had before, and so I somehow expected a smaller man to step through the door, but as I turned he ducked his head slightly to clear the doorway, turning his hat in his hands.

I motioned to a kitchen chair and moved away to see about tea, and then surprised myself by offering him a shot from the bottle. "I could use a shot myself," I told him. "The day's almost over. Why don't you call it quits and join me?"

If Cheevers wondered what the penalty might be for drinking with a resettlement candidate, regardless of what may or may not have been in his briefcase, he paused only briefly, and I watched his mind work, his eyes on the moonshine.

"It has been a long day," he said.

"A number of them," I agreed.

We sat in silence for several minutes.

"I know you want to bargain," he said, finally, and he sounded tired. "The position of B.C. Hydro is that we will not bargain." He took a swallow from his glass and gave an involuntary shudder. "But we will negotiate."

I laughed. "What's the difference?"

"Once, I thought I knew," he answered, and held his glass out for another shot. He swirled the liquid so it made a small whirlpool. "I shouldn't be doing this."

"No, I suppose not," I said, but later I wondered if he was referring to the shot in his glass or the job he'd taken on.

"Thank you, Mrs. Strautman. Ursula," he said as he left. He shook my hand and his blue eyes met mine with a warm glow only partly alcohol-induced. Nice man, I thought. A wife. Kids.

By the time Ed came in dinner was not yet made, and Cheevers had left. The bottle was empty.

"I think we're his new best friends," I said to Ed.

"You didn't settle!" He looked alarmed.

"Oh, no. But he told me all about his family, and his job, and a whole mess of other things he probably shouldn't have said."

"Like what?"

"Like that this thing hasn't been so well-thought-out. That resettlement doesn't take into proper account the fact that so much land will be lost; there won't *be* that many places to resettle. There are two thousand people to place, he said. Two thousand. I feel sorry for him, Ed."

"You can't worry about him." He was looking at me and at the empty bottle.

"Of course not. Give Sprate another call, will you? Tell him we need those numbers."

After that it was a waiting game. Sarah came and went, her usual moody self. I saw Isobel almost every day, and worried about her; she seemed diminished, somehow. Ed had stopped playing cards but kept himself busy doing odd jobs for those still friendly. There were a handful, though, that kept their distance, cold shoulders that got icier as time went on. It was as if a cancer had invaded Bear Creek, small tumours here and there, threatening to spread. At the post office one morning I ran into Flora, who'd married Roy Epp in '56. I had always supposed she had looked to Bear Creek as a place to live out her days as part of the extended Epp family. I never liked Flora much, but I was nevertheless surprised by her tone.

"It's a backwards place," she said dismissively, squint-

ing at me, holding her mail in a fist on her hip. "No electricity, even. You're crazy not to take the money."

"How much did they offer for your place?" I asked.

Her eyes narrowed and she pressed her lips together.
"That would be confidential."

In fact, all settlements were confidential, but that did-
n't keep most people from talking about them. When the
Klaussen place finally went for almost $20,000, there
were some unhappy people in Bear Creek who had settled
for less and saw the Klaussen property as inferior to their
own.

"At Hydro we try to compensate for specific situa-
tions as well as land value," Cheevers explained when he
next arrived at my door. "The old folks have particular
needs, while for young people, it's easier to start over.
Not that you have many young people anymore."

He looked at the kitchen table, conspicuously absent
of bottles, and then laid his briefcase on its surface and
snapped open the clasps. His hands shook slightly. He
held the Hydro offer out to me, a neat envelope with the
name Strautman typewritten on its face. It looked stark-
ly official, and it struck me that ours was nothing but a
name on a list in an office, the final dollar figure the
only thing that mattered. I don't know why the thought
hadn't occurred to me before.

My voice was cold when I spoke. "We don't want to
look at Hydro's offer until we get our appraisal figures,"
I said, holding up my hand. His eyes searched mine,
looking, no doubt, for the camaraderie we'd shared
before. I wasn't giving him a thing. He shut the envelope
back in his briefcase and closed the lid. He looked away
and gave an almost imperceptible nod before leaving
quietly.

Later, I found Isobel on her front steps, weeping.

"What's the matter?" I sat beside her.

"I asked Cheevers what was going to happen to the graveyard. I guess I thought they might move the graves to higher ground or something, which would be upsetting enough. But he told me they'd be laying cement over the whole thing. They'll be drowning them! Oh, I know they're dead. But you know. Somehow all of these people, our relatives, our neighbours, under water…" she trailed off.

"What about Jack?" I asked quietly. Jack had, in death as in life, breached convention when it came to his final resting place. The Spanish cherry caught a breeze in its branches as I glanced at it, a gentle shrug.

"Cheevers didn't know. Not his department," she said. Her forehead was drawn into tight lines, and her eyes were wet. My brave friend, hard of spirit, gentle of heart, pillar to the weak.

"Oh, Iz," I said.

"Ursula," she looked at me, her voice despairing. "I'm going to have to settle. We're all just going to have to settle."

When I returned from Isobel's, Ed was back from the post office and was sitting on the porch. He'd called Sprate, he told me.

"What did he say?" I asked.

"Monday," he replied, and I sat beside him on the step. I told him about Isobel and the graveyard. I told him about Cheevers bringing by Hydro's offer for our home.

"I wasn't ready to see it," I told him, and he nodded.

"Monday," he said again.

I went to bed that night feeling defeated. "What's a

five-letter word for exhausted?" I asked Ed. "Tired," he mumbled sleepily as he drew me close. "Just plain tuckered out."

"End of the rope," I whispered. "Past the point of no return."

"Shhhhh." He told me.

Sarah began staying closer to home, and I suppose I was too distracted to ask why. We were making bread together the Sunday before our appraisal was due.

"Sarah, if you keep pounding the dough like that, the bread's going to end up like a rock. There's kneading, and then there's beating up on it," I told her.

Sarah kept pounding, speaking in short, hard sentences as the bread went fold, slap, thunk. "It's. Not. Fair," she said.

"What's the matter, hon?"

"Barb's folks don't want me there because they're mad at you. About you and Gramps getting an appraisal. And Barb says it doesn't matter anyway, we won't see each other ever again after this place is gone." She punched the dough with both fists and began to cry, then, angry tears of a betrayed adolescent. And she was betrayed. What could I say?

I made a fist, shook it at the dough, and began to keep pace with Sarah and you know, it *did* feel good. Fold, slap, thunk. Fold, slap, thunk. Soon we were in unison, our own percussion section as we sped up. We began to giggle, not looking at one another, just laughing into the bread dough we pummelled, faster and faster. By the time Ed came to the door the dough was flying and we were both covered in flour.

"I met Mr. Cheevers on the way home," he called out

cautiously, and the land negotiator appeared in the doorway beside him, peering through the cloudy air. I brushed the tears from my eyes with the back of a floury hand. Monday was tomorrow. We wouldn't be negotiating, but Cheevers looked so ill at ease I asked him in.

"Stanley!" I said, as if greeting an old friend. "Come, I'll get the bottle."

Perhaps he thought I was making fun of him, reminding him of his earlier indiscretion. Perhaps he knew of the rumours wafting up and down the lake with the smoke and bad feelings. Clearly uncomfortable, Cheevers turned away. "I'll come back at a better time," he mumbled. Sarah and I, caught up in the moment of our hilarity, barely registered his departure.

When he had gone, we looked at one another and dissolved further into laughter, sinking together to the floor in a small, multigenerational puddle. "You look ridiculous," Sarah told me, waving a hand weakly in my direction. I stuck my tongue out at her in a most ungrandmotherly manner.

It was good to laugh like that, I thought later, especially because of the things that happened in the next few days that were not laughing matters. First, Sprate came with the appraisal, which was less than we had hoped. Then Cheevers came with the Hydro assessment, which was less than half the appraisal.

"We won't settle for that," I told Cheevers, waving the appraiser's papers in front of his face. "It's an insult!" My face was inches from his.

"It's a generous offer, Mrs. Strautman," he said, taking a full step backwards. I must have noticed then that he did not look as neat and pressed as he did before, that his hands shook, but it didn't register. It was the shift from our first-name arrangement that really irked me at that moment.

"It's an insult, *Stanley*," I countered, emphasizing the familiar name.

I thought I saw him flinch, but perhaps that, too, is hindsight. Perhaps all of my perceptions—the rumpled crease in his pant leg, the pallor of his face—are just hindsight, now. "I'll be back in forty-eight hours," he said. "Think it over."

The next day Bill Androsoff, the *Vancouver Sun* reporter, came back. I was sitting on the porch, enjoying the sun's rays as they warmed my face. There was a crossword on my lap and a pencil behind my ear, and my eyes were closed as I tilted my head towards the warmth. It was a perfect Bear Creek day. When I heard the step in the yard, I opened one eye just enough to see him, then closed it again.

"Mrs. Strautman?" He stood several feet from the step, thinking I was asleep.

I spoke with my eyes closed. "What's a four-letter word for upheaval?" I asked. There was silence for a few moments.

"Move?" he asked finally.

"Hydro," I answered. "But that's five letters, I suppose. It's all the same anyway." I opened my eyes and waved him into a chair. He sat, notebook closed on his lap.

"I'd like to talk to you about the resettlement program, and how you're feeling in view of the news," He said.

I looked at him, waiting. I hadn't left the house all morning.

ANNE DeGrace

"Have you settled?" He asked.

"Not yet. Stanley Cheevers is due back today."

Androsoff looked uncomfortable. He appeared to be gathering his words. "There was a fire up the lake last night," he said at last. "That hotel, the Grizzly Bear? It burned to the ground. Just a pile of ash today. The owner is just beside himself. Says it's a Hydro torch job. Then they couldn't find Cheevers."

"My God. Stanley was in the fire?"

"They found him later, in his hotel room. He'd shot himself."

There's nothing like death to wake you up to life. I stood on my porch after the reporter had left, looking out towards the lake, thinking of Stanley Cheevers in his lonely hotel room, who knows what on his conscience. Thinking of his wife, his children. I thought of Isobel and the graves she could not protect. The sudden animosity of our neighbours, and the weighty inevitability of the flood. Newspaper photographs of people watching their houses burn. You can only fight so far, and for so long, I thought. There are precious days to be spent.

A new negotiator showed up a couple of weeks later, and we settled for our private appraisal figure, almost to the penny. It was as if the events up the lake had shaken everything, right down to the hard line. Hydro's new man made it very clear, though: he wasn't bargaining; he was just negotiating.

The last evening before Sarah left we walked, the three of us, down to the wharf where we sat on the end, feet dangling. Ed had a pocket full of flat stones, and we took turns skipping them across the water. The evening was peaceful, the lake calm. The smoke drifted lazily, heading southward.

"It's not like you won't see us again," I said, looking at Sarah, thinking how much she looks like Win. I was thinking about the flow of families, and the pull of place. "It just won't be here."

Sarah skipped a stone, counted: one, two, three. She didn't answer; there was nothing to say, I suppose, or maybe too much to begin. Ed was quiet, but then, he's never been one to talk much. From above, an osprey called. The last pebble skipped across the water silently and faded into the smoke like a sigh.

1967

When I got the job holding the hose for the house burnings I figured: hey, it's a job. It's not like anything I could say or do will make any difference to this backwater called Bear Creek. It's all going to be under water—thiry-five feet of water—in a few months' time, and by then we'll all be long gone. And me, Paul Doyle, sixteen last week and wanting cash for all kinds of things, it was a good opportunity. Past years, I'd be spraying trees in the spring, picking fruit in the fall, pruning, picking and packing—an endless cycle. Man, the number of times I'd go to bed at night after a day of picking and then pick all damn night again in my dreams, only to wake up and have to do it all over again.

But with B.C. Hydro buying folks out—they started a couple of years back, in '65, when that treaty was signed for the dam—lots of folks were gone before the trees even blossomed and now lots of trees are gone, too, leaving rows and rows of stumps. Last night at dinner my mum said to my dad: "John, it's like living in a war zone, destruction and smoke everywhere. It's a wasteland." And my dad said, "yup," and looked at me, because it's what my mum says every day. "How was your day, Paul?" he asked me, to change the subject. It wasn't much of a change, though, because my day involves burning down houses.

"We did the old Klaussen place," I said. "Went up like kindling."

Mum glanced at me, a look I couldn't read, and then returned to cutting up her pork chop, knife sharp against the china plate. "Poor old Tom," she said. "Glad he didn't stay around to see the old homestead go. He was born there, you know."

"He's got that job in Castlegar, been making that trip from here at 5 a.m. every morning for two years. Bet it's a relief to be closer to the job," offered my dad. Dad likes to put a positive light on things. "How's the car fund coming?" He asked me.

"Coming," I said.

From the beginning of all this Dad knew first hand how each person felt about leaving. He always said it's amazing how much people can tell you in a five-minute ferry trip. This past month, a lot of the people he's been taking out are crossing for the last time, sometimes in tears, all their stuff piled up on pickups. Some spend the whole way looking back, he told me, and some just look straight ahead. Me, I'd be looking forward. Besides, the view looking back isn't exactly pretty. What you see are the stumps of trees and piles of brush and the remains of burnt houses. And the smoke hangs there, sometimes all day. My mum says we'll be smelling it in our clothes for months after we're gone. I will for sure. There's black under my nails I don't think will ever come out.

Like I told my buddy Ken: it's a job, somebody's going to do it, might as well be me. That was a few weeks back. We were sitting on the wharf after supper. The smoke in the air made the sunset really red and cast the whole valley in an eerie glow.

"It's a dirty shame," said Ken, chucking rocks into the water, and I knew he was echoing what his parents— what everybody—had been saying for months. There's not a thing we can do about it, they'd say, but it's a dirty shame. Ken wasn't looking forward to the move to Edgewood. "We're all going different directions," he said. "It's like this place never existed."

When we walked back in the half-dark, we passed the Wylie house with an X on the side. It swam against the whitewash in the fading light. "They gone?" he asked me.

"Yesterday," I said.

The way they do it is this: Hydro offers a price and when the deal is closed, folks have a set time to move out. Sometimes they'll go as soon as the papers are signed, sometimes they'll hang on 'til the last minute. Once that time is passed, Hydro goes in and marks the side of the house with a big black X. My parents and I walk through Bear Creek's few streets in the evenings, and I can tell by the new Xs where I'll be working tomorrow. Since my dad runs the ferry, we'll be the last to go when the time comes, just park the ferry on the other side and drive away. They won't need to mark our house with an X, because there won't be any other houses left.

The bulldozer comes in first and pushes down the smaller barns and sheds. The houses go up where they stand and the dozer goes in later, making piles of unburnable debris. I hold the big cloth fire hose— 400 feet of it, water pumped up from the lake—and make sure the fires don't spread.

One or two houses did get moved, and Gerry Weber and a bunch his friends spent two days drinking and moving, in pieces, the old schoolhouse to upper Bear Creek, the ridge of land that'll be above high water when the dam goes in. Gerry was drinking for strength, Mum figured. She said the whole thing hit Gerry more than anyone, especially the school, which is funny because I heard it took him forever to graduate. Everyone says that the Webers were never exactly a smart bunch.

For the last dozen years or so, we'd been bussed to Castlegar for school, across on the ferry and then twenty miles of dirt road, in all kinds of weather. The school-house was used for meetings, like the ones we had when all this dam stuff began. At first, folks thought they could fight it, but like Isobel Armstrong said to my mum at the store, it's too big for us. And it is: it's the whole river, with five dams and a lot of American money.

Anyway, like I was saying, we were bussed to Castlegar, and while I hated the trip at 7 a.m. after a full hour of chores, it's one of the things I'm actually going to miss. On the last bus ride into Castlegar for high school, at the end of June, our driver Barry Schroeder, who's a real ham, was singing at the top of his lungs all these old songs, "Good Night Irene," "School Days." We'd decided to drown him out on the way back, sing our own songs. Even without power in Bear Creek, excepting the generator at Fischers', we heard the new songs through our transistor radios: the Beatles' "Help!" and The Monkees' "Last Train to Clarksville."

By the time we were belting it out on the last trip home on the old bus, it was "Take the last boat to Bear Creek and I'll meet you at the landing" and "We all live in a yellow schoolbus, a yellow school bus, a yellow schoolbus." Mr. Schroeder began speeding up, trying to get us home, I guess, before we drove him nuts.

"And our frieeeeends are all abooooaaard," we wailed as the bus hurtled around a corner on two wheels, and then hung there, still moving, but sideways for what felt like an eternity but was probably a second, leaning over the edge of the bank that tumbled down to meet the lake. "RIGHT!" yelled Mr. Schroeder, and we all lunged to the right side of the bus, which promptly swung back and righted itself on the road. We hadn't even slowed down. Nobody made a sound the rest of the way.

These are some of the other things I'll remember: listening to music on a red-and-white portable record player in the Shannons' back shed with the line strung from the Fischers' generator next door. Counting deer on the road to school. Keeping tabs on the bears in the orchard every fall, trying to get the fruit before the bear did. Swinging off the rope into the swimming hole on an August day. My bedroom in our house. I carved my initials in the soft cedar wood at the back of my closet. On the shelf I lined up models of airplanes I carved out of pine and painted. Some of them, the first ones I did, were pretty bad, but I kept them all. I hid notes under a floorboard for someone in the future, some kid who would occupy my room when I'd grown up and moved away. Some kid who might want to know about who lived there before.

I kept a coyote skull on the table beside my bed. I didn't kill that coyote; lots of kids hunted and trapped, but we didn't arrive until the 1952 and my parents weren't the hunting or trapping type. We came from Alberta, where my dad had inherited a small farm he worked for a few years, but he had terrible hay fever there, a real problem for a farmer. Pete Shannon is Dad's uncle, my greatuncle, I guess; he told Dad there was some land for sale here in Bear Creek, told him it was a wetter climate, so we came out and rented for a summer, and my dad's problem cleared up. Next year we sold and moved. Now Mum runs the store and post office and Dad runs the ferry—or at least Mum ran the post office until they closed it a couple of weeks ago. Anyway, by the time we had settled in, none of the orchards were doing so good, at least not enough to make a living.

I found the coyote skull the first time I walked out in

the woods. I didn't know any kids or anything and I guess I was too shy to just go up to them. I must've been five years old. So I was digging around in the woods just back of our place and what do I find but this skull, all brown, and no other bones around it. So I picked it up and brought it inside. My mum didn't even flinch. She crouched down with me and we admired its curves and hollows together. Then she said she thought we should boil it to get any germs out of it and then leave it in the sun. So there it was the next day, bleaching on the fence post, and that's how I met Kenny, who stopped dead in his six-year-old tracks on his way by our house when he saw it.

"You can touch it," I told him, and he said "Yeah, so what, I've got one just like it at home." I can remember it clear as day. Ken's been my best buddy since then, and we've had some good times, hunting for arrowheads, fishing for Dolly Varden and Steelhead, knocking over outhouses. Good times.

Like the time we wanted to have a campfire with some girls up at the lookout and cook some food but nobody had any money, so we snuck into the Schroeder henhouse for a roaster. There was Kenny, slipping in the hen shit, wings flapping and feathers all around, after this one fat chicken he was determined to get. Lucky for us there was a preacher down to Bear Creek from up the lake, and most folks were at the schoolhouse for the service, including the Schroeders. It never mattered what church the preacher was from, everybody went, but we teenagers were often let off the hook.

Those birds let up such a racket, it was a surprise nobody heard from the schoolhouse. It was so loud we didn't even hear Duke barking, tied up on the porch.

When he finally busted loose there was Ken with his arms around the bird and one leg over the barbwire fence, me safely on the other side the whole time. Ripped a hole from his crotch to his knee trying to scramble over, but he didn't let go of the bird. Kenny cut the head off with the axe kept in the schoolhouse shed and we laughed when it flopped around, though it made my stomach flip. It took a long time for the water to boil to get the feathers off, and lucky Kenny knew what he was doing with that thing, 'cause I sure didn't. We had a fine chicken roast later up at the lookout.

Ken didn't get to kiss Janet, a girl we both kind of liked, but we ate well. It might have been the way he was sitting, his legs crossed like that all night because of the hole in his pants, that sort of put her off. Me, I was too shy anyway. I never even told Ken I liked her too.

Ken's been gone a month. His family moved up to Edgewood, and we're moving to Trail, so I guess that's that. I gave him the coyote skull. "I always wanted one of these," he said as he traced his finger along the pattern of cracks that ran through the narrow crown. By the time he held it, ten years after I'd found it, it had lost several teeth.

Isobel Armstrong—everyone calls her Isobel—left last week to live with a niece back in Manitoba. Mrs A.—Isobel—was like the queen of Bear Creek, and led the fight with Ursula Strautman, when folks thought there was still a fight against Hydro. The day before she went, the few of us that were left watched as the workers poured cement over our little graveyard, a big slab that will keep the dead in their place, as Isobel said to Ursula, like a joke, but she wasn't smiling. It takes a long time to pour that much cement, but those two stayed the whole time. I came back towards the end when the workers had finished, thinking to hang around and scratch some little message in a corner somewhere—not enough to offend anyone, just something to say I was here. Ursula and Isobel were still there, and so I sat down behind a tree like I was watching the sunset or something. They didn't notice me.

"When are they cementing down Jack and Ace?" Ursula asked. Isobel Armstrong may not have won the battle for Bear Creek, I heard my mum tell my dad, but she won the battle to keep those graves on her property.

"Tomorrow morning," Isobel replied. "I'll be gone by afternoon. Tom's going to give me a ride to Nelson." Tom Klaussen would drive up from Castlegar then. Tom always did have a soft spot for Isobel.

"Thanks again for the porch chairs, Iz. They'll be nice at the new place. We spent a lot of hours in those chairs."

"Solving the world's problems," she agreed. "I didn't want everything to go at auction."

I waited forever for those two to leave, but they just sat there on the little grassy hill above the cemetery, arms around each other, until it was dark. I went home before they did, and when I got back the next morning, the cement was too hard to make any impression at all.

It's taken a long time to get to this point. Some folks were upset about it all, but others were okay about leaving. Fruit trade has been down, too many wet summers to really regain the crop levels. The packing shed, which one bumper year shipped 12,000 crates of apples, 7,000 of cherries and 5,000 of peaches has been getting emptier and emptier as the years went by. Life's changing anyway, some say. It wouldn't have gone on much longer. At the end, there were 33 homes, 128 people. Hardly any little kids anymore.

By the last years, most were getting work elsewhere, at nearby mills or working in the woods logging or planting or somesuch. Some, like my dad, still had trees but didn't rely on them so much, and when Pete Shannon retired, my mum took over running the post office and the store. I have an older sister, Jenny, away at nursing school. My folks want to see her graduate, and that takes money, Mum says.

Me, I'm thinking when we move I'll make more friends if I have a car. Dad reminds me that even if I buy some old junk heap for next to nothing I'll have to get a licence and insurance. It's not like Bear Creek, where kids just drive around our old roads as soon as they can reach the pedals. I don't know what insurance costs but I figure I'll have almost three hundred dollars saved when this is over, and I figure I can find a car for that much.

Sometimes I ride back and forth on the ferry, and I've been doing that more lately with my friends all gone. When you've been standing in the heat and ash all day, you get pretty gritty. I'll sometimes go for a quick dip and then lean, dripping, against the ferry cabin, feeling the wind dry my skin, talking to Dad. Yesterday on the way back there were two cars, Ed and Ursula Strautman in their old truck, and Mr. Turnbull in his company truck. I waved to Mr. Turnbull, who is boss of all of us on the crew, and he waved back, smiling. Usually Dad waits a bit on the far side and peers down the shoreline for the telltale puff of dust that says someone else is coming. Three cars fill the ferry, and if he heads off with just two, nine times out of ten someone will honk his horn for a pickup before we're a quarter way across, and of course they have to wait. But when one of the bigshots is on he just goes. They're paying him extra.

It's a short ride across but most folks get out and stand and stretch, and that's what Ursula did right away. Ed got out, too, and leaned against the cab and looked out over the lake. Mr. Turnbull just rested his wrists over his steering wheel and stared ahead. So I watched while Ursula went up and leaned in the window of the Hydro truck.

"As you know, Mr. Turnbull, we'll be leaving day after tomorrow," she said to him. Even over the motor, the Bear Creek ferry is so small you can hear everything.

There was a pause, Mr. Turnbull looking at Ursula through the open window. They've had run-ins before, those two. He didn't look unfriendly, exactly, he just looked sort of closed, like a shut door. He's had a lot of people hammering on that door, demanding this or that, just plain angry, and it's like the wood's just gotten thicker. He nodded at her, to say he was listening.

"You're not to set fire to our house until we're well out of sight. I mean that. I know we're about the last, but you wait until the next day, even, if it comes to that. Hear me?"

I saw Mr. Turnbull nod at her, a slow up and down motion of his chin. If he spoke, I couldn't hear him from inside the cab of his truck. Ursula seemed satisfied. By the time she got back in her own truck, we were docking.

It's weird being the only kid in town. The only reason we're still here is because of the store and the ferry, and we're gone tomorrow. The Strautmans are here I suppose because, as my mum says, that Ursula is so stubborn there's no way she'll make it easy for them. She did hold out forever for the best price she could get, and I heard from Mum they've got a pretty nice place to move to in Beaton. So it's down to us and the Strautmans and the Hydro guys who are setting fires and clearing trees, strolling around in their orange overalls. Mr. Turnbull's really a nice guy, Dad says, a nice guy with a nasty job. He's been nice to me, giving me the job, me and a few other local kids, but they're gone now; like I said, I'm the last one.

And yesterday Mr. Turnbull came up to me and asked how I was doing and how was my family and told me I'd been doing a good job. "Heard you're wanting a car," he said, and patted me on the back. "I'll have your pay-cheque ready Tuesday. You get a good one, hear?"

"Yes sir," I said.

Yesterday afternoon we barged the last of the stuff down to where we have a truck waiting to take it all to Trail. There was really nothing left at the store, and the last mail delivery was last week. Some stuff, shelves and things, got picked up from store owners in other places. Mum took the Bear Creek post office sign and, even though it's government property, slid it in with the stuff on the barge as a keepsake. Some stuff got moved up away from high water into the schoolhouse in upper Bear Creek, things maybe someone could use sometime but are just too good to burn. You have to act fast if you want to keep something. Before Gerry Weber left, he and his wife, the second one, went down the lake for a day to set up their new place. By the time they got back their barn was gone, with the other half of the stuff stored inside they were going to take with them. You should have heard Gerry Weber then. The Webers, as my mum would say, have always been a loud bunch.

Mr. Turnbull got an earful, and now the Webers are trying to get compensation, listing all sorts of things my dad says were never in that barn or even in Bear Creek.

So it's all gone. Most of our furniture is gone, just our beds and some kitchen stuff and odds and ends to go tomorrow. Some will go down on the barge, and the last stuff will go with us on the truck. I spent the evening packing up my stuff. All my wooden airplane models, even the bad ones. All my books and comics: *Archie, Classics Illustrated*, Ripley's *Believe It or Not*. When I got into bed it was just me and a bed and five cartons stacked along the wall. My feet echoed on the floorboards. It sounded weird, like a house under water. From the living room, where Mum and Dad were packing, I could hear them talking.

"Pack this?" My dad's voice.

"It was from Ursula. She was the first one over when we moved in. I always loved the label. That's why I kept it." I know now that she's talking about the Mason jar that has sat on our kitchen windowsill since I was five. Sometimes it held lupins, sometimes odds and ends. It had a homemade label on it that said:

Welcome to God's Country
– He should be so lucky!

There was a little painting below, about as long as my thumb, that showed the mountains and the lake.

"It had canned cherries in it. Biggest cherries I ever saw," my mother's voice went soft. I got out of bed, pulled on my jeans and walked outside before she could start crying. I hate it when my mother cries.

I walked up to the lookout, following the path that must've been there from day one. Might have once been a trapper's path, or even an Indian path. I wasn't worried about bears, all that smoke and noise around all the time, I figured they were hiding out about as far away as they could get. But as I came out of the woods and out onto the outcropping that looked out over the lake, I could see a shape, something that didn't belong there, and I felt my heart jump to my throat. Then the shape moved and divided, and Ed Strautman said: "That you, Paul?"

"How'd you know it was me?"

"Just a guess."

I sat down beside Ed and Ursula on the smaller of the two sitting rocks. We sat together without saying anything for a while.

I had almost drifted to sleep there on that rock in the warm smoky air when Ursula asked me: "Looking forward to Trail?"

"Yup."

"It's a dirty shame, isn't it?" she said, and I thought of Kenny.

"Yup."

"You all packed?"

"Yup." If she was looking for conversation, she was looking in the wrong place. I didn't want to talk. I didn't know what to say.

"Did you know I was born here, Paul? I was the first baby born in Bear Creek." Of course I knew that. Everybody knew that. I kept quiet; she sounded spooky.

The moon through the haze looked larger and more yellow than it should have.

"When I was a girl we had German classes in the schoolhouse right after Sunday School. We had apple schnitzing bees," she said, "boxes of apples and everyone helping with the cutting and drying. The smell, sweet, on our hands, in our clothes, it was in everything."

Old Ed cleared his throat, and I thought he'd say something, but he didn't.

"Oh, we've had our births and deaths. We've had our storms and floods. And we've sure packed a lot of fruit, haven't we?"

"Guess so," I said.

Ursula Strautman knew everything there was to know about Bear Creek. She'd been here, like she said, forever. But also she and Isobel Armstrong and some other ladies wrote a book about Bear Creek. I guess they wanted to get some things down on paper before it all disappeared. When we got those books—every family got one—we all went around getting folks to write in them, like a high school yearbook. Ursula gave me one of my own. In it, she had written:

> To Paul Doyle with fond regards from Ursula
> Strautman. Thanks for all of your help in the
> Garden! March 27, 1966.

I used to help the Strautmans dig up their kitchen garden in the spring. Ed had been having trouble with his back. Now he got up stiffly, and Ursula rose and stretched. I didn't know what the time was, but I figured it must be pretty late. She'd been talking for a while, and my foot was asleep.

"We'll be leaving tomorrow. You'll make sure they won't strike that match until after we're gone, won't you, Paul?"

"Yes, ma'am," I said, and she tousled my hair. I hate that. But I could still feel her hand there, even when I was back in my bed in my empty room trying to sleep.

I slept in, which kind of makes sense since I was up so late, but I couldn't figure out why Mum hadn't woken me up sooner.

"I was packing up the last things, Paul," she apologized when I found her on the lawn, lowering a box. "Sorry, I guess I lost track of time. You won't be late if you hurry. There's oatmeal, still warm."

There were several boxes on the front lawn. We were supposed to leave at the end of the day, after I'd finished my last day of work. Two more houses: the Strautmans and ours. The Strautman house was scheduled to go up first at 9 a.m. When I got there, Mr. Turnbull was pacing and the guys were standing around. I walked up to Terry, who had been hired on at Nakusp to work the Bear Creek demolition.

"Hey, Terry, what's up?"

"They were supposed to be out by now. Lady says her husband threw his back out lifting a box, can't get out of bed. I dunno, Turnbull says we're on a schedule, we have a deadline, and anyway they've had a bunch of extensions. Don't think he'll burn it down with them inside, though."

I could see Ursula through the window, moving about. She came out on the porch and waved. "Hi Paul," she said. "Tell these guys not to wait around 'less they've got a stretcher." One or two of the guys laughed. I caught Mr. Turnbull's eye and didn't. I wanted to go in, ask if I could help or something, but there was a thickness in the air, and it wasn't smoke. It was something else. We hung around for a while, and then Mr. Turnbull told me to go home for lunch. His voice sounded tight.

"He's got a contract," Terry offered again as I passed him, heading towards home. He was opening a black plastic lunch box. The smell of warm tuna fish wafted upwards. "He has to get this all finished up on time. Don't make any difference to me, so long as I get paid."

At home Mum was making peanut butter and jam sandwiches. There were boxes at her feet, open and waiting for our lunch things. Our new house was waiting for us in Trail, most stuff already moved in. We'd be gone with the last of the load late this afternoon. Dad said we'd go out for dinner when we got to Trail, an hour and a half's drive. It was kind of a big treat for us; it's not like there was ever any place to eat out in Bear Creek.

"I went to see Ed and Ursula off at the wharf, but I heard Ed's laid up. I want you to take these sandwiches over," she said. "Eat yours first, though."

"Aw, Mum…" I began. I didn't want to be taking the sandwiches past Mr. Turnbull, like I was aiding the enemy or something.

"Just do it. Tell Ursula I'll be right along to see what need's doing. I just want to get the last of our things out for your father and the truck."

When I got back with the sandwiches, Mr. Turnbull was coming down off the step, Ursula right behind him. Ed Strautman was standing up in the doorway, looking pale. The guys were loading up a company truck with boxes. I was surprised, because they weren't supposed to be moving household effects. Like us, most of the Strautman stuff had already gone, so there were just some boxes and the bed to go. I watched while Terry and Jake slid the bed frame onto the truck and went back in for the mattress. When they came out, Terry passed me and said, "Get the bedding, Paul."

When I walked up the steps, Ursula was standing with her hands on her hips. I was suddenly kind of afraid of her, but then I saw the corners of her mouth were turned up, like part of her was enjoying this.

"I do like to see those boys work," she said, accepting the sandwiches. She handed one to Ed, and lowered herself onto the step. "There's a pot of tea on the counter. Get it for us, would you, Paul? And a cup for yourself." I remembered my mum's words about how Ursula was stubborn and wondered if they were faking Ed's back problem, but his expression didn't look like he was faking. He remained leaning in the doorway. "Can't sit down," he told me with a pained smile, and then: "Thanks, Paul," when I handed him the cup of tea I'd poured. I'd forgotten Terry had asked me to get the bedding until I saw him and Jake heading back to the house as I handed Ursula her tea. She smiled at me. "Better get to work, eh?"

"Yeah," I said, grateful to be released, especially because of the way the guys were looking at me.

It felt strange to be gathering up the sheets, still-warm from where Ed had been lying on them, heaped on the floor where Jake and Terry had left them when they dismantled the bed. I picked them up from the worn linoleum and tried to fold the sheets by spreading them out on the floor, which was dusty with the bootprints of the workers. I had a lot of chores at home, but folding sheets wasn't one of them, and I didn't know how to go about it.

"Here, let's do it together." Ursula came into the room, smiling that way she does, and picked up two corners. "Now, you pick up the other two," she said, and I did. Then she began to hum. It was echoey in the empty room, the light streaming in the curtainless windows, dust swirling in the air.

"One two three, one two three, hmmm, hmmm," she hummed a waltz tune and danced her way towards me until our fingers met. "You can't let me dance alone, Paul

Doyle," she said. She tucked her two corners between my thumb and fingers and caught the folded end. "Now, one two three, one two three." I watched the loose skin under her bare arms sway as she moved.

By the time we'd folded the mattress cover, the bottom sheet, the top sheet and the quilt, she had me dancing, too, even though I had no idea what I'd do if Jake and Terry came back in. When the last sheet was done, Ed was standing in the doorway, smiling. "Time to go, my dancing princess," he said, and she left me with an armful of folded bedding and danced into his arms, which he gingerly drew around her, the careful movements of someone in pain.

When we got the Strautmans into the truck with all their stuff on the back, it was getting late. There was still this house and our house to go and a Hydro deadline that wouldn't budge. My mum had arrived to help with the last of the packing and to ease Ed into the seat, and as I waved she moved down the lane to see them off at the wharf, where Dad waited to ferry them across. I stayed behind waiting for Mr. Turnbull's instructions, my eyes watching the ferry as it pulled away.

Not five minutes had passed before I heard Mr. Turnbull shout "Hold on, boys," and I turned around to see the house going up. Jake and Terry had gone ahead and lit the fire, not waiting for Mr. Turnbull's okay. I could see him yelling at them over the roar of the flames from where I stood, nowhere near the hose or the pump, which in any case had not even been started up.

The house went up fast, the whole thing a ball of flame in minutes, black smoke pouring out. The Strautmans couldn't have been more than halfway across. Ed would be facing forward, I thought. He was so stiff he probably couldn't turn his head. But Ursula would have seen the flames as they rose through the dry empty house, as they crackled the painted X on its side.

When we'd finished with the Strautman house, Mr. Turnbull came up to me and told me my work was done.

"Your final paycheque," he said to me, handing me an envelope. "There's a little extra in there, to help with your car fund. You've been a good worker, Paul."

I walked home to find Mum and Dad sitting on the step. The last of our stuff was all on our truck parked down at the ferry, which sat idle. Nobody was coming or going from Bear Creek now. The next trip would be for us.

It was after seven by then, much later than we'd ever figured on getting away. We'd forgotten about our dinner out, and in any case, Mum said she wasn't hungry. I went in and washed up, drying myself with the towel Mum had left for me on the hook. The house was creepy with nothing in it, and I walked through the rooms, echoes sending chills down my spine, my footfalls too loud. I changed into clothes Mum had left out and tucked the sooty overalls and the towel into a paper grocery bag, leaning it against the doorframe before stepping through to join my parents on the step.

"They won't burn it down tonight," my Dad was saying, but as he said it I could see the orange overalls of the crew walking down the lane towards our house. Behind them, smoke rolled lazily up from the rubble of the Strautman house. The bulldozers wouldn't go in until everything had cooled down. My mother sighed, a sound I couldn't quite read. Unlike Ursula, she actually wanted to see our house go up. She needed to, she told us.

"It's like it's not real if I don't see it, John," she had

told my father, who nodded at the time as if understanding. I suppose I did, too. I mean, after working all
these fires, what's one more? Once they were gone, it was
almost as if they had never been there. You could imagine you had dreamt the house, like it wasn't ever real. So
you watch it, and then you really know. You wouldn't
always be thinking it was standing there, waiting for you
to come back to it.

"We'd like to finish today, Mr. and Mrs. Doyle," Mr.
Turnbull said as they approached.

"Be my guest," said Mum, and she stepped away from
the porch. "Come on, you two."

We stood at the end of the drive, my mum holding
her cardigan wrapped around her, although it wasn't
cold, my dad with his hand on her shoulder. I stood
with my bag at my feet, feeling strange not to be working with the guys, and strange to be watching as they
walked into the rooms of my house, strategizing the
places they would set with paper and gasoline. When
the thought struck me, it was with a sharp knock to the
chest, as if I'd been hit with a rock.

"Wait!" I yelled, and sprinted into the house, past
Terry and Jake, and into my room at the back.

The board was loose, with a full finger width of space
between it and the board it joined. It had always been
covered by a little hooked rug my grandmother had
made, but now it lay exposed. I had it up in seconds,
while Jake and Terry stood in the doorway, waiting.

"Just a sec, okay?" I said over my shoulder, and they
drew away, setting down the can of gasoline and the
matches and stepping onto the porch. I could hear them
explaining to Mr. Turnbull that I wanted a few minutes.

I pulled out the papers, messages I had left for some

kid in a future that wasn't going to happen. There was a drawing I had made when I was five years old, my name written below. *Paul*, it said. At five, that was all I knew how to write. The picture might have been a coyote skull, if you knew what you were looking for. Underneath, my mum had written the date: June 12, 1956.

There was a photograph of my dog Patch, a brown-and-white mongrel I had loved until he died of old age when I was twelve. He was buried out back, no cement to hold his grave down. He sat inside the white frame of the photograph looking out, one haunch cocked sideways, a goofy grin on his face. I could remember his brown eyes, the way they looked at me when he wanted something I was eating.

I turned a shard of ribbon quartz over in my hand that had been tucked between the papers: an Indian scraper, for animal hides. Once I had a whole collection: arrowheads, pounding stones. I couldn't remember why I had saved just this one. I tucked it back under the boards.

There was a note written in 1964, when I was thirteen. I remember writing it, and it made me embarrassed then, kneeling there, to read it. *I love Janet Sherbansky*, it said. *I would do almost anything to kiss her.* I could remember her lips, I realized, but I couldn't remember where the Sherbanskys had moved.

For some reason, that got me going. The rock in my chest, the lump in my throat, a swelling that burst forth in tears that ran down my cheeks, but instead of thinking about the papers in my hand or the empty house around me, I thought of the impossibility of stepping outside looking as if I'd been crying. Without really thinking, then, I grabbed the can and an armload of paper scraps and kindling, threw them all in the corner of my room and dowsed them with gasoline. I wasn't allowed to set the fires, just to hold the hose, but this was my house and I wasn't working for Mr. Turnbull anymore.

It started slowly, not with the whoosh I had expected, and I looked at the papers I held in my hand. I tucked the photograph of Patch into my pocket and fed the rest into the fire. The smoke was billowing from the corner by then, black as the flames licked the wallpaper. I picked up the can from where I'd set it in the doorway and backed out.

"It's going," I said as I passed Jake and Terry by the door. It took a minute to register, and then they looked back in alarm. I handed Terry the can. "See you around," I said. My face was smudged with the smoke from the fire I had started. If my tears were visible, I didn't care anymore. When I joined my parents in the road, my mother rubbed gently at the runnels on my sooty cheeks with her thumb, then turned back to watch the flames rise.

Epilogue

May 2005

The slab of concrete that covers the old cemetery takes me seventy-two paces to walk its length, thirty-seven its width. How practical an engineering feat, an effort to ensure that neither bones nor stories would float to the surface. There is no plaque, no grave marker, nothing to tell the low-water walker that this is the Bear Creek cemetery, 1904–1965.

To the south, the lake reflects the passionate blue of a spring sky. The light on the water is a scatter of diamonds, sharp against the spring green of trees, the cut of rock. To the north the lake bends gently, a graceful bowing to the mossy flank of mountain.

By June, when the dam increases its flow, this will all be under water. Now, I can see the bones of tree stumps, rows traced through the sand. Here, the foundation of a house has left a depression; there, an empty stretch that may have been a road lies like a whisper. The remains of a wharf, pilings like broken teeth, stretches beneath the water from the shore.

My grandmother, Ursula Hartmann, was born in this place in 1905; it has been a hundred years since her birth. My grandmother, my mother, now me: a flow of daughters, settling into the places we belong. And so I have returned, at low water, to walk the ghost streets of this village. Today I am fifty-five years old.

Looking upwards to the forested hillside, I can almost hear our childish shouts as we coursed down the snowy slope on makeshift sleds in winter, our whispers as we played at Indians in summer. There is a tree on the upper ridge, above the high-water mark, so large four of us could circle it, arms outstretched, fingers barely touching. It still towers above the old townsite below, where the water begins its slow ascent.

The weather is shifting, and with the change in wind comes the smell of rain. As I make my way from the cemetery to the shore I imagine things as they were. Here was a house and a porch where people gathered to play fiddles and spoons. Nearby I see shoots of asparagus poking up through the grass like small miracles: the remains of a backyard garden. Most have been topped by deer. I find two with tops intact, and their taste is sweet and fresh and nothing like the sad bundles bound by purple bands in the supermarket.

A small shout of white in the sand attracts me, and I turn over and over the wedge of china, a plate perhaps. Dinners served. Butter passed. Gravy poured. I tuck it into my pocket, continue on, make my way along the beach. My mood softens as I listen to the water lap at the pebbles, and I find a flat rock, good for skipping. It's hard to see the rock as it skips across the water now pocked by rain, yet I believe I count three splashes—no, four. We spent a lot of time skipping stones when I came here as a kid.

Summers in Bear Creek we fished for trout. We had forts in the woods. We hiked up to old trappers' cabins; the boys shot rabbits and squirrels. We swam in the swimming hole when the lake was still icy in early summer, then braved a plunge off the wharf towards the end of August. Every summer we put on a play or a concert in the old schoolhouse, retired from active duty in '61 when Bear Creek kids started being bussed to Castlegar. Barry Schroeder was the last bus driver, parking the old yellow school bus on his property and taking the kids across on the barge. Some winters, the road was so bad we barely made it. I can still smell the wet wool of three dozen mittens gripping the bars of the seats in front as we swayed with the movement of the bus.

The air has turned suddenly cold as the wind sweeps southward down the lake, and now the lake is slate grey and brooding. I inhale the sharp scent of water, fill my lungs with the perfume of earth and rock. By the time I reach the rocks at the far side of the beach it has begun to rain, and my jeans are soaked through. The rest of me is dry, thanks to the wonders of Gortex, and I'm grateful for that. I think of the folks of Bear Creek on a rainy day like this: in oilskins in the early years, later in green or yellow slickers, big rubber boots stamping off the wet. Then a wood fire and a card game on an old, pitted kitchen table lit by an oil lamp. I can smell cookies, hot chocolate. It's my Oma's house I'm seeing, smelling.

I walk up alongside Sanders Creek, the smaller of the two creeks. On the way, bear sign: a tree stump ripped apart for insects, great claw marks across the soft wood. It takes some time to follow the path up to the road on the upper bench, still maintained by the ones who came back: people who, like me, were young when Bear Creek came to its end: Howard Weber and his wife, Barbara, Sid and Linda Milner. And old Tom Klaussen, who only comes in the summers now. A little settlement well above the high-water mark. Here, some of the old fruit trees still bear apples, good for pies at least, and there is one cow that roams freely, communally owned. There is Linda's grey horse that she named Ace after the legendary beast buried on the old Armstrong property. There was a separate slab of concrete poured for the horse and his master, Jack. B.C. Hydro did that much at least.

Boat is still the best way to get here, the logging road from Edgewood being often impassable. Transportation in Bear Creek is mostly by foot or ATV, and a blue jeep held together with chicken wire and duct tape that always has the keys left in the ignition. Like the old days, nothing has, or needs, a licence here. There is still no electricity, but we have cell phones, now, and one generator to charge batteries for these and for vehicles and flashlights. It's a quiet sort of civilization.

As I reach the road I hear the rattle of a motor and here are Howard and Barb, grinning through the rain at me: they've been checking up on Ace and the cow.

"Sarah!" they call, and there are soggy hugs all around. "What weather, eh?"

Later, in their cabin, mugs of strong tea in our hands, Howard scolds me: "You should have told us you were coming, I could have opened up your place, made sure you had dry wood." As he's saying this, Barb is already filling a box for me: bread, jam.

"I'm not staying," I tell them. "I just needed some time out. Just needed a walk, I guess." I laugh at myself, and Barb looks at me more closely.

"You'll be back in the summer, though," she says.

"Oh, yes," I tell her.

"And the girls?" She means my daughters, both grown, with lives of their own.

"Yes. I think so."

The tea is warm as it slips down my throat, and steam rises from my jeans as they dry on my legs in front of the fire. The rain beats a rooftop staccato, while outside the lake rises silently, one inch at a time.

Acknowledgments

It takes a community to raise a child, and it takes one to raise a book as well.

Thanks to mentor Verna Relkoff, whose unflagging encouragement and practical editing made me a better writer; Steve Thornton, who from the beginning held me to a higher standard; my writing group: Susan Andrews Grace, Jennifer Craig, Joyce MacDonald, Jana Danniels and Nicola Harwood; friends who read the early manuscripts and offered insights and advice: Jacqueline Cameron, Cyndi Sand-Eveland, Kathy Witkowsky, Joan Lang, Ruth Porter, Tim Kendrick, Eileen Delehanty Pearkes, and Marilyn James; Irene Mock for sage advice; Shawn Lamb at the Nelson Museum, who is always there for me; Rose Rohn, who wrote the book about Renata that so inspired me to write about Bear Creek, and her son Bruce Rohn, with suitcases full of photographs and a passion for history; Wally Penner, who, one low water day, introduced me to the place he loved; my agent, Morty Mint, and the serendipity that put us together; the formidable team at McArthur & Co; and to all those who shared information and memories for specific stories—there are too many to list.

And of course, and most importantly, thanks to my family.

Thanks also to the Columbia Basin Trust through the Columbia Kootenay Cultural Alliance, and to the Nelson and District Arts Council.